A Gift
from the
Cottage
by the
Loch

BOOKS BY KENNEDY KERR

Loch Cameron

The Cottage by the Loch

A Secret at the Cottage by the Loch

The Diary from the Cottage by the Loch

Magpie Cove

The House at Magpie Cove

Secrets of Magpie Cove

Daughters of Magpie Cove

Dreams of Magpie Cove

A Spell of Murder

Kennedy Kerr

A Gift
from the
Cottage
by the
Loch

bookouture

Published by Bookouture in 2024

An imprint of Storyfire Ltd.
Carmelite House
50 Victoria Embankment
London EC4Y 0DZ

www.bookouture.com

ISBN: 978-1-83525-181-2
eBook ISBN: 978-1-83525-180-5

For Simona, hairdresser par excellence. And to Kelsie, for everything.

PROLOGUE

Bel looked at the envelope in her hand.

'I'm sorry, Bel.' Her boss, Emma, shrugged. 'Nothing I can do. They've gone into administration.'

'How... how long?' What she meant was, *How long do I have?*

'You need to clear out your desk today. We all have to.' Emma put her hand on Bel's shoulder. 'I'm sorry,' she repeated, awkwardly.

Emma had never exactly been a friend. It wasn't like that at HandyPhone – not in the customer service team, anyway. You came in, sat in your little nook, made your calls. Then you went home. Breaks were strictly timed and monitored during your shift, and there wasn't a lot of office chitchat or laughs in the kitchen, as there seemed to be at other workplaces.

Bel stared at the divider in front of her, which was high enough so that she couldn't see anyone else if she was sitting at her desk. When she'd been made Customer Services Manager, she'd suggested lower dividers between the banks of cubicles, so that employees could see each other. She'd only been at Handy-Phone two years, at that point. She still had enthusiasm.

Her suggestion had been politely ignored. *Conversation lowers productivity*, Emma had told her when Bel had followed it up. That was six years ago. Bel had tried other things to make the working environment nicer. She'd suggested bowling and drinks nights out, office quizzes, ergonomic chairs, longer breaks. None of it had got the green light from management. And, over time, Bel had stopped trying.

'So, us talking to each other wasn't the main problem the company had.' Bel raised an eyebrow. 'Maybe we could have had the odd karaoke night, or a vending machine. Maybe that wouldn't have been the end of the world after all.'

'What?' Emma frowned at her.

Bel looked at the thick stack of envelopes still in Emma's hand. There were people working here who really needed their job. She needed it, but at least she had Andy. She wasn't a single mum, like Donna, or caring for her dad like Raj was.

'Nothing. Do they really need us all to go? I could suggest some people to stay. A skeleton staff. I mean... if they've been bought by another company, then they'll need to keep the phone lines open, won't they...?' Bel trailed off, trying to think of something that would keep Emma from having to hand out all the envelopes.

But Emma shook her head.

'Sorry, Bel. It's not up to me.'

'You're home early.'

Andy's voice sounded on edge. Bel guessed he was in the kitchen. He often worked from home, though his schedule was changeable. She frowned, realising that music was playing. *Odd.* Andy usually liked quiet when he was working.

'Yeah,' she called back, taking off her coat and kicking off her shoes. HandyPhone had a dress code for managers: black skirt, white blouse, court shoes, tights. Even the tights had to be either flesh tone or black, removing the possibility that Bel might express a miniscule glint of personality with some pink hold-up stockings or a pair of orange-and-black striped Halloween tights.

It wasn't as though she loved the job. She hated it, in fact. She hated the stupid uniform – as if anyone cared what a lowly customer services manager at a mobile phone company wore! – she hated the overly bureaucratic rules, and she hated the fact that she hadn't been able to make any discernible improvement to any of her staff's lives in the six years she'd been their manager. Yes, she'd tried. But she hadn't succeeded. The road to hell was paved with good intentions, as the saying went.

Bel had worked at HandyPhone for eight years, and she didn't think she'd ever enjoyed a day of it. But it was a job, and not everyone had one, these days. Plus, every time she'd brought up the subject of finding something else, Andy had made barbed comments about paying the mortgage. So, she'd stayed.

Andy was a freelance quantity surveyor, in charge of managing budgets and supplies for large building projects. He had the larger salary, but he still made them split everything – including the mortgage – down the middle. *I pay for all the fun stuff on top*, he'd always said, even though Bel couldn't remember the last fun thing they'd done.

She walked into the kitchen in her stockinged feet. She had no idea what to do now. She supposed she'd have to start looking for another job in customer services, but the idea filled her with dread.

A cup of tea first, she thought. *I'll sit down, and have a moment to think.*

Andy was standing by the kitchen island as she walked in. His laptop was open, and the music was still playing. He looked rattled at Bel's sudden appearance. It was 11.20 a.m. She wasn't due back for hours.

'Hey.' She went to the kettle, saw it was a quarter full, and flicked the ON switch. 'I've got bad news.' She looked back at Andy, who was still standing in the same position by the kitchen island. He looked more than rattled now: it was as if he was captured in stone. Bel frowned. 'Andy?'

'Yeah,' he said, looking to the door to the hallway.

They used to have a small kitchen, but they'd had it extended in the lockdown. Being in the building trade, Andy had known some builders who were happy to do the work, even though everything was supposed to have ground to a halt. Half of Bel had been worried about the risk of contamination, but half of her had been pleased that Andy had designed a beautiful, high-ceilinged extension. It had large glass Crittal doors and exposed brick walls, and when it was finally all finished – three months after the deadline – Bel had enjoyed finding beautiful accessories for the space: a couple of large Ficus plants in smart black pots, some birds of paradise, expensive scented candles. Andy had insisted on a modern, poured-concrete floor, and though it had been a pain at the time, when it was done, Bel had to admit it looked amazing.

Bel followed Andy's gaze to the door.

'What's up?' she asked, frowning – he was cagey, like a spooked cat. 'I've got some bad news, anyway. I...'

The door to the hallway opened, and a woman, wearing just a towel – one of Bel's favourite bath sheets, the white fluffy ones she took such care of – walked into the kitchen, her bare feet leaving damp marks on the concrete floor.

'Oh,' Bel said, staring at the woman. 'Oh,' she repeated. It was all she could think of.

There was a silence. Bel knew she should say something. Something clever or biting or witty, just like people did in the movies when this kind of thing happened. But, this wasn't a movie, it was her life. And it had suddenly, completely, fallen apart.

ONE

Bel was exhausted. But she had finally made it to Loch Cameron.

She pulled up outside the little white-washed cottage, pulled on the handbrake and slumped over the steering wheel. *Here I am*, she thought. *Hundreds of miles from home. What the hell am I doing here?*

Bel hadn't even known where she was going when she had got in the car. But, after the woman had walked into the kitchen, it felt as though everything had moved very fast.

She hadn't said anything to Andy. She didn't need to ask what was going on: it was all there in his face.

She had run out of the kitchen and up the stairs to her and Andy's bedroom, where she made herself not look at the bed – their bed, where presumably he had just been with the woman in the towel – and threw some clothes into a holdall. Then she went into the bathroom, found her travel wash bag and stuffed some essentials into it, trying to ignore the fact that the shower was still dripping.

That woman had just been in her shower. Using her stuff. And that woman – whoever she was – had been wearing one of her extra-large, fluffy, luxurious bath sheets. Bel had bought them a few months before from an upscale homewares shop, on sale. She couldn't afford them at full price, and she'd been so pleased with herself when she'd found them.

She loved those towels. Now, she could never touch them again.

Bel had run down the stairs, grabbed her handbag from the hallway and hightailed it out of the house. Andy had run after her, but she had thrown her bags into the car and locked the doors.

'Bel, come back. Be reasonable!' he'd shouted through the car window.

She'd just wanted to get away, so she'd ignored him and driven off, her hands shaking.

But, now, she was furious at what he had said.

Be reasonable?! Was he actually serious?

For the first hour, she'd just driven. She'd hardly known where she was going until she found herself on the motorway, heading north. North was the only home she had left now, because that was where her sister, Sally, was. She couldn't think of anywhere else to go.

She'd stopped for a coffee, gone to the ladies' and splashed cold water on her face.

What are you doing? she asked the Bel in the mirror. *Focus. You're in shock.* Bel blinked at her reflection. *I can't believe he would do that to me. After all this time.*

Another thought occurred to her. *How long had Andy been seeing this woman?* She had no way of knowing. She'd assumed at first that she'd caught the two of them on a one-time thing, but that had to be highly unlikely. Andy worked from home a lot anyway, being freelance. *They could have been together every day – in my bed – when I was at work, for all I know,* she thought. *Oh, God.*

Bel closed the car door and burst into tears again as the realisation hit her.

She sobbed for a long time, sitting in the driver's seat of her car. Eventually, she took in some deep breaths and managed to calm down. She stared out the windscreen at the trucks and cars going past on the road. So many lives. She wondered if anyone else had just lost their job and their relationship in the space of a morning.

Probably not.

She'd bought a sandwich while she was inside, and so she ate it and felt a little better.

What was she going to do now? Going back was unthinkable. She couldn't walk into that house again. And it wasn't as if she had to go back for work. So where was she going to go? She didn't have any particularly close friends she could stay with in Essex, where she lived, and she didn't want to be there, anyway.

Bel wanted to put as much distance as she could between her and Andy, and she realised there was only one place she could go.

She picked up her phone and called Sally.

Loch Cameron is nothing like Essex, Bel thought, as she drove slowly into the village. The sudden riot of colour from the hanging baskets of bright flowers lifted her spirits after a five-hour slog of a drive up the motorway to Scotland, which had been followed by a further three hours along smaller, twistier roads that cut through green and purple hills and past deep, still lochs, to reach her destination.

The closer Bel had got to Scotland, the better she'd felt. Loch Cameron seemed like the obvious place to go, since her sister Sally lived nearby with her partner, Bess. Bel had visited the village a few times and always found it a calm and serene place, which was what she needed right now.

Bel reflected on how quickly life could turn on the tiniest of moments. When she'd woken up that morning, she'd had a partner and a job. By lunchtime she had neither.

She'd called Sally from the car, her voice breaking.

Take a breath and tell me what's wrong, Sally had said, sounding worried when she answered the phone to Bel's choked cries. Bel couldn't even say *hello* properly. She'd burst into tears more times than she could count while driving.

She'd pulled onto the hard shoulder and stopped the car; it wasn't safe for her to drive at that moment. Then, word by excruciating word, she'd told her sister everything.

Right. You're coming here, Sally had said. *No arguments.*

I don't have to, Sally. You don't have to solve my problems for me, Bel had argued weakly.

You're my little sister. I'm hardly going to leave you to suffer alone, Sally had replied briskly.

In that moment, Bel didn't have it in her to fight. *Okay.*

The only problem is that we've got builders in at the moment doing the extension and the whole place is a mess. So I'll find you somewhere nearby to stay. I'll sort it out, don't worry. Just drive, and I'll text you the details.

Thank you, Bel had whispered.

So, she had driven north. An hour later, her phone had pinged with an address in Loch Cameron, along with a contact phone number.

This is a cottage I've heard good things about. When you get a minute, call Gretchen Ross. She manages the lettings. I've paid for two weeks up front, but you can stay longer if you need to. Let me know when you get there.

Bel was grateful. She really was. But she felt a little apprehensive about seeing her sister. There had been tension between her and Sally for almost as long as she could remember. Since their mother had passed away, Sally had decided that it was her responsibility to take over looking after Bel. It had gotten worse after their dad had also passed away.

Bel had been close to her dad. She missed him so much.

It wasn't that Bel didn't appreciate her sister's help. She really did. But, quite often, Sally's intense protectiveness – and her bossy, efficient manner – made Bel feel a mess; like a child who wasn't allowed to do things for herself, because she couldn't be trusted to do a good job. Sally had always been the same, even when their dad had been alive. She'd said, often, that Bel and their dad were too alike: dreamers who never got anything done.

Living so far away from Sally for the past few years hadn't necessarily been the worst thing, if she was honest. Sally had got a job in a whisky distillery in a remote Scottish village, and Bel had stayed in Essex. Sally had been torn about leaving, but Bel had told her to go. She would be fine, looking after herself.

And, she'd thought she was fine. Until now.

I guess I do just mess up everything, she thought, as she drove along. She *was* grateful that Sally had swooped in and sorted out a place for her to stay, but there was a part of her that wished she'd never called her sister in the first place, that wished she'd just decided to hole up in a roadside motel for a few days until she figured out what to do.

But she hadn't. Maybe she was too used to relying on Sally, still.

Or maybe you shouldn't beat yourself up about asking for help when your world has just fallen apart, she thought.

Andy had called her while she was driving, and then again, when she didn't pick up. Then he had texted.

We need to talk.

I don't bloody think so, she thought as the text message

flashed up on the car's internal display. It was linked to her phone, and meant she could get messages and talk as she drove. She dictated her reply.

You cheated. It's over, isn't it? Isn't that what happens?

No. It doesn't have to be that way.

Furious, she'd called him, intending to tell him where to go.

I've left you and I'm not coming back. So, leave me alone, she'd said.

Just listen, Bel. You owe me that, he'd wheedled.

I don't owe you anything at all, she'd retorted, but she had listened, wondering what he thought was going to happen when he finally stopped to listen to her.

That had always been part of the problem. Andy had talked, and Bel had listened. She was good at it. She didn't *mind* listening – in fact, she enjoyed it. Bel had always found others interesting, and she didn't mind giving someone else the space to express themselves. She was well aware that what had happened in her and Andy's relationship was that they always talked about and thought about and prioritised *Andy's* thoughts: his issues, his problems, his priorities. Was that his fault? Perhaps not. But it was what had happened, nonetheless.

This time, Andy had explained over the phone that he'd been so unhappy in their relationship. He was lonely, he'd said, and had needed company. Needed sex. And they hadn't done anything apart from roll away from each other to opposite sides of the bed at nighttime for years.

Years.

And it had been killing him. But this didn't have to be the end of their relationship. Perhaps they could seek counselling, or have an open partnership.

An open partnership. So that she could keep paying half the

mortgage and Andy could keep on ignoring her in bed? Presumably that was what he meant.

I think not, she thought, angrily. *I think absolutely not.*

Quite how Andy had the nerve to suggest that he had some kind of remarkable sex drive that she'd never been able to fulfil was laughable. This was a man whose rare moments of enthusiasm were limited to buying new ergonomic slippers, or watching TV documentaries called *Nazi Megastructures* or *Engineering the Aqueduct*.

You didn't ask why I was home early, Bel had said.

She'd heard his words – understood them, and understood Andy, even – but she had also felt a strange calm settle over her, and as she let him talk, she had gathered that calm around her like a robe. She, too, had been unhappy. Desperately unhappy and lonely, feeling like a ghost in her own house, for years. Really, for most of their relationship, after the honeymoon period wore off and she realised that the traits she had found so appealing in Andy when they'd met – confidence, being thorough and taking charge – were, in fact, badly rooted arrogance and an almost relentless criticism of everything she did.

She'd never known anyone complain as much as Andy. Once he continued to berate her for buying the wrong sized bath mat until she cried. Another time he'd lost his temper so badly at an airport – because Customs had broken the zip on his new suitcase – that he'd kicked and swore at the suitcase until Bel had wished that the ground would open up and swallow her. She had realised, in that moment, ahead of two weeks in Cyprus together, that she had no idea who she had married. Because the man she'd married had been calm, confident, sweet and attentive. Not this toddler having a temper tantrum in the airport in a foreign country.

If they never had sex anymore it was because he had never really wanted to in the first place. She'd realised that on that holiday in Cyprus, too. Putting aside her misgivings about the

suitcase incident, she'd been excited to be away together somewhere so romantic and be able to revel in each other – in their
bodies, in the sun and the heat and the ocean. But Andy had
been curiously cold towards her even then. He hadn't wanted
sex. He hadn't been that interested in the beach, and he'd
complained about their apartment. She wondered at the time
what it was that he really wanted, because it obviously
wasn't her.

What? Andy had sounded appalled that, for the first time,
Bel didn't seem interested in listening to his problems.

I lost my job at HandyPhone, she'd said. *Made redundant.
With immediate effect.*

Oh.

That was all he had to say. Not even a sorry, not even a
whisper of sympathy.

I'm going to stay with my sister for a while, Bel had added.

Right. He'd sighed. *Might have guessed.*

His tone was derisive, but she didn't rise to it. Andy had
never liked Sally. Perhaps it was because Sally had had zero
patience for his constant complaining.

I guess that's another thing she was right about, Bel thought
as she'd ended the call.

When she had calmed down a little, she had called
Gretchen Ross. An elderly woman had answered the phone –
Bel could hear it in her voice – but Gretchen also sounded
perky and completely with it. She had given Bel directions – go
through the village and up the narrow road at the end. There
was no sign to Queen's Point, but she'd know it because of a
sharp incline and a twist in the road that took you up the hill to
a raised outcropping along the side of the loch itself.

Queen's Point was a rough tongue of rock that poked out
from the edge of the land, and when Bel followed the tiny road
as Gretchen had indicated, she found a number of whitewashed
cottages there, all looking over the loch.

I'll get a neighbour to leave you a key under the flowerpot, dear, Gretchen had said. *I'll get him to leave you a pint of milk and some bread, and there'll be some tea bags in the cupboard. You make yourself at home. Sounds like you need some rest.*

Gretchen had clearly been able to tell from Bel's tone that she was stressed. Bel hadn't explained her reason for coming other than that she wanted to visit her sister, who Gretchen knew. *Sally's sister! Ah, what a pleasure to have you stay*, she'd said. There was something in Gretchen's warmth that was so kind and genuine.

Thank you. Bel had teared up again; this time, at Gretchen's kindness.

TWO

The cottage was much nicer than Bel had expected. In fact, it had all been such a rush that she hadn't thought too much about what the cottage was going to look like inside on her drive up north – she was in shock, still, about what had just happened. Bel was aware that her mascara was smudged and she must look exhausted. She was exhausted. But, at least there was no one to meet her and judge her appearance. Sally and Bess were going to come over the next morning. Sally could go in to work late – she was a director at the whisky distillery – and Bess was a self-employed handywoman, so she could be flexible with her day. But, until then, Bel was alone, hundreds of miles from almost everything familiar, without a job or a partner – or a home, for now.

It was still Wednesday. A day that wouldn't end: a day she fervently wished had never happened.

Bel dropped her holdall in the hallway of the cottage and put the key with its Loch Cameron Distillery keyring on a narrow side table covered in a large lace doily. If, after talking to Gretchen on the phone, she had expected that the whole cottage would be swamped in old-lady paraphernalia, she was wrong. In fact, the cottage was clean and tidy, with white walls, a neutral carpet in the hallway, and smelt fresh and airy – not mousy and damp, as she had half-imagined on her drive up.

Thank goodness. She didn't think she had it in her to deal with any new problems today.

At the end of the hallway, a cosy living room surprised her by being wallpapered in a modern, bold wildflower pattern, with a pink vintage-looking chaise longue facing a comfy white sofa, and a couple of upholstered fabric chairs that added to the cottage feel. A standard lamp stood in the corner, and a beautiful Victorian tiled fireplace acted as the focus of the room, with a mantelpiece above it that held four vintage pink glass candlesticks with white dinner candles.

Turning to the right, Bel walked into the little cottage kitchen, off the lounge, where she found a scrubbed pine kitchen table, a couple of mismatched chairs and a vintage blue leather chesterfield sofa. She ran her fingers over its aged, chipped texture in appreciation, taking in the rest of the room.

At one end of the kitchen there was an old-fashioned cast-iron range cooker, with a copper kettle sitting on top. At the other, where she stood, a gorgeous old Welsh dresser, full of vintage crockery, mostly mismatched. Bel was charmed by it all.

She opened the cupboards and peeked inside: pots, pans and cutlery were plentiful, as well as various crystal vases and serving plates she doubted she'd ever use. Reaching up to a cupboard at head level, she located tea bags and a packet of unopened biscuits. Finding a mug in another cupboard, she set it on the counter, picked up the kettle and took it to the sink where she filled it with water from the tap. After hunting around for matches for a moment, she found what she realised was a battery-powered stove lighter in a nearby drawer and lit one of the gas rings on the hob, placing the kettle on top of it and hoping she'd done it right.

In the fridge there was a pint of milk, just as Gretchen had promised, and next to the bread bin Bel found a handwritten note which said: *Loaf of bread and some buns in here. Enjoy, and welcome!*

She guessed the helpful neighbour must have written the note, and opened the bread bin, realising that she hadn't eaten anything since stopping at the motorway services hours ago, when she'd made herself eat a sandwich in slow, careful bites so she didn't pass out from hunger at the wheel.

Suddenly, her stomach rumbled, and Bel reached in to the bread bin for the paper bag containing buns. Taking one out greedily, she stuffed it into her mouth. It tasted of orange zest and butter; it was as soft as a cloud. Maybe it was because Bel was suddenly, ravenously hungry, but she couldn't remember tasting anything as delicious for a long time. *Hunger is the best sauce*, her dad used to say, her heart aching a little as she remembered his voice.

The kettle started to whistle, and she grabbed a tea towel so that she could take it off the hob safely, without burning her hand. There was no point in hurting herself. Today was quite enough, as it was.

Having made her tea, she sat down at the kitchen table and ate two more buns. Gradually, she started to take in what had happened that day.

She had lost her job, which she had hated.

She had found out that her long-term partner had been cheating on her, and she had left him after years of unhappiness.

She had left her home, which she liked, but which had also never felt like hers.

She was alone in a cottage in the middle of nowhere, wondering what the hell she was going to do now.

Bel laid her head on her arms on the table and wept.

THREE

Bel awoke to the sound of a lawnmower outside her window. She sat up in bed, her hair stuck to her face and her eyes puffy from crying herself to sleep the night before. She didn't remember what time she'd fallen asleep, but it was definitely past midnight. Even though she'd been exhausted from the Day From Hell, it had been difficult to turn her brain off last night. She presumed there had come a point when she'd just passed out.

There was an old-fashioned clock next to the bed: brass, with a round face and Art Deco numbers. Bel reached for her glasses, put them on and peered owlishly at it, waiting for her eyes to wake up and focus.

8.10 a.m.

'Are you kidding me?' Bel muttered as the lawnmower roar intensified and then quietened slightly. Someone was clearly outside in the little cottage garden, going from side to side, which would account for the way that the noise was almost cyclical. But it was way too early for mowing lawns. Wasn't there some kind of law about making noise before 9 a.m. in residential areas?

She wondered if she could ignore it and go back to sleep. She was still absolutely shattered from the day before, and only half awake. Bel lay back down and pulled the covers over her head, hoping the thick patchwork eiderdown would dampen the noise outside. However, after a couple of minutes of lying there and not sleeping, Bel realised that not only was she more awake than she'd been before, but that she was also absolutely livid about being woken up.

Now the lawnmower sounded as if it was idling right outside her window, and in the distance, just audible above the mower's chugging roar, she could detect voices.

'Right. That's it,' she muttered, throwing off the covers. Clearly, this person had absolutely no consideration for other people.

She hadn't given packing her bag much attention the day before, and she'd fallen asleep in a T-shirt and some of her big, comfy cotton knickers. She smoothed a hand over her curly brown hair and pulled on her robe, which was an old pink one with a teddy bear pattern.

Bel had worked in customer services for eight long years at HandyPhone, and not once in that time had she lost her temper with a customer. That was saying something, because Handy-Phone was a terrible company and its customers were often furious about the fact that they'd been billed incorrectly or couldn't upgrade their phone when they wanted to. Perhaps it was because Bel sympathised with the customers that she never really became annoyed by their complaints. She got it. She knew HandyPhone was terrible. They had every reason to complain. This innate calm in Bel meant that she was very good at her job, remaining stoic in the face of sometimes virulent abuse at the other end of the phone. Sally might have thought she was a dreamer, but being calm was often a very good thing.

It was also a quality she had exercised all those years with Andy, as he complained about everything. Andy, for whom something was always wrong, whether it was his back, his neck, the bed being the wrong kind of hard or soft, his soup too cold, his jeans just that little too short.

But, right now, Bel had had enough.

She charged out of the bedroom with its quaint painted cast-iron bedstead, patchwork quilt and soft floral flannel sheets that had felt so comfy to get into the night before. Flinging the front door open, she stalked outside and down the little paved pathway. There was a lawn at the front of the cottage that now looked neat and freshly mowed – it had looked rather more overgrown when Bel had arrived the night before, now she came to think about it – but there was no one to be seen.

Incensed, Bel followed the grass around the corner of the cottage into the garden behind it, which was surprisingly large and filled with an explosion of wild flowers, rose bushes and various other blooms and shrubs Bel couldn't identify. She'd never been much of a gardener. It had always seemed like a nice thing to be good at, but she'd never had the time, or anyone to teach her about plants. In fact, her dad had been a keen gardener, but he'd been gone a long time now. Bel felt her heart contract as it always did when she thought of him: the best man she'd ever known. Sometimes, she thought her dad was the *only* truly good man she'd ever known.

But it wasn't time to think about her dad now. In fact, Bel reflected briefly, if her dad had been there, he probably would have asked her what she was doing, half-dressed at 8.30 in the morning, furious at someone she'd never even met. *Cupcake, don't be hasty*, he might have said, raising a finger gently to admonish her impulsive nature. But her dad could never really tell her off – he was too kind-hearted, and he'd adored Bel.

She had been so different, before he died. Excitable, bossy, a little pouty when she didn't get her way – or argumentative when Sally tried to lay down the law. All that had died with him. It was as if Bel gave up any fight she had left.

But it seemed she still had some in her, after all.

The lawnmower, still ticking over, stood right outside her bedroom window. Bel felt rage wash over her again. How dare this person be so thoughtless as to leave it there? She scanned the garden, but it was empty. Following the sound of the voices, she crossed the lawn, realising that the garden wrapped around the whole cottage, and that there was another part to the other side.

'What the hell d'you think you're doing?' she interrupted the two men who stood at the side of the house.

One was an older man, perhaps six feet four or five, with a long ginger beard and longish scraggly hair. He was probably in his sixties, although Bel was bad at estimating ages, and looked for all the world like a Viking or a character from one of those big fantasy movies that were always on TV. The other man was younger, perhaps in his late thirties or early forties. He was leaning on a spade, his heavily muscled arm on display as he did so. He wore a once-white T-shirt, khaki work trousers and work boots. He was about six feet tall – not as huge as the Viking, but still a powerfully built man. He had a shorter beard – what was it with beards? Bel thought. Were all Scottish men sporting one nowadays? – but his head was shaved. Tattoos covered his arms, and she could see the edge of one on his neck, just under the neckline of his T-shirt. She had an unpredictable urge to turn back the roll of fabric and see what it was.

'Morning.' The man with the shaved head gave her a long, unsubtle look from head to toe, and smiled lazily at her. 'I'm doing the garden, like I always do. Every week. What are you doing?' He seemed, if not unsurprised by Bel's sudden appearance, then certainly to be taking it in his stride.

'You're mowing right outside my window. You woke me up! It's not even nine o'clock!' Bel raised her voice, still furious. She pointed at the bedroom, which featured the same old-fashioned blue-painted sash windows as the rest of the cottage. They looked pretty, but Bel knew from her dad's house, which had also been an old cottage, that they weren't that great at keeping noise or the cold out.

'I didn't know anyone was in. Gretchen didn't say anything.' The man stood up, stopping leaning on the spade.

'Well, I am. I arrived yesterday. It was all a bit last minute, I guess she didn't have time to tell you,' Bel snapped. 'But I had a very long day yesterday, and I'm very tired, and I'd really appreciate it if you could just go away and leave me in peace.'

'Well, I've got to finish the garden. It'll look weird if I leave this part unmown.' The man frowned at her. 'And then I was going to do some weeding and trim the hedge, sort out a few of the rose bushes. But I guess I can leave that until next time.' He shaded his eyes from the sun.

'I'd appreciate it if you did,' she replied sharply.

'Far be it from me to upset a lady.' A smile played at the edge of his mouth. 'Especially when you got all dressed up to come out and yell at me.'

'That's mature.' She put her hands on her hips and met his eyes, one eyebrow raised. 'Obviously, I'm in my dressing gown because – if I didn't make it clear just now – *you woke me up.*'

'Not a morning person, I see.' He raised his eyebrow in return. 'I wouldn't have someone like you down for teddy bears. You seem like more of a Tasmanian Devil type. Or perhaps a dominatrix.'

'Yes, in fact I've got a PVC catsuit on under here,' she replied drily. 'You got me. I've got a fifty-year-old City trader nailed to the wall in there.'

'That's why you're here, is it? Needed a remote location to torture men. In that case, I'd definitely better behave myself.' He broke into a sudden, wide smile.

But Bel couldn't return his jollity. She exhaled, thinking of the real reason she was standing in a remote Scottish village at this particular moment in time. She looked away, blinking back tears.

'No. That's not why,' she said shortly. 'Look, I'd just appreciate some quiet. Okay?'

'Okay. Sorry, I... I didn't mean to disturb you.' The man's smile faltered, and a flash of something – concern? – lit up in his eyes. 'I'm Christian McDougall, by the way.' He held out his hand.

'Oh. Isabel Burns. Bel.' She shook his hand, more as an automatic reaction than from any desire to be polite and play nice. She was still annoyed, but now she felt slightly on the back foot. If Christian really hadn't known she was there, she supposed she had no right to be angry with him.

'This is Angus. He lives in the cottage over there,' Christian added, nodding to the Viking. 'You guys are neighbours.'

'Oh, I see. Hello.' Bel shook Angus's hand too. She was rapidly feeling embarrassed about standing in the garden in her bare feet, wrapped in her aged bathrobe.

'Good mornin', Bel. Nice tae meet ye.' Angus gave her a twinkly smile, and she felt a little better. 'Welcome tae Loch Cameron. Sorry if we woke ye up. It willnae happen again, aye, Christian?' He raised a craggy eyebrow at the other man.

Christian held up both hands in mock defence. 'No, no, of course not. I'll come later next time. I just started doing Gretchen's old place first because it was empty. Now that I know you're here, I'll start somewhere else. I come every Thursday, just so you know,' he added. 'I don't want you to feel like I'm intruding. I'll try and fade into the background. You won't know I'm here.'

Bel thought that Christian, with his wide, thickly muscled shoulders and arms, shaved head, beard and tattoos, was incredibly unlikely to *fade into the background*, unless the background was a prison, a garage or a tattoo parlour. However, she nodded. 'Thanks,' she said, and re-tied the slightly ragged belt of her bathrobe, wanting something to do with her hands to stop herself feeling quite so embarrassed. 'Well... I'd better get back in.'

'Nice tae meet ye, dear. Pop by for a cuppa when ye have a minute.' Angus smiled warmly at her. 'Mine's the cottage with the green door. No numbers up on Queen's Point. I'm usually home.'

'Okay. Thanks, Angus.' Bel couldn't quite get her head around this being her reality for now – this time yesterday, she'd still been at work. It was as though she was in some kind of strange alternate-reality TV show she hadn't volunteered for. Like the ones where people went on the run for money.

I'm on the run from my life, she thought, as she walked around to the cottage's front door and closed it behind her. *Never mind the money.*

Oh, but she was tired.

Bel padded into the kitchen, made a cup of tea, ate the last bun from the bag and drank the tea. Then, she went back to bed.

This time, she slept.

FOUR

In the dream, Bel was standing at the edge of Loch Cameron.

On the loch, a small boat bobbed in the water. It was connected to a rope, and she held the rope in her hands.

As she pulled the rope and as the boat grew closer, Bel realised that the figure in the boat was her dad.

'I've missed you, cupcake,' her dad said. He was just as she remembered him: the same laugh lines around his eyes, the same kindness in his smile. The same tiredness written into his expression from the long years working in the biscuit factory. He'd started working there aged sixteen and had still been there when he'd died of a heart attack.

'I've missed you too, Dad,' she replied. In the dream, she felt the roughness of the rope in her hands, chafing her skin. She tried and tried to pull the boat ashore, but it wouldn't come.

'It's no good, cupcake,' her dad said. 'I've got to stay out here.'

'No, I think I can pull you back in,' Bel said, her arms straining. Her hands burned. 'I can do it.'

'Cupcake. You've got to let me go.'

. . .

'So, how's the cottage?' Sally placed a tray of coffee and cake on a low table between the two large black sofas in her and Bess's living room.

Unlike the cottage Bel was staying in, Sally and Bess lived in a new house development in a nearby village, Aberculty. Sally and Bess's house was spacious where the cottage was cosy, and modern and full of clean lines where the cottage was quaint. But Aberculty wasn't as picturesque as Loch Cameron, with the sweeping view over the loch Bel had from Queen's Point, and the fairy-tale castle on the other side. It had loomed in the mist that morning as Bel had driven slowly along the high street to get out of town.

'It's actually really nice. Good suggestion.' Bel took a mug of coffee from her sister and sipped it gratefully. She realised she was enjoying having the cottage to herself. As much as she loved her house, she hadn't felt at home there for a long time. *It was Andy's show home*, she thought. *But the cottage is a home. I felt it as soon as I walked in.*

'I need to go to the shops, though,' Bel added. 'Get some supplies in.'

She was trying not to think about her dream. Bel and Sally's dad had died ten years ago, and Bel still missed him every day. He'd been their rock, and when he'd died Bel knew that it had contributed towards her falling into Andy's arms. Without her dad, she'd felt rootless. There was suddenly a hole in her life, a space where once there had been someone who supported her, who was there for her. With him gone, she'd fallen for Andy, the first man who had been nice to her. *And I shouldn't have*, she thought.

'Hmm. There's a village shop in Loch Cameron where you should be able to get the basics. Or we can drive to an out-of-town supermarket if you want more. Depends how long you're staying.' Sally raised an eyebrow. 'You haven't really explained what happened between you and Andy. Not that I'm not happy to see you, obviously.'

'I know. I'm sorry for coming out of the blue.' Bel smiled as Bess walked into the room, leant forward and kissed Bel on the forehead. 'Especially with all the building work going on. Bad timing on my part.'

Bess tutted. 'You don't exactly plan a breakup to coincide with the most convenient time for everyone else. Life happens. Glad you're here, though. We were worried.' She laid her hand on Bel's shoulder for a moment and gave her a wink. 'Your sister hardly slept. I had to read her four chapters from *Murder on the Orient Express* to get her to nod off. At least our bedroom is the one place in the house that doesn't feel like a bomb's hit it.'

'Sorry. I'm okay.' Bel watched as Bess sat next to her sister, reaching for her shoulders and giving them a gentle rub. Bel wondered when the last time was that Andy had ever touched her so gently or kindly. She couldn't remember. He'd certainly never read to her in bed when she couldn't sleep. 'The house will be amazing when it's finished. I remember what it was like when we had the kitchen extension done.'

'I know. Worth the pain.' Sally rolled her eyes. 'I've decided I'm just not looking at the mess. There's no point trying to tidy up around the builders. Fortunately, they're some of Bess' mates so at least they're decent guys to have around. No arse cracks or sexist jokes.'

'That's good.' Bel smiled, trying to summon up positive vibes: Sally was the kind of person who became really excited about home improvements. Bel had always thought that must have been part of why she was attracted to Bess in the first place, being the local handywoman.

'Yeah. But we're not here to talk about that.' Sally returned her attention to her sister. 'Come on. What's happened?'

'Well, I've left him. In a nutshell.' Bel sighed, then recounted the events of the day before. 'I just didn't know where else to go,' she finished, lamely. 'I just knew I had to get out of there.'

'That damn...' Sally swore under her breath. 'How dare he cheat on you?!'

'I know. It's crappy.' Bel took a long gulp of coffee. 'I just wonder if I could have done something different... Is it my fault, somehow?'

'God, no. I never thought he was good enough for you, Bel.' Bess leaned forward and took a slice of cake. 'You know that. He was never very attentive. So critical of you, too. And I've never forgiven him for that time we were visiting, remember? And Sal had her bad back? You had to make him give up your bed for us. He wanted her to sleep on that bloody futon. No one puts Boo on a futon.' Bess stroked Sally's forearm gently, as Sally smiled at the memory.

'I know. I was so angry at him too, that time.' Bel shook her head. 'It's like he was at the back of the queue when they handed out the book on how to be a gentleman.'

'I don't think he ever got that book, babe.' Bess shook her head. 'Damn, even *I* got it. And I wasn't in the damn queue.'

As if he knew they were talking about him, a text from Andy flashed up on her phone.

We need to talk. When are you coming home?

She turned the phone over and set it to silent.

'Is that him?' Sally asked.

Bel nodded. 'He wants to talk. I don't.' Hurt bloomed in Bel's heart like a bruised rose. It was just so painful; she was still in shock, even though she'd had some sleep and she was far away from Andy now. She looked down at her hands. 'I don't know what I'd say.'

Bess snorted. 'Fair enough. I wouldn't want to talk to him either. Apart from to give him a few home truths.'

'Yeah. But she has to be practical, babe.' Sally turned to Bess. 'They own that house together. Bel, you don't want to leave him alone in it too long. Before you know it, he thinks it's his. You've got equal stakes there. That's your money.' She turned back to Bel with concern in her eyes.

'I know. I just need some time to think.' Bel looked up. 'What with losing my job on the same day... I mean, you hear about this kind of thing, but you don't think it's going to happen to you.'

'Yeah. It's spectacularly bad luck,' Bess agreed. 'But you did hate that job.'

'I did.' Bel sighed, taking a piece of cake, a lemon drizzle, which was delicious. 'But it's still weird not to be there. I feel... sort of pointless.'

She thought about how a rose looked when you had stomped on it: the way the soft, velvety petals browned and stained. Something so beautiful, spoiled so quickly. Not that she thought of herself as beautiful, or that her life had been particularly wonderful, either. But, spoiled, nonetheless.

'Nice, isn't it? Crochet coven.'

Bess watched Bel take a bite of the cake. 'Crochet coven?' Was Bess in some kind of rural cult she hadn't known about?

'My crochet group. We meet every week, sell lunch for the community, raise a bit of money for the mother and baby group, have a chat, do some crochet,' Bess explained.

'Oh! I see. Amazing.' Bel took another bite. 'It's yummy.'

'Yeah. June made that one. You'd love her. Ex-nurse, all business, apart from she's got a heart of gold. Listen, didn't you used to do hairdressing? Why don't you go back to that?' Bess leaned forward, pouring herself a coffee from the cafetiere.

'Yes, that's a good idea,' Sally agreed. 'You could get a job in a salon again. You used to enjoy it.'

'I did, but that was so long ago,' Bel protested. 'I haven't worked in a salon for years. I'm too old to be a junior again.'

'Just a thought. I mean, I know you kept it up on the side, or at least, you used to. It's been a while since you cut my hair.' Sally raised an eyebrow. 'Remember when you used to dye it rainbow colours? You did it for me for Pride a couple of times.'

'Yeah. That was fun.' Bel smiled sadly, unable to shake her feelings of grief. 'Took hours though, didn't it?' In fact, she'd always cut hair, if people asked. She did regular haircuts for quite a few people she worked with. She cut Andy's mum's hair every month, and once every couple of months she volunteered at a homeless shelter giving free haircuts as part of a local Back to Work programme. She didn't mind not being paid. It was just something she could do, so she did it.

She turned over her phone and saw there were three missed calls from Andy.

We need to talk, he'd repeated.

'Him again?' Sally asked, raising her eyebrow.

'Yeah. We need to talk, apparently.' She hugged her arms around herself in a protective gesture.

'Do you want to talk to him?' her sister asked.

'No.'

'Don't, then.' Sally shrugged. 'Talk to him when you're ready. It doesn't have to be on his timetable.'

'Well, you know what, he didn't want to *talk* when he was banging whoever-she-was in our house.' She got up and started pacing around.

'Exactly. You don't have to talk to him until you're ready,' Bess agreed. 'You can block him on your phone. You can unblock him when you want to.'

'Maybe. He'll lose it if I do that, though.' Bel stopped pacing and picked up her phone. She considered calling Andy back, but then she thought about how she had felt when that woman had walked into her kitchen, just wearing a towel, and she put the phone back on the table. No. He could wait.

'Then he loses it,' Bess said, her voice steady. 'Andy's

emotions are not your responsibility, Bel.'

'Or his lack of ability to control his emotions,' Sally added. 'He's like... a big grown-up child. What did he think you were going to do when you walked in and found him with another woman? Why is it up to you to be reasonable? Bloody men.'

'Also, I hated that job. Placating angry phone customers who were perfectly within their rights to be angry about a crappy company. Andy always implied I should stay there, because it was reliable. I don't know why I did... I guess I got used to listening to him. Thinking he was right...' Bel started to cry. Emotions welled up inside her, needing an outlet.

'Bel. Hey. It's okay.' Sally enveloped her in a hug. 'Oh, bless your heart. Come on. Let it out.'

Bel sobbed into her sister's shoulder, overwhelmed with bitter tears. She couldn't stop thinking about her cubicle at HandyPhone, and the long years she'd spent in it, her view obstructed by its high blue partitions, hating her life but not doing anything about it. It was such a *waste*. That was the feeling. She'd wasted years of her life in that cubicle and she'd wasted a similar amount of time in a relationship that felt exactly the same. Restrictive. Boring. Dead.

'You guys probably needed to talk for a long time. But you avoided conflict. It's easier to sit side by side on the sofa every night and binge-watch one detective series after another, never have sex and resent each other, right? Eventually, though, you can't do that anymore. Be grateful you're moving past it. Let him go, if that's your choice,' Sally said as she rubbed circles on her sister's back.

'But get half the house,' Bess added. 'Sal's right about that. So, maybe play nicey nicey for now until you get that sorted.'

'That's good advice,' Sally agreed.

'I know,' Bel said, muffled in Sally's shoulder.

Sally was right. Life had a way of bringing the pain, even if you tried to avoid it.

There had been signs that things were wrong between Bel and Andy, but she had ignored them.

Andy and his suitcase at the airport had been a sign. Andy losing his temper and kicking a panel loose in the bathroom door because she'd bought the wrong size bath mat had been another sign, but Bel hadn't listened. So, she guessed she'd had to walk in to that fiasco yesterday. Because, otherwise, she would have gone on and on with her life with Andy and HandyPhone – and it wasn't a good life, she could see that. She'd known it for some time. She wasn't an idiot. But it had all just sort of crept up on her when she wasn't looking.

Her dad had died. Sally was away working, and Bel didn't feel as if she had anyone to lean on. And then Andy had come along, being sweet. She'd been a junior hairdresser at the time, and he'd come in to get a haircut. He'd made her laugh.

In fact, after she'd met Andy, she'd had a very vivid dream about her dad. She had dreamt that she was standing at the end of an aisle in a church, in a wedding dress. Andy was waiting at the front of the church. Her dad stood next to her. He'd said, *Do you really want to do this, cupcake?* And she'd said, *No.* She'd woken up next to Andy, her heart beating wildly. Yet when Andy had asked her to buy a house together, she'd said *yes*, feeling unmoored from reality.

Bel had always believed that her dad had become her guardian angel since he'd died, and that he sent her signs. If she followed the signs, she felt as though she was taking the right path. Sometimes, if she didn't follow the signs, then her dad had a way of shouting louder until Bel took notice. That dream was one of the times she should have listened to her dad. But she hadn't.

'The thing is, even though I hated HandyPhone... and Andy and I weren't happy... I just feel kinda like... I lost it all, you know? Everything you're supposed to have. The house. The job. The man. What have I got now? Nothing.' Her voice broke and she started crying again. At least, before yesterday, she had felt like her life was together. She knew who she was.

'Babe. Come on. You haven't got nothing. You've got exactly what you had yesterday, which is yourself. No one can ever take that away from you.' Bess joined them in the hug. 'And you've got us. Always.'

'And, look, a relationship is nice, but it's not the goal.' Sally smoothed Bel's hair back from her forehead and looked her sister in the eye. 'Love should be something you find with yourself first.'

'Easy for you to say. You guys are rock solid.' Bel wiped her eyes with her sleeve.

'Right, but that didn't just happen overnight,' Sally replied. 'We worked at our relationship. I'm not saying you didn't work on yours either, but...' she trailed off. 'I guess what I'm saying is, it's possible that you could spend some time being there for yourself for a while. Okay? Maybe that would be a good thing.'

'I agree, Bel.' Bess let go of Sally and Bel, and picked up her coffee with a sigh. 'Spend some time with us. Hang out in the village. Let yourself just be for a while. We've got you, okay? Get to know who you are again.'

'I don't want to go home. So, okay. I guess I'm staying a while.' Bel sniffed, a smile lurking at the edge of her mouth. 'It's good to see you both, you know.'

'Are you kidding? Bess is so pumped you're here. Now she gets two of us to fuss over.' Sally rolled her eyes affectionately.

Bess elbowed Sally in the ribs and gave her a stern look.

'And I'm glad, too. I missed you, little sis,' Sally added, in a dutiful tone. But, she smiled, too.

'I missed you too,' Bel admitted with a smile. It was good to be with Sally and Bess, despite the fact that she and her sister could butt heads from time to time: she still felt safe and *held*, somehow, there. Held in a way that she realised no one had done for a very long time.

FIVE

'Mornin'.' The young woman behind the counter looked up as Bel walked in, a friendly expression on her face.

'Morning,' Bel replied, not particularly wanting a conversation. She walked to the racks of clothes and started idly flicking through them. She'd brought a few outfits, but only one pair of pyjamas and no summer shoes. She'd also only packed four pairs of knickers. So, when she'd been walking along Loch Cameron's little cobbled high street and seen Fiona's Fashions, she'd realised it might be necessary to do a little shopping.

She'd got up that morning and wondered what to do with herself. She could call Andy and talk about the state of their relationship, but the idea filled her with dread. She considered watching TV all day in her pyjamas, which was appealing, but as the sun streamed through the windows of the little cottage, Bel thought, *Wouldn't it be nicer to go out? Just a walk or something. Get a coffee and then think about what the hell I'm going to do with my life.*

As soon as she'd left the cottage and felt the morning sun on her skin, she knew she'd made the right decision. The light glinted on the loch and set off a million sparkles on its flat, silky surface; so much that Bel had to shade her eyes from its diamond brilliance. It was absolutely breathtaking. Here and there, boats bobbed on its surface – from such a distance, Bel couldn't tell whether they were fishing boats or just people out to take in the views.

Queen's Point, with its white stone cottages and gardens full of wildflowers, had a calm quality that Bel wanted to breathe in. Perhaps it really was the air that made her feel so centred: it was so clean and fresh that she felt as if she'd accidentally stumbled onto an exclusive spa resort. Birdsong filled the air, and the smell of roses wafted gently past her nose.

She'd walked down the narrow road from Queen's Point and found herself at the end of Loch Cameron's little high street. Walking along it, nodding a polite hello to the people she passed – people seemed to say *hello* here, even to strangers – she counted a butcher's shop, a bakery, a little bookshop – which she was tempted by, and decided she might pop in later – a shop selling whisky, Fiona's Fashions and a hairdresser's, Curl and Wave, which had a CLOSED sign in the window.

She had paused thoughtfully outside the hairdresser, looking in through its tall windows at the two sinks with black leather chairs, the rather tired black-and-white checkerboard tiles on the floor and the faded pictures of women's hairstyles in the window, which didn't look as if they'd been changed since the nineties.

Bel had loved working in a salon. Andy had been the one who had persuaded her to leave, and HandyPhone had come along as a stopgap until she found another hairdressing position. Eight years later, she had still been there. The money was better, and she'd been seduced by that, to some extent. But the real reason was that Andy didn't like her being a hairdresser, even though that was how they had met.

In the early days of their relationship, she'd been so flattered that he'd taken an interest in her that she'd figured she had to pay attention to what he said. *God knows why*, she thought crossly as she flicked through a rail of T-shirts. *He was a bloody idiot.* Yet back then she'd listened when he'd said, *Baby, I don't like the fact that you cut men's hair. You know they're just coming in because they want to sleep with you.*

She'd explained that she could ask just to cut women's hair. It was a unisex salon, but that was a possibility, even though she quite enjoyed cutting men's hair.

No, baby, I don't think you should be doing it at all, he'd said. *All that standing on your feet. The chemicals. It's not good for you. I'm just saying this because I care. Because I love you.*

Why? Why had she given up something she loved?

She knew why. She'd met Andy when her darling dad had passed away. Andy had been there in the darkest of days, holding her, cuddling her, letting her cry. He'd been such a rock and she'd been so grateful. And her confidence had been low. She'd been grieving. She'd needed someone, and there he was.

But as time went on, Bel realised that what she'd mistaken for support and kindness was really the fact that Andy loved her to be miserable, to have to depend on him. And he'd tried as hard as he could to keep her from feeling joy, all the time they were together.

Bel picked up a couple of packs of cotton panties and took them to the counter.

'Hi. I'm going to keep looking for some other things, but I'll take these. Can I leave them here?' she asked the young woman behind the counter.

'Sure, of course. What else're you lookin' for? I'll be able tae tell ye what we have.'

'Oh, right. Well, I guess I need a couple of casual outfits. Summer sandals that are comfortable. Ah... a hoodie, maybe? It gets cold sometimes.' Bel shrugged. 'I don't know. Maybe some other things, I'm kind of living by the seat of my pants right now. No pun intended.'

The young woman chuckled. 'No' a bad way to live, some-times. I'm Fiona, by the way. This is ma shop.'

'Oh, Fiona's Fashions Fiona?' Bel nodded. 'That's so cool. It must be fun, running your own business. I'm Bel. Just staying up on Queen's Point for a while.'

'The Ross cottage?' Fiona gave her a shrewd look.

'That's right. I guess there aren't many houses to rent for holidays in Loch Cameron.'

'Aye, an' it makes no sense. Apart from there's the Inn, o' course. People stay there. An' there's a campsite on the other side o' the loch. But, no' many rental properties for holidays and short stays. Most people have never heard of Loch Cameron, I suppose. An' the ones that do find it never want tae leave.' She chuckled again. 'Stayin' long?'

'I'm not sure yet. For a little while. I can see why people wouldn't want to leave. It's beautiful. If you don't mind me asking, though, it must be a little difficult running a business somewhere like this? There can't be that many people needing new boots or a new T-shirt? Or, are there? I don't know.' Bel leaned on the counter.

'Well, it's got its challenges, to be sure. But you'd be surprised. I have ma regulars, the locals. There's always someone needin' somethin'. An' I have a busy online shop too. So, a lot o' my business comes from that. Plus, the Laird's very good about givin' all of us business owners low rent, an' for the first couple o' years I was tradin' he gave me a grant.'

'The Laird?' Bel frowned. 'Oh, wait, I think I remember my sister talking about this. Lord Cameron. He owns the land, right?'

'Laird's what we say, but aye. The land's belonged tae the Camerons for hundreds o' years. He's the landlord for most o' the properties. He lives in the castle you'll have seen. Cannae miss it.'

'Hardly. It's like something out of a movie.' Bel smiled. 'I didn't realise someone actually lived in it.'

'Och, aye. Nice guy, too. No' that old. Fairly easy on the eye.' Fiona winked. 'Though, if yer thinkin' aboot tryin' yer luck, I'm afraid tae say he's got a very glamorous American girlfriend. Nice girl, mind ye, so we cannae hate her.'

'Oh, no. That's the last thing I'm thinking about.' Bel blinked, having temporarily put Andy to the back of her mind. It had felt good not to think about him for two minutes. 'Believe me,' she added with a sigh.

Fiona shot her a curious look. 'Anythin' ye want tae talk aboot? I know we're strangers, but I'm a good listener,' she said, her eyes crinkling at the corners.

'Oh gosh, that is kind. But you don't want to hear about my troubles.' Bel looked out of the window onto the high street, avoiding Fiona's eyes. She felt tears welling up and frantically willed them away. She didn't want to start blubbing in public.

'Well, I'm sorry there *are* troubles.' Fiona reached over and patted her hand. 'Look, if you're stayin' a while, you can always pop in for a chat. Sometimes it helps tae have an ear. Someone who isnae connected tae anythin'.'

'Thanks. I might take you up on that.' Bel wiped her eyes surreptitiously, hoping it wasn't obvious that her feelings had threatened to overtake her. 'I'm just here for a while. My sister is quite local, so I'm taking some time to hang out with her.'

It wasn't exactly a lie – Bel would be spending time with Sally and Bess. It just wasn't the main reason she'd come.

'Ah, that's nice. Live in the village, does she? Your sister?'

'No, but nearby. She and her partner live in Aberculty. Sally Burns.' Bel's full name was Isabel Burns. Her mother had liked Isabel, apparently, but her dad and Sally had always shortened it to Bel. And since Sally and Bel's mother had died when they were three, that was the way it had been, most of her life.

'Oh, Sally's your sister! Ah, that's great.' Fiona grinned.

'Well, in that case, I look forward tae seein' ye at our quiz night. The next one's on Sunday at the Inn. Yer sister always plays tae win, aye.' Fiona laughed.

'Oh, right. Yeah, she reads a lot. She was the smart one.' Bel smiled. 'I was the practical one. Good with my hands.'

'Aha. Well, I'm sure ye've probably got some quiz skills, aye? It's always fun. Gets pretty competitive, mind ye.' Fiona raised an eyebrow.

'I'm not surprised, if my sister has anything to do with it.' Bel changed the subject. 'So, there's a hairdresser's next door? I was thinking I might see if they had any scissors I could buy. I need to cut my hair.'

Bel had considered making an appointment, but she also had an idea that a little hairdresser in a remote Scottish village might not know how to deal with mixed race hair. Sally and Bel's dad had been black and their mum had been white. Both girls had brown hair and while Sally straightened hers, Bel's was curly. She wore it long, and often put golden blonde high-lights through it. She usually cut it herself, but she hadn't brought any hairdressing scissors with her. Plus, she was curious about the salon, in the way that a book lover would be interested in the little bookshop along the high street. Hair had always been her passion. How many locals came in for a trim or a perm or a fade, she wondered?

'Aye, Curl and Wave. They're hardly open, though. The lady that ran the salon, Bella, she got ill a couple of years ago. For a while she was only opening now and again. ME. Terrible thing. Some days she feels okay, but a lot of the time she can't leave the house. She's had tae let the salon go, now. Poor lamb.'

'Ah, I'm sorry to hear that,' Bel said. 'I've heard ME can be so difficult. And she had to close the business because of it too?'

'Aye. People understand, of course. But it means now that if ye want a hairdresser, ye have tae go to Aberculty. There's a barber there, but it's no good for ladies' hair. I've no' had a trim for about two years, an' I work next door.' Fiona tutted at her split ends. 'Just look at that. I'd do it myself, but I dinnae know what I'm doin'.'

'Well, I could do it for you,' Bel offered. 'I trained as a hairdresser. I still do cuts for my friends, here and there. If you want.'

'Really? Oh, that'd be grand!' Fiona beamed. 'Really? Ye wouldnae mind?'

'Not at all. I do need some proper scissors, though. I... I didn't pack any,' she said, not wanting to explain further. 'I'll get hold of some, I guess I could order some online? And come and do it for you.'

'That'd be amazing! An' I know quite a few ladies who'd want their hair doing too, if ye were interested. We'd pay ye, of course.'

'I guess I could.' Bel was slightly taken aback – she'd gone into Fiona's Fashions for a few new pairs of knickers and a warm hoodie. She hadn't expected to be offered work at the same time.

'Well, maybe ye should take over the salon! Then I could come in for a cut whenever I wanted!' Fiona chuckled. 'It's available to rent. Very fair rates. The Laird supports small businesses, like I said.' She gave Bel an appraising look.

Bel blinked in surprise at the suggestion. 'Oh, no. I'm just here to see my sister. I couldn't do that.'

'Why not?' Fiona asked. 'Think big.'

'Well, I couldn't just... up sticks and move here forever.' Bel frowned. So far, everything she'd done had been in a panic. She was literally in Fiona's shop because she didn't have enough knickers to get her through the week, never mind the presence of mind to start a business. Yet, as soon as the idea was in her head, she loved it. For a second, she allowed herself to imagine running the little salon. Two sinks, two stations: just enough room for her, and maybe an assistant.

The idea of being her own boss lit a fire of excitement in her stomach.

'Well. Never say never.' Fiona shrugged. 'I took a chance on this place an' it was the best thing I ever did.'

'Well, I'm not planning to stay.' Bel thought about her house back in Essex. Sooner or later, she'd have to go back. It was her home. Or, at least, it had been.

'Aye, well,' Fiona raised an eyebrow, 'life's what happens when we're busy makin' plans, so they say.'

'I can't argue with that.' Bel felt her phone buzz in her pocket. She took it out and looked at it.

BEL. PLEASE CALL ME. WE NEED TO SORT THIS OUT.

She sighed. 'Sorry, Fiona. I've got to take this,' she said, and pushed the shop door open to make the call in the street. Now was a good a time as any to talk to Andy, she supposed: there was never going to be a time when she felt eager to talk to him. Those days were over: in fact, they had been over for a long time.

She screwed up her courage and pressed the call button.

SIX

'Bel. Thank God. Are you okay?' Andy's voice was fractured and tired.

'I'm fine.' Bel looked out over the glassy, calm loch in front of her, drawing a sense of peace from its presence. She didn't ask how he was. She didn't want to know.

'I thought... you might have done something stupid,' he said. 'I was worried. I didn't know where you were going.'

'I'm fine. I'm with Sally and Bess,' she said, instantly irritated at his phrase. *I thought you might have done something stupid.* Like she was some kind of brainless idiot.

Bel knew what he meant. He was worried she had killed herself.

Even though she was heartbroken by what had happened, the idea that Andy thought she would kill herself over losing him made Bel snort involuntarily. It just showed that he didn't know her at all. Not that she didn't have the utmost sympathy with people who were driven to such extremes of misery, but the idea that Andy thought his infidelity was enough to make her lose the literal will to live struck Bel as utterly ridiculous. It was as if she had walked into the freezing waters of the loch and they had awoken her from her shock and sadness.

And that's one more reason why you should have ended that relationship a long time ago, she told herself. *Because, actually, you're not heartbroken about losing Andy. And you also don't miss your job at all. It was more that's what you thought your life was supposed to look like, and it was suddenly pulled out from under you.* She stared out over the loch. *That's what it is. That's what I feel.*

'Oh. Good, I'm glad.' Andy let out an audible breath. 'Bel. I'm so sorry you saw... what you saw. The other day.'

'You're sorry I saw, or sorry you did it?' she shot back, feeling the power of the loch course through her. Even though she was standing on the shore, she felt as though she as somehow drawing power from the water, up through her feet and into her body. There was a steadiness in Loch Cameron that helped her feel grounded. And when she took in a deep breath of the clean air, she felt it untangle her jumbled thoughts.

'You know what I mean. Don't make this harder,' he sighed.

'I'll make it as hard as I want to, thanks,' Bel replied, levelly. 'I lost my job and came home to find you having sex with another woman. Tell me what I should go easy on you for. I'm listening.'

'Don't be like that, Bel. You must have known,' he said, weakly. 'We haven't been happy for a while.'

'Of course I didn't know!' Bel raised her voice, pacing up and down the high street outside the closed hairdressing salon. As she paced, she looked through its windows, at the dated mirrors and the cracked vinyl countertops. The whole place was crying out for renovation. 'How was I supposed to know you were cheating on me? What, you thought I knew, but I was just carrying on, not saying anything? What kind of monster would that make me?'

'Fine, whatever. You didn't know. But you knew we were both unhappy,' Andy insisted. 'And you didn't do anything about it.'

'Yes. We were unhappy. I was unhappy. I am unhappy.' Bel was glad, though, that as she spoke to Andy it was anger that was carrying her through, not sadness. Anger made her feel strong. 'And, no, I didn't do anything about it apart from try to make it work. Try to be happy. Try to be who you wanted me to be.'

'I never wanted you to be anyone other than yourself,' Andy protested. 'Who did I want you to be?'

'Oh, come on,' Bel raised her voice, irritated. 'You never liked me hairdressing. You didn't like it if I expressed an opinion other than agreeing with you. You made me stay at HandyPhone.'

'I never made you do anything you didn't want to do, Bel,' Andy argued. 'You're an adult. You could have got another job anytime you wanted. And I didn't make you give up hairdressing. But you have to admit you made more money at Handy-Phone. And you didn't have to be on your feet all day, with your hands in strange men's hair.'

There it was. That same jealousy there had always been. Jealousy that was completely unwarranted: Bel had never been the flirtatious type. Andy had been her one long-term relationship, and even though it hadn't been a happy union for many years, she still hadn't looked elsewhere.

But now, it didn't matter anymore.

'Whatever. Why are you really calling me, Andy?' Bel gazed back out over the loch. A group of mallards dabbled in the reeds at the edge of the water, whilst, further out, a lone canoeist traversed the loch from one side to the other. She concentrated on breathing in and out steadily, feeling the clear air fill her lungs and clear her mind.

'Well, I wanted to check you were still alive,' he said,

humourlessly.

'I'm alive.'

'Fine. Well, in that case, what happens next? Are you coming back? Are we still together?'

'Are we still together? Are you mad?' Bel snorted incredulously, again. 'Do I really need to answer that?' The thought was ridiculous, and that, in itself, told her everything she needed to know. She didn't want to go back to Andy, even though she had lost everything. But the loss was her life, or the life she had thought she had. It wasn't him.

'I didn't know if you wanted to go to couples' counselling,' he said flatly. 'I would, if you wanted to.'

'No. I don't want to go to couples' counselling,' she said. 'I'm done.'

As soon as she said it, Bel felt a weight fall from her. She had needed to say that. She'd spent the past couple of days thinking about everything; she'd second-guessed herself so many times, thinking that maybe she should go back and try and rebuild what she'd lost. But, now, she knew she didn't want to.

'I'm done,' she repeated, feeling the truth of the words. 'It's over, Andy. And I want to sell the house. Or you can buy me out of it, either way. But half of that house belongs to me, and I want it. As soon as possible.'

There was silence at the end of the line.

'Bel... you know I don't have that kind of money just lying around,' he said after a long pause. 'Don't be stupid. I can't just produce that because you ask for it.'

'Then we'll have to sell the house,' she said coolly. 'Your choice, Andy. But I'll be getting in touch with a solicitor, so that we can do this properly. And I'm not stupid. Goodbye.'

She ended the call, and looked back at the salon. For a moment she imagined herself inside, standing at the mirror, talking happily to a client. Salons had been her happy place, once.

Perhaps one could be, again.

SEVEN

'Question three. Which World War One poet also wrote the book *Memoirs of a Fox-Hunting Man*?' A spry older man, probably in his early seventies, read solemnly into the crackly microphone. He wore bottle-green cord trousers and a faded cream, red and mustard tartan shirt, open at the collar, with a pair of reading glasses halfway down his nose.

Bel was late for the beginning of the quiz, and slipped into a seat next to Sally just as the murmur of chatter rose, as the quiz teams discussed their answers.

'Sorry I'm late,' she whispered to her sister.

Sally waved her hand impatiently at Bel as she wrote down the answer on the quiz sheet. 'Siegfried Sassoon. Honestly, the questions are getting easier every month.' Sally tutted under her breath. 'Hi, Bel.'

'Hi, sweetie.' Bess gave her a peck on the cheek. 'Your sister'll become a better sibling and partner after the quiz is over. Drink?'

'I'll get one. What're you guys drinking?' Bel looked towards the bar, which was relatively quiet, since the quiz was in full swing.

'I'll have a glass of red, thanks. Sally's a diet coke.'

'You're not having wine, Sal?'

'Driving. Plus, got to concentrate.' Sally flashed her a brief smile.

'Right.' Bel took off her jacket and went to the bar. An elderly woman with a smart platinum bob smiled as she approached.

'What can I get ye, dear?' she asked.

Bel gave the drinks order and added a glass of white wine for herself.

'Haven't seen you before, have I?' the woman, wearing a lilac tweed skirt and a smart cream jumper with what looked like an amethyst brooch at the neck, enquired politely.

'No, I'm Sally's sister. Bel.' Bel pointed to Bess and Sally's table, where her sister was whispering something in Bess' ear. They were both giggling. 'Just here for a visit,' she added, vaguely.

Who knows how long I'm here for. I don't know what I'm doing.

'Oh, how lovely!' the woman exclaimed, beaming. 'I'm Dotty. I run the Inn here with Eric, ma fella. That's him up onstage, doin' the questions.'

'Oh, I see! Lovely to meet you, Dotty.' Bel's stomach rumbled; she hadn't had anything at the cottage that resembled a dinner. 'Could I have a couple of packets of crisps, as well? I'm starving.'

'Oh, no! We cannae have that. I'll get ye somethin'.' Dotty looked concerned. 'We've got sandwiches, chips, soup, that kindae thing.'

'A sandwich and some chips would be amazing, actually,' Bel confessed. Her stomach growled again, as if in agreement.

'I heard it that time! Sounds like ye got here just in time. Ham an' cheese do ye? I can put a bit o' salad in it if ye want. Or make it a ham an' cheese toastie.' Dotty laughed.

'Ham and cheese toastie and chips sounds perfect. Thanks, Dotty.' Bel was touched at Dotty's warmth.

'Nae bother. I'll bring it over for ye.' Dotty nodded. 'Ye much of a one for quizzes like your sister?'

'Not really. I just came to be sociable and get out of the house.' Bel handed Dotty some cash and surveyed the bar. 'Looks busy, though. Lots of competitive people in Loch Cameron, I guess.'

'Aye, indeed. Ten teams tonight,' Dotty explained with a nod. 'There's a cash prize an' a trophy. People get more het up about the trophy, it hastae be said.' Her eyes twinkled.

'Haha. I can imagine.' Bel knew what Sally was like if there was a potential trophy on offer. She'd been top of all the sports teams at school, whereas Bel had always been picked last. Art had been Bel's passion, or anything crafty, and whereas Sally had been super focused on sports and her studies, Bel was the one with hundreds of friends. Then, when she'd found hairdressing, she'd realised there was something she could do that utilised her artistic eye and let her work with people too.

The teams were varied. Some of them were two or three people, like Bess and Sally and her, but some seemed to comprise a whole gang. Bel noticed a large group in the corner who had pushed two tables together and were loudly debating the answer to something. They were mostly men, and Bel realised that many of them wore the same kind of leather jackets. They bore a slogan or badge of some kind, but she couldn't quite make out what it said.

Bel lowered her voice. 'Who are they?'

Dotty frowned. 'Hmm. That's the local motorcycle club,' she replied. 'They've been comin' to the quiz for the last few months.'

'Motorcycle club?' Bel stared at them again. Many of the men had tattoos and piercings; many wore beards. Mostly, they wore a uniform of jeans or leather trousers, dark T-shirts and the odd leather waistcoat. 'In Loch Cameron? I thought that was something out of American movies in the eighties.'

'No, dear, it's very much still a thing.' Dotty looked philosophical. 'I cannae say I approve of the way they look, or the noise they make when they ride through the village, but they havenae made any trouble... *as yet*.'

'Wow!' Bel didn't have quite the same preconceived notions of biker gangs as Dotty did, but she was surprised to see one out in force at the Loch Cameron Inn quiz night. Still, *it takes all sorts*, she thought: something her dad used to say.

She picked up Bess' wine and Sally's coke to take them back to the table and turned around, just as Christian McDougall walked up behind her.

'Agh!' she blurted out, watching helplessly as the top inch of coke splashed out of the glass and onto her jeans. She swore, then blushed at Christian's surprised expression. This was the second time they'd met, and she'd been angry both times. She wasn't exactly making a great impression, even though of course she didn't care about making a good impression on Christian McDougall.

'Oh, no... I'm sorry!' he chuckled. Carefully, he reached out and took both glasses from her and set them back on the bar, picking up a paper napkin from a pile and handing it to her. 'There. It's not a big spill. You'll be okay.'

'I know that. Goodness.' Bel was thrown off balance by his tone. Was he being patronising? Her time with Andy had made her hypersensitive to that. He had just the day before called her stupid. She wasn't stupid, and she didn't need to be patronised by some big oaf in a pub in Loch Cameron, of all places. Who, Bel realised, was wearing a black T-shirt with the same logo as the biker gang in the corner.

'Well, I just meant it's okay. You haven't ruined your outfit. You still look very pretty.' He cleared his throat and looked away, and Bel wondered if he'd meant to say that. 'Christian.

We met the other day, at your cottage? I had the lawnmower that was too loud.'

'I remember.' She frowned, rubbing the wet spot on her thigh with the napkin.

'So, you're here for the quiz?' he asked, leaning on the bar.

Bel couldn't help notice his huge biceps and muscled forearms, though she looked away quickly. 'Just keeping my sister and her wife company. You?'

'With some friends,' he said, turning to give his order to Dotty. 'Ten pints of shandy, thanks, Dotty.' He turned back to Bel. 'Otherwise, we'll never get on the bikes,' he added.

'So, you're in a biker gang?' Bel asked. She had to admit she was a little curious.

'Yeah. A few years now.' He looked over at the men in the corner and grinned. 'It's fun. Good guys.'

'What do you actually do? Dotty seems to think you ride around terrorising the neighbourhood.'

'Ha. Hardly. We go on rides – the landscape's stunning around here, so there are some great routes. All across Scotland, really. We talk about engines a lot. Various charity activities. Hang out. It's a community thing, really.'

'I remember hearing that bike gangs had criminal connotations. You know, all those seventies movies,' she said, Dotty's comments in her mind.

'Are you asking if I'm a criminal?' Christian raised his eyebrow.

'No. That would be rude.' Bel felt a blush stealing up her neck and onto her cheeks.

'Yes, it would,' he agreed, a smile tugging at the edge of his mouth.

'And I'm not a rude person,' she added. 'Admittedly, I was a bit rude the other day. I was just really tired. I didn't have the best day, beforehand.'

'Sorry to hear that.' He picked up a square beer mat and

picked at the edge of it. 'And don't apologise. I'm a bear if I get woken up early too,' he grinned, and Bel was struck by how his whole face changed. Christian was a man who, if you didn't know him or speak to him, looked like someone you wouldn't want to meet in a dark alley. Or a well-lit one. But when he smiled, a goofy expression lit him up and Bel had to grin back. 'Though, I have to say, you are a much scarier morning bear than me.' He made a growling sound and made claw-like shapes with his hands.

'*You* have a bear-like quality about you,' she said, suddenly reckless and oddly swept along in Christian's silliness. '*I* definitely do not.'

'No, maybe not now,' he conceded with a shrug. 'Now, you're a beautiful lady panther or something. Yesterday morning: Grizzly Bear. Though I do recall you were wearing pink pyjamas or something.' He giggled. 'Now I'm judging myself for still being intimidated.'

Dotty had been filling two round drinks trays with pints of brown shandy – bitter, topped up with lemonade – and she cleared her throat as she placed the last one down.

'There you are, dear. Will there be anything else?' she asked politely, interrupting their conversation.

'Well, I better get back,' Bel picked up the drinks again. No one had ever called her a *beautiful lady panther* before. That was definitely a first. Was Christian flirting with her, or were they just having a nice conversation? She'd never been able to tell when people were flirting. Maybe that was what had annoyed Andy so much when she was hairdressing. She'd always just thought people were being nice, talking to her, having a bit of a laugh and a joke while she cut their hair. That was all part of getting your hair cut, just like asking about people's holidays.

Christian was paying for the drinks. 'Right. Good luck.'

As she walked away, she looked back briefly. It was instinct;

she wanted to look at him. He was an attractive man, in a rough and ready kind of way. She'd never really been attracted to that type before, but she found herself letting out a sigh as she gazed at his muscular back under the tight T-shirt.

Bel set Sally and Bess' drinks on the table and sat down herself before she realised she'd left her glass of wine on the bar.

'You've missed the whole round!' Sally hissed. 'What were you doing up there?'

'Forgot my drink. Hang on,' Bel muttered, and went back up to the bar to get it.

'Just getting my wine,' she waved at Dotty.

'Nae bother, dear.' Dotty came over and leaned over the bar slightly conspiratorially. 'I saw ye havin' a good blether with that Christian,' she said, a little expectantly.

Bel wondered what she was supposed to say – *yes, and he called me a beautiful panther, which was unexpected but nice*? She nodded instead.

'He does the gardens up on Queen's Point. I was just saying sorry because I was a bit rude to him the other morning. That's where I'm staying, in the rental cottage.'

'Oh, I see. In the Ross cottage, aye. No, dear, I was just wantin' tae say, be careful with that one. There've been some funny goin's on in the village since that gang have been around, an' I wouldnae want a nice girl like you getting' caught up with the wrong types. If ye know what I mean.' Dotty gave Christian and his friends a quick, arch glare.

'Funny goings-on?' Bel frowned, wanting to know more, but a group of people came to the bar; Bel realised that Eric, Dotty's husband, had announced an interval. Dotty looked like she was going to say more, but got called away to serve the queue that had formed rapidly. Bel took her glass of wine back to the table where Sally greeted her with a frown.

'We could have used you while you were gossiping at the bar,' she tutted.

'Ignore your sister. She's just cross because the bike gang are thrashing us,' Bess announced cheerily. 'Was that one of them you were talking to? Sleeping with the enemy, is it?'

'Hardly. He didn't give me any of the answers, if that's what you mean.' Bel sipped her white wine.

'Did he give you his number?' Bess asked.

Sally nudged her with her elbow. 'Hey! She doesn't need some guy's number. She's going through a traumatic breakup.' Sally turned to Bess. 'He didn't, did he?'

'No.' Bel looked over at the tables in the corner where Christian was laughing at something one of his friends had said.

He looked up for a moment, as if knowing her gaze was on him, and their eyes met. Bel blushed, and looked away. But not before there had been a spark of connection between them.

'Uh-oh.' Bess followed Bel's line of sight, noticing the slight blush on her cheeks and the way she'd looked down, hurriedly. 'You wouldn't mind if he did, though, would you?'

'I would. Well, I wouldn't care, either way,' Bel protested.

Sally looked scandalised, but Bess just laughed.

'Oh, Miss Isabel,' she chuckled. 'There's hope for you yet.'

EIGHT

Fine. You win. I can buy you out.

It was a brief text, but it made Bel stop in her tracks as she walked over the quaint blue painted iron bridge that led to the grounds of Loch Cameron Castle. That morning, Bess had offered to meet her at the castle; she'd suggested they take one of the castle tours together. The castle wasn't always open to tourists, apparently, but it was at the moment, and Bess had the morning free. As she was self-employed, doing painting and decorating, plumbing and electrics jobs for people in the local villages, she tended to have a more flexible work schedule than Sally.

What? She looked at the text again. It *was* from Andy. Did he really mean that?

It had been a week since their phone call, and since then Bel had heard nothing. That hadn't been a bad thing: she *welcomed* hearing nothing from Andy. She had been sleeping in each day, making herself nice breakfasts and eating them in the garden, looking up the flowers on a nature identification app she'd downloaded onto her phone. The weather had been unusually sunny the whole week, and so by the time midmorning came around, the cottage garden was an absolute sun trap.

Slowly, Bel had been recovering from the shock of that one day where she had lost everything. Those small daily rituals – breakfast, walks, nature, the clean air of Loch Cameron – had been helping her come back to herself. There was still some way to go, though, because she felt as though she had forgotten who Isabel Burns really was.

Are you serious? Bel replied to Andy. Out of interest, she'd looked on a property website the day before and compared the value of similar properties to hers and Andy's. Since they'd done the kitchen extension and renovated the rest of the house, plus the fact that the housing market in their area seemed to be doing well, it was worth a decent amount more than they'd paid for it five years ago. Bel tapped out a number which represented half of what she estimated the equity in the house to be, and followed it with a question mark.

Not too far off that. My solicitor has advised this much, he replied, following it with a number not too different to the one Bel had just sent.

She stopped in the middle of the bridge, taking in a breath. It was a pretty large sum.

I'll continue with the mortgage in my name only, if we do this, Andy messaged. *You'd sign the house over to me. I buy you out with this much, and that's it.*

She replied, cautiously.

I'll need to get a solicitor my end before I formally agree to anything. But, in principle, let's proceed.

She didn't know what had prompted Andy to do this, but she wasn't going to look a gift horse in the mouth, as her dad used to say. Andy had relatives who may have been able to help him out with a loan: his family were quite well-to-do.

If you're sure that you aren't coming back, then it seems the sensible thing, he replied. *At least we're not married.*

Be grateful for small mercies, Bel thought and raised an eyebrow, looking up as a car hooted at her from behind. She realised she was standing in the middle of the bridge, and stood aside to let the car pass. She waved apologetically; the man behind the wheel of the Jeep gave her a friendly wave back.

That morning, over her coffee and toast, she'd been worrying about how much longer she could stay at the cottage without having a job. Now, everything had changed. Or, possibly, depending on whether Andy changed his mind or not. She didn't like the fact that her fate could depend on his decisions but, she reminded herself, it didn't have to. She was still in charge of her life.

She started walking again, following the signs for the footpath up to the castle. On the other side of the bridge, tall bushes hid what Bel assumed were private castle grounds, and a well-kept gravel pathway curved along the edge of the loch. She took it, admiring the view over the loch to the village which was now on the other side.

It was such a cute little village. The Loch Cameron Inn was bedecked with colourful hanging baskets, and the railings alongside the loch also held long baskets of trailing flowers. From where Bel was, she could also see the tiny village primary school and the community centre next to it; she could even spy her cottage up on Queen's Point, along with the rest of the little houses that were arranged slightly higgledy-piggledy on the raised promontory over the village.

From this distance, she could also see Fiona's Fashions and the closed hairdressing salon, Curl and Wave, next door. She pondered the salon as she walked along the gravel path, making a turn up some steps – *100 steps to Loch Cameron Castle* – according to a wooden sign.

She climbed, taking in the view. A cloudless blue sky caressed the grey turrets of the castle ahead of her which slowly appeared. To her left, ornamental gardens swept downwards towards the loch, with topiary trees cut into the shapes of animals: a squirrel faced a deer, and to its left, a swan looked on. There were rows of sharply trimmed privet hedges, in intricate patterns, and in the squares and triangles created between the hedges, evergreen trees spread their branches. Wide stone steps led down from the terrace outside the patio and, at the bottom of a grassy hill, joined a long stone wall that ran around the whole edge of one side of the castle.

A path with steps led down through the centre of the gardens. Bel wondered what it must be like to live in an actual castle, and to have those gardens to look out on every day. *Pretty sweet*, she thought.

What Bel was also thinking was that she could buy the salon. Or, rent it, since Fiona had said that most places were rented from the Laird. As long as Andy was serious about buying her out of the house, then she'd have a lump sum coming to her soon that would be more than enough to cover rent and get a business up and going.

She neared the top of the steps and took a minute to turn and look back over the view. *I could live here*, she thought, as wild as that was. Just a week or so ago she'd been living in Essex and thinking her life was never going to change. Now, as she stood with the wind buffeting her hair, staring out over Loch Cameron to the far purple and green hills on the horizon, she realised with a jolt that her life *had* changed and, now, anything was possible.

You are in the new timeline, she thought to herself, repeating something she'd read on social media. A tarot reader she followed had put up a new post that morning. *You are in the new timeline. You have made the shift. You have changed your reality. Don't doubt yourself now.*

Above her, hawks circled in the morning sky, their cries ringing out across the loch. *Dad. Is that you?* she wondered.

She'd dreamt about her dad again the night before. This time, he'd been making tea in the cottage kitchen. She'd dreamt she'd woken up and walked in, finding him spooning loose tea into the porcelain teapot with the sprigged flower pattern.

Hello, cupcake. Thought you'd like some company, he'd said, smiling at her.

In the dream, she had the same thought she always did when she saw her dad – that she thought she'd never see him again, and yet here he was. There was such relief in that feeling; it was so good to see his face again.

She'd woken up as he'd handed her a porcelain cup of tea, smiling. His words stayed with her as she'd got up: *I'm always here for you, Bel.*

Bel jogged up the final steps that opened out onto a long gravel drive, leading to the castle. With the dream still fresh in her mind, she felt him with her still, and it was a nice feeling. She believed he would have approved of her new plan.

NINE

'Morning, petal.' Bess gave her a peck on the cheek and a hug. 'Lovely day for it. I think you brought the sunshine with you from down south.'

'Well, I don't think it has anything to do with me, but thanks,' Bel grinned. 'Thanks for taking the tour with me too. I always fancied having a look around Loch Cameron Castle.'

'No bother. I've never actually had the formal tour. Been up here a few times, with the May Day Party and various shindigs over the years.' Bess hefted her backpack over her shoulder as they approached the castle's heavy wooden doors. 'But Hal doesn't keep it open a lot of the time. It's his home, so I doubt he wants nosey tourists looking in his bathroom cabinets that much. Plus, I've got to stay out of the house today. They're pouring the new concrete floor.'

'Oh. Sounds right up your street. Didn't you want to stay and help?'

'Nah. Rather spend some quality time with my sister-in-law.' Bess gave Bel a squeeze as they walked along. She'd always been more affectionate than Sally, even though Sally was Bel's actual sister. Bel knew that Bess had always felt somewhat protective of her, and she didn't mind it at all. When Sally and Bess had got married a few years back, Bess had taken her aside and told her that, as far as she saw it, Sally and Bel's parents weren't around anymore, so she considered it her responsibility to look after them both.

'What's he like? The Laird?' Bel asked as they entered a large entry hall. A glamorous-looking woman about Bel's age was sitting at a table on their right tapping at a laptop; a phone and a mug of coffee sat next to her on the table, and a hand-lettered sign decorated with drawings of flowers in a frame said: TICKETS.

'Nice. Cares. Good guy.' Bess opened her arms for a hug as the woman squealed, getting up from her table. 'Zelda Hicks. Looking divine as always,' she greeted the glamorous-looking woman.

'Bess! It's been too long, baby. How are you?' Zelda exclaimed; Bel realised she had an American accent. She was impeccably dressed in vertiginous black platform heels with red soles, a black pencil skirt and a white T-shirt with the logo of a 70s rock band on it. She had long, poker-straight black hair in a high, sleek ponytail and red lipstick. Altogether, Bel was surprised that someone so glamorous was working the ticket office at Loch Cameron castle. By contrast, Bess and Bel were both wearing jeans and hoodies. Bess wore hiking boots, and Bel had pulled on her trainers that morning. She hadn't bothered with any makeup either, pulling her shoulder length curly brown hair into a messy topknot, and now she was regretting it.

'I'm fine, thanks. This is my sister-in-law, Bel Burns.' Bess touched Bel's shoulder. 'She's up here staying for a while. Not with us, though – we've got the builders in. She's actually staying at Gretchen's old place.'

'Oh wow, you're staying at the cottage?' Zelda shook Bel's hand energetically. 'I redecorated that place when I stayed in it a couple years ago. That was how I started in interiors,' she explained, waving at her laptop. 'That's what I do now.'

'Oh... I thought...' Bel looked around at the vaulted ceiling of the entry hall, which featured heavy wood panelling and a number of oil paintings; rural scenes and pictures of the loch hung alongside portraits of men and women with period costumes. Or, Bel reflected, just the clothes of their time.

'You thought this was my job? No, I'm just helping Hal out while I'm here. My boyfriend. Well... my partner, I guess. That's what we say to sound more adult, right? I always think boyfriend and girlfriend makes us sound like we're in grade school.' She chuckled.

'Oh, the Laird? I see.' Bel caught Bess's eye; she could tell her sister-in-law was dying to dish some gossip about all this.

'Yeah. For my sins,' Zelda winked. 'Okay. So, two tickets.' She tore two slips from a book. 'Good for all day. Hal's coming down to start the tour at ten thirty.'

'Great. Thanks, Zelda.' Bess handed over the money. 'I haven't seen Hal in a while. He okay?'

'I'm bonny, thank ye, Bess.' A tall, bearded Scotsman dressed in a Black Watch kilt, knee length black socks, designer trainers and a black T-shirt that showed off his enviable physique strode into the room. 'Comin' fer the tour, are ye?'

'Bel, this is Hal Cameron, Laird of Loch Cameron,' Bess introduced them, and Hal shook Bel's hand warmly. 'Hal, this is Sally's sister, Bel. Staying for a while.'

'Hello, Bel. Lovely tae meet ye,' he said.

Bel liked him immediately, though he was nothing like what she would have expected a Laird to look like, especially with the fashionable, modern kilt and T-shirt.

'Sally's sister, aye? Ye have the resemblance,' he nodded. 'Stayin' long?'

'Not sure.' Bel smiled a little vaguely, not wanting to have to explain herself, even though Hal seemed nice.

But he nodded, and exchanged looks with Zelda. 'Zelda came here fer work, an' ended up stayin' longer than she expected,' he said, his eyes lighting up as he looked at his love. 'Loch Cameron has quite an effect on some people.'

'Well, we're here for the tour, so do your best to scintillate us,' Bess said with a grin.

'That I will.' Hal nodded seriously. 'Zelda, is there anyone else comin' today?'

'There's a bus load of German tourists just pulled up.' Zelda had gone to stand at the door and was watching a coach pull up onto the gravel drive. 'They've pre-paid. Remember, I told you last night.'

'Ah, right. Ye did,' Hal made a face at Bel. 'I'll be back. Better go and be the welcoming landowner,' he said, and followed Zelda out of the front door.

'Well, he is not what I expected,' Bel whispered as she and Bess walked through into the Great Hall.

'Ha. I don't see it myself, not my type. But I guess he's good looking, for a guy,' Bess shrugged.

'Umm… yeah,' Bel giggled. 'Zelda's gorgeous too. They make a great couple.'

'Both sweethearts too,' Bess nodded. 'So, what d'you think?'

The Great Hall was hung with muskets, swords and other old weaponry, hung in neat patterns. Bel stopped to read a sign that indicated the weapons had been used by the Cameron clan in tribal wars. She wondered if they'd been cleaned, or whether they still held the blood and guts of whoever the Camerons had fought.

'Wow. This is quite something.'

'Yeah, it's quite the thing,' Bess chuckled, looking up at the swords and claymores. 'Not many people can say they have this in their front room.'

'Or this many paintings. I don't have one oil painting of an ancestor, never mind hundreds,' Bel whispered; it was echoey in the hall. Large oil paintings in ornate gold frames hung everywhere – portraits of Hal's ancestors, many of whom shared Hal Cameron's intense blue eyes.

'They make a handsome couple, don't they?' Bess inclined her head towards the entrance hall where they could hear Zelda and Hal making small talk with the tourists. 'He's a good guy. I'm often up here giving him a hand with the archaic plumbing in this place, or doing something needs doing at one of his properties. If it wasn't for Hal Cameron I'd be seriously out of a job.' Bess picked up a photo frame of four Scottish noblemen and their ladies with serious expressions, frowned at it and put it down again.

'Should you be touching things?' Bel hissed.

Bess shrugged. 'I practically work here,' she said.

The hall also contained a variety of display cases holding valuable-looking vases and other trinkets. Bel stared into one full of antique china; a note indicated that it had been a present to the Laird – Hal's ancestor – from Queen Victoria. She raised an eyebrow. *How the other half live*, she thought. She wondered what it was like living in Hal Cameron's timeline.

'Sorry to have kept ye!' Hal swept into the Great Hall, leading the coach party behind him. 'Let's get goin', shall we?'

Hal led them up a sweeping staircase, balustraded with intricately carved wood. The carpet was a deep wine red. Bel ran her fingers over the fantastical creatures that roamed over the banister as they walked up the stairs.

'So, Bel, what d'ye do, when you're not on holiday in Loch Cameron?' Hal asked as he led the tour into one bedroom featuring a four-poster bed, and then another. The walls were hung with silk, slightly watermarked, and there were grand marble fireplaces in each room.

Bel imagined waking up in one of these beds and having a maid make up the fire, like she'd seen on those period dramas on TV; even on a sunny day, the castle was draughty. She imagined how cold it would be in the winter, and how cold it must have been before the advent of central heating. Not that the castle's plumbing was all that great these days, according to Bess.

'Well, I'm kind of between jobs. I used to work in customer services for a phone company, but I'm actually a hairdresser. Or, I trained as one, anyway,' Bel corrected herself.

'Oh, that's interestin'. We all have tae go over to Aberculty for haircuts since the salon closed,' Hal repeated what she already knew. 'I'm over there every month keepin' this under control, an' my beard trimmed. Zelda's rules,' he chuckled, running a hand through his curly brown hair.

You are in the alternative timeline, Bel thought, feeling slightly out of her body as she considered what she was about to say. She'd always privately scoffed to herself when people said things like *you create your own reality*: it all seemed rather new age-y and twee. *Come on, now*, her doubt nagged at her. *It's a crazy notion. You can't run your own business, just like that.*

But, I can. I can do that. I believe in myself and there's no reason I can't.

Bel cleared her throat. Here she was, in a Scottish castle, about to make a crazy suggestion to its laird. *Who's in the alternative timeline now?* she asked herself.

'Hmm. Well, actually, I know this is a bit out of the blue, but I was wondering if you could tell me what the rent would be on the salon. If you're looking for a new tenant, that is,' she added hurriedly, her heart pounding.

Hal cocked his head to one side thoughtfully. 'Are you serious?' he asked. 'The salon?'

'Kinda, yeah. I just found out I've got some money coming my way, and I also just lost my job. It sort of feels like fate.' Bel bit her lip. 'I mean, I have no idea how I'd do it. I've never run my own business before. And it's been a while since I worked in a salon. But...' she trailed off, hearing her doubts fall out of her mouth.

Hal was frowning at her.

Why are you saying these things? she thought, furiously. *Stop it. Just tell him you can do it.*

Bess, who had been chatting with one of the German tourists, waited for them to catch up.

'Did I just hear you talking about the salon?' she asked. 'Bel. You should totally do that. It's a brilliant idea!'

'Thanks. I think it would be good.' Bel forced herself to sound positive. Once upon a time, she had been a sassy little girl who took no prisoners and went for what she wanted. Losing her darling dad had changed her. But that confident little girl was still in there somewhere.

'I agree.' Hal reached into a pocket in his kilt and took out a business card. 'We can chat through the details, but I'd love someone to reopen the salon. We need it in the village. I can't tell you the number of complaints I've had about it only being open now and again. I offer a grant to new businesses, and two years reduced rent. Basically, I'll make it as easy as I can for you to run your business, Bel, if that's something you wanted to do.' Hal handed her his card. 'Think about it.'

He strode to the front of the group, who had questions about the books in the library that they had wandered into. It was a light, airy room, with a full-sized harp in the corner and velvet sofas that Bel could imagine sinking into with a book and a coffee on a rainy day, and admiring the view from the long windows out onto the gardens.

'Oh my goodness, Bel! I had no idea you were thinking about moving here!' Bess squealed, taking Bel to one side. 'Sally is going to be beside herself! Can I call her? I'm going to call her,' she said, as she got out her phone.

'Look, I haven't decided anything yet,' Bel protested. 'There's no need to call Sally. Not until I know what I'm doing.'

'Okay, okay.' Bess rolled her eyes, and put her phone away. 'You know I'm going to tell her tonight though, right?'

'Yes, you can tell her tonight. That I'm *thinking* about renting the salon, that's all.' Bel laughed at Bess's disappointed expression. 'I need to get more information. And I can't do anything if Andy doesn't buy me out of the house. He's said he would,' she explained, showing Bess the text. 'Obviously, that means I have to believe him, and goodness knows how long it might take for that to happen. But, I'm cautiously optimistic.'

'Wow, Bel! That's fantastic!' Bess studied the texts from Andy. 'Why d'you think he's offered that so quickly? D'you think it's because he wants to move his new lady in?' She handed Bel's phone back to her.

'Maybe.' Bel hadn't even considered that idea, and her face fell as the idea hit home.

'Oh, love. I'm sorry. Forget I said that.' Bess slapped her forehead. 'Ignore me, that was a thoughtless thing to say.'

'No, it's okay.' Bel considered the idea. Of course, it was possible that Andy and his new woman might want to live together. But so soon? Bel had only been gone a week.

That made her wonder again how long Andy had actually been seeing this woman. Was it months? Years, even? The thought made her stomach turn. Not because she still wanted Andy. But because of the betrayal that would mean. The lies. The number of times that he had gone behind her back.

'I... I guess I find it hard to imagine them being together in my house, you know? It's just weird. And hurtful, even though I know things between Andy and I weren't good for a long time. It's not him, per se, I feel I lost. It's more like, that is – was – my home. She's using all my stuff. I lost my home, my job... and now he's moving her in? I mean, good luck to them, I guess,' she shrugged, but her heart felt heavy.

'Sorry, babe.' Bess walked beside her as they followed the group along a long corridor and down some back stairs. 'I know it's hard. But, if it helps at all, I think you did the right thing by leaving.'

'I know.' Bel waited for the queue to pass in front of her, and walked into the castle's large kitchen, which was decked out with gleaming copper saucepans and a huge, old black range oven. 'I don't miss him. I didn't love him anymore, Bess. I'm not sure I ever did.'

'I don't think you did, either,' Bess agreed. 'And you know I don't think he was good enough for you. I never did.'

'I know. And you were right,' Bel said, admiring the copper pans.

Bess smiled. 'I'm always right.'

TEN

'That's Gretchen, over there. Playing Bridge.' The home care assistant pointed to a games table in the corner, where a quartet of elderly women were having a heated discussion about something, and laughing loudly. He rolled his eyes theatrically. 'Can you tell them to keep it down? Some of the other residents don't have their... energy,' he added, smiling.

'I'll try, but it looks like they might laugh in my face,' Bel chuckled, toting her carrier bag full of packages over to the table in the corner.

'Gretchen? Hi, sorry to interrupt. I'm Bel. We spoke on the phone? I'm staying at the cottage,' Bel gave the women at the table a self-conscious wave. 'You said to pop by. I brought your post, too.'

After her trip to the castle with Bess, she realised it was good for her to get out of the house each day. She needed other people to retain perspective, even if she wasn't going to discuss her problems with them. Getting out and about – and not staring at the walls of the cottage – reminded her that life went on, despite whatever had happened. Yes, Andy had had an affair and their relationship was over. But the sun still rose in the morning and set at night. She didn't want to wallow.

When her dad had passed away, Bel remembered feeling resentful when the sun rose the day after he died, that it was disrespectful to his passing. But it had to, of course, like it always did, and Bel had grown to find that fact reassuring. Things might change and loss happened, but she was still alive, and the world was still there.

'Oh, Bel! Why, yes, of course. How lovely.' Gretchen's brow furrowed. 'I'm sorry. Did you tell me you were visiting today? I'm usually quite good at remembering, but sometimes things slip away from me.'

'No, I just thought I'd pop over and bring you these.' Bel placed the bag down somewhat gratefully on the floor next to Gretchen's chair. 'Don't let me interrupt. I just wanted to say hi, and thanks for organising everything at the cottage so last minute.'

'Oh, not at all, dear. Not at all. It was just a matter of asking Angus to pop in and give the place a quick once-over.' Gretchen put her cards down on the table. 'Bel, this is Mavis, Muriel and Evangeline. Girls, make room. Bel, pull up a chair.'

'Well, just for a minute.' Bel picked up a spare chair from the neighbouring table and placed it at an empty corner of the square table the women were sitting at. 'If you're sure. I don't want to spoil your game. Oh...' she laughed, catching the eye of the care assistant she'd spoken to on the way in. 'That man says can you keep it down a bit. You were getting a bit rowdy.'

'Oh, spare us,' Gretchen muttered, giving the man a saccharine smile and a wave. 'When that boy is old enough to shave, he can give me orders. Not before.'

'He's probably in his late twenties,' Bel reasoned, sitting down.

'Men in their late twenties know nothing about anything,' Mavis scoffed. She sat tall in her chair, a tight purple-tinted

perm clinging close to her head like a helmet. She wore a white
tracksuit and trainers and had picked up her glasses to hold in
front of her eyes like a magnifying glass, looking Bel up and
down as if she was inspecting a horse. 'How old are you? Old
enough to know anything?'

'Thirty-five.' Bel had learnt from hairdressing that quite
often, feisty older ladies like Mavis could come across as rude,
but they were just testing you, and you needed to be assertive
and feisty in return. 'I guess that means old enough to sit at the
table, but not to tell you to be quiet?' she countered, giving
Mavis a twinkling smile.

'Good answer. Nice to meet you, dear,' Mavis chuckled,
and put her glasses down.

Muriel, next to her and in total contrast of demeanour, gave
Bel a wide smile. 'Don't mind Mavis. She thinks she's the
Queen Bee around here, just because her grandson works in the
High Court. Jonathan this, Jonathan that. It's all we ever hear
about.' Muriel stuck out her tongue at Mavis.

'I'll thank you to keep a civil tongue in your head,' Mavis
said icily. 'Jonathan is a legal assistant, you know.'

'I do know, because you've told us about a million times,'
Muriel replied. 'I'm Muriel, and it's very nice to meet you, dear.
Are you staying at the cottage long?' she turned to Bel, ignoring
Mavis, who looked furious. Muriel had curly white hair in a
kind of triangular bob that started flat on her scalp and spread
out to the sides, almost like a cartoon character. She wore her
glasses – pink frames, on a gold chain – around her neck on top
of a lilac sweatshirt with lace detail.

'I'm not sure. Maybe,' Bel replied, liking Muriel immediately but not wanting to get into the whole story.

'Ah, I hope so. Loch Cameron's a lovely village. I lived there
for a time, many years ago,' Muriel continued. 'Is Dotty still
down at the Inn? And Eric? I haven't seen them for years.'

'Yes, they're still there,' Bel said, inadvertently thinking about how she had spent the rest of the quiz night at the Inn trying to avoid Christian McDougall, and how Bess had kept trying to send her to the bar for more drinks whenever she saw him go over. They hadn't spoken again that night, but she'd caught Christian's eye a couple of times and had looked away, blushing.

'And this is Evangeline,' Gretchen interrupted. 'Evvie is our resident palmist. Go on, give her your hand,' she encouraged Bel.

'Oh. I've never had that done before.'

'Hello, dear.' Evvie gave her a wink, her dark brown eyes warm and surrounded by wrinkles. 'It's all right. I don't have to look if you don't want me to.'

'No, it's all right. You just took me by surprise. Go on.' Bel held out her hand and Evvie took it in her knotted, brown hand.

'Hmmm,' Evvie turned Bel's hand up to the light. 'Well, I can see there's a break here. Not a heartbreak, as such... just an ending.' She looked speculatively at Bel. 'You're thirty-five, you said?'

'Yes.' Bel was instantly taken aback. A *break?* That was a little close to home.

'Hmmm. So, that break's happened about now. And it's on your heart line, so it was a relationship. But you're not that broken-hearted about the person. It's more that you have to love yourself a little more...' Evvie frowned, and traced her finger along Bel's palm. 'Anyway, you don't need to worry. Plenty of love here for you. A new someone. Coming in soon, too.' She released Bel's palm.

'Ooooh.' Muriel leaned forward. 'Do mine, Ev.'

'Muriel. You're eighty-three. There's no point, unless you want to know when you're going to die,' Evvie sniffed. 'I've told you a million times.'

'Rude.' Muriel, however, didn't look particularly offended.

'Well, that's good news about the new love on the scene,

dear.' Gretchen turned to Bel. 'Has there been heartbreak? Not that you need to tell us. We're just four nosy old biddies.' She gave Bel a penetrating stare, nonetheless.

'I just separated from someone,' Bel confessed. 'I do feel it was the right thing, though. That's why I'm here. Spending some time with my sister and her wife while I decide what to do next.'

'The break,' Evvie said, smugly. 'I knew it.'

'Yes. And you're right, actually, Evvie. I don't think we ever truly loved each other. But it was still hard. I lost my job on the same day.' Bel felt the by now familiar rush of grief rise in her, and pushed it down with some effort.

'Oh, dear,' Evvie frowned and took Bel's hand again. 'Hmm. But you weren't meant to be doing that job. You clung on to it because you didn't believe you could do something else. But you have another skill. Something that brings you joy.'

'I do. Hairdressing,' Bel confessed. 'Wow, Evvie. You're really good at this.'

'I know,' Evvie said, without a hint of self-effacement.

'I've actually been thinking about starting my own salon. In Loch Cameron,' Bel said.

Hal Cameron had emailed her the details of the salon rental after she visited the castle, and she'd been researching how much it would cost to re-fit the salon and modernise it, as well as pay herself a salary for the first year while the salon built up its clients. Then, there were all the other costs: utilities, stock, training, health and safety. But she'd made a spreadsheet and was planning it all out carefully. Really, she needed Sally's help with the financial planning side, and her sister had said they could sit down together at the weekend and look at Bel's plans.

'Oh, please do that,' Gretchen clapped her hands. 'I mean, we have someone on-site here to keep us coiffed and beautiful.' She performed a starlet-esque toss of her grey head. 'But I know Loch Cameron is absolutely crying out for someone to reopen

Curl and Wave,' Gretchen's hair was done up in a complicated bun, stuck with pins. Bel estimated that her hair must be at least as long as her mid-back, if not longer.

'Well, if my ex can buy me out of our house, then I think that's what I'm planning to do,' Bel said. Every time she talked about the idea, she got more confident about it. 'I mean, I think I need a bit of a refresher training. But that's doable.'

'I'm sure that's possible, dear.' Gretchen looked thoughtful. 'We wouldn't be without our hairdresser, and once a week we have a beautician and a complementary therapist come in as well. Last time, Mavis had her nails done and she couldn't pick anything up for a week,' Gretchen giggled.

'That's not true. I managed perfectly well,' Mavis huffed. 'They were just a little long, that's all.'

'She looked like a hussy,' Evvie remarked, drily.

Bel couldn't help laughing at the outraged expression on Mavis's prim face. Being at the care home reminded her suddenly of her days in the salon, way back when. She had had a lot of elderly customers, particularly women, and had always enjoyed their gossip.

'Not that being a hussy is anything to be ashamed of.' Gretchen raised an eyebrow. 'Many's the time I was called a hussy for being a single mother, or having lovers rather than get married, or being a single working woman. Evvie, *really*.'

'Oh, get off your high horse, Gretchen,' Evvie huffed. 'You know I was only joking.'

'Hmmm.' Gretchen gave her friend a gentle nudge. 'Anyway, Bel. Why don't you carry that bag of books to my room for me?' She patted Bel's hand.

'That's what's in the packages? Books?' Bel looked down at the linen tote bag, stuffed full of packages.

'Oh, yes. I worked in publishing all my life, you see. And even when I retired, I sort of remained someone who people sometimes like to send new books to. For my thoughts, or reviews, or what have you.' Gretchen shrugged. 'Most of them end up in the little library here, but I must say it's a nice way for us to keep our book group happy. Some of them I keep, if it's an author I like.'

'I see.' Bel nodded.

'Well, come on, then! Let's go,' Gretchen stood up slowly, and Bel instinctively held out an arm for her, which Gretchen took gratefully. 'Ah, thank you, dear. I'm not as quick on my feet as I was. It's the tango I miss the most,' she chuckled.

'Only if I'm not interrupting your card game. I feel bad that you didn't finish it,' Bel protested. 'Really, there's no rush.'

'Oh, it's fine. Mavis and I were losing anyway.' Gretchen *tsk*ed. 'I can't stand losing. Girls, I'll see you at dinner.' She waved.

Bel picked up the bag of books. 'It was lovely to meet you all,' Bel said, letting Gretchen lead the way. 'Maybe I'll see you soon.'

'Hope so, dear,' Muriel trilled. 'Byeeee!'

'They seem nice,' Bel said, as she and Gretchen made their way slowly out of the room and into a long hallway hung with photographs of woodlands and beaches.

'Ah, they're nice enough,' Gretchen admitted. 'Not much in common apart from the fact we're all old now, but that's life for you. At least there are men here. And, some that aren't dead from the waist down.' She smiled at an elderly man who was walking past with a walking stick; he smiled back, and looked away shyly.

'Gretchen!' Bel giggled, once he was out of earshot. 'You flirt!'

'I'm not dead yet,' Gretchen shrugged. 'Might as well get it while you can.'

ELEVEN

Having the idea to open your own hair salon was one thing, but making it happen was quite another, Bel was learning quickly.

She had made the decision in the middle of the night, after seeing Gretchen at the care home. She wasn't sure exactly what had made her act on the idea, but she thought it was something to do with those four women: Gretchen, Evvie, Mavis and Muriel. All were in the twilight years of their lives, but Bel had the sense they had lived full lives. Bel thought that Gretchen would not have hesitated to take the plunge and open her own hairdressing salon if that was what she wanted to do.

So, what's stopping you? Bel had asked herself, as she'd lain, wakeful, in the cosy bed, covered in the padded, flowery quilt.

Nothing.

There wasn't anything getting in the way of her achieving a long-held dream, apart from her own fear. And, now that some of the biggest things that she had been holding on to – a relationship, a house, a job – had been pulled out from under her, that fear had lost its teeth. What else was there to fear when you had already lost everything?

She had decided, then and there, that she would open the

salon. At least, she would try it. If it failed, if there weren't
enough customers, if she wasn't as good a hairdresser as she
thought she was – well, then, at least she would have given it
a go.

If you don't try, you'll never know, cupcake, she could
imagine her dad saying.

Once she'd decided to go for it, everything had fallen into
place remarkably quickly, as if it was meant to be. Hal Cameron
had granted her the lease on the salon, and she'd got the paperwork to sign by email that morning. Though that was the least
of it. She had to register herself as a business in Scotland, and
register for tax. She'd never been self-employed before. As well
as that, Bel had spent the morning opening a business bank
account. She didn't have the money from Andy yet, but Bess
and Sally had lent her the money she needed to get everything
going at the salon, since Hal had wanted her to begin the lease
as soon as possible.

The money Andy had promised her was a good amount. It
was more than enough to get her started, and she'd set a good bit
of it aside as a deposit on a house, as and when she was ready to
think about buying something in the village. Seeing as property
in Loch Cameron wasn't half as expensive as in Essex, she
would be in a good position when the money came in. She'd
estimated to Bess and Sally that she'd be able to repay them for
a very short-term loan in a couple of weeks.

Bel felt as if her whole life had suddenly become immersed
in filling in forms, but it was worth it. However, as well as all the
relentless form-filling, Bel had realised that she had to arrange
for the salon interior to have a complete overhaul. The décor
was incredibly dated. The sinks at the wash stations were
chipped and stained, the coral-pink wallpaper was peeling off in
places and there were still black-and-white posters of models
with haircuts from the nineties in the windows.

Now that Hal had given Bel the keys to the place, Bess and

a couple of her plumber friends were ripping out all the sinks and putting in clean new ones, as well as – with Hal's permission – replacing the salon bathroom with a new white suite Bel had being delivered. Bess had assured her that it would be a couple of days' worth of work, and then she could get started on the internal décor and the flooring, which needed serious attention.

Bel had offered to help, but Bess had given her a wry smile as she'd taken the salon key from her that morning.

'Best to just let us get on with it, sweetheart,' her sister-in-law had advised as she'd headed off in her overalls. 'It'll be a huge mess. Me and the lads'll have made good headway by the afternoon, though, if you want to come over then.'

So, having been refused access to her salon for the morning, Bel was planning the rest of the re-fit. It was convenient having Bess on hand to do the decoration and the technical stuff for her, rather than have to wait months to get different tradespeople in on the project. And, in the case where she needed a few extra pairs of hands, Bess had friends she could call upon to help.

Bel had an idea for the type of look she wanted at the salon – clean, modern and cosy, but not too girly. It was a unisex salon, and, unlike the coral-pink walls the owner of Curl and Wave had favoured, Bel wanted something sophisticated but understated. Therefore, she'd decided on all white walls, white sinks and white leather chairs. Also, the salon itself wasn't large, so it was a good idea to maximise the space as well as let in the light, airy brightness that was such a key feature of Loch Cameron.

She wanted the salon to be somewhere that felt luxurious and yet familiar for her customers: a place where they could relax and enjoy a break from their normal lives. In short, Bel wanted her salon to be for them what Loch Cameron had been to her, so far: a place of comfort.

In fact, Loch Cameron was fast becoming more than that for Bel, she was realising: for her, it was a place of refuge, where she had started to rebuild her life. Her rational self – the part of her that had told her that staying at HandyPhone was a good idea for all those years – said *a hairdressing salon is hardly a place of refuge, Bel. Don't be dramatic.* But, in her heart, she knew what the salon meant to her. It was the first thing she had had that was ever truly hers, and it was all part of her new life.

She also knew that rational voice wasn't really hers: it was Andy's voice, and it was the voice of everyone who had ever told her to stop being silly and stop dreaming and stop being who she was. It was the voice of fear, and she decided to stop listening to it. Gretchen Ross, if she had ever had a similar voice in her head, had for damn sure never listened to it. So, Bel wasn't about to, either.

Bel was taking a break from her paperwork and making coffee when there was a knock at the door. She went to answer it, expecting the postman with more packages for Gretchen, but Christian McDougall stood there.

'Oh!' Bel said, surprised.

'Morning. Just wanted to let you know that I'm working in the garden today,' he said, almost apologetically. 'I will be using the mower at some point, but I didn't come too early, right? I didn't want a repeat of last time.'

'Morning. Sorry. I should have said that.' Bel was suddenly aware that she was wearing a pink crop top and marching jersey shorts that were super comfy around the house, but not necessarily what you wanted the local hot biker gardener to see you in first thing in the morning. *Have I even brushed my teeth?* Bel worried suddenly, and surreptitiously held her hand to her mouth, breathing into it quickly and taking a sniff. 'That's fine, of course. Carry on. I promise I won't shout at you.'

Christian held out a bunch of peonies and roses to her. 'From the garden. Thought you'd like to have some in the house,' he said, looking away shyly. 'I picked them as a peace offering in case you were going to rip my head off again.'

'Now I feel awful for being such a gorgon.' Bel took them, awkwardly, and her hand brushed Christian's. 'They're lovely. Thank you.' There was a tingle of electricity as her skin met his; she instinctively pulled her hand away, and, in doing so, dropped a couple of the roses on the doorstep. 'Damn. I'm so clumsy,' she muttered, blushing, and stooped to pick up the flowers.

Christian dropped to his knees at the same time, and Bel, temporarily thrown off balance by having him so near to her, found herself reaching out for him, to steady herself. Her hand landed on his knee, which, because he was wearing shorts today, was exposed. In the brief moment before she moved it, Bel noticed how warm Christian's skin was; how tanned he was, and that tattoos covered his calves.

'Oh... sorry,' Bel muttered, standing up so abruptly she became a little dizzy.

'It's okay,' Christian picked up the flowers and handed them to her. 'No harm done.'

There was an awkward silence; Bel wished someone would come to interrupt them, and end what was possibly the most self-conscious moment she'd ever experienced. Where was the postman when you needed him? Or nosy neighbours or the locals Bel often saw walking along the dirt path in front of the cottage?

'Well, thanks for these,' she repeated, feeling even more stupid. It wasn't like her to be struck dumb; at HandyPhone her whole job had been charming difficult people over the phone. She was adept at conversation. So why was she lost for words around Christian McDougall?

'No trouble, really. There are so many flowers out here, I

actually have to cut some of them back. This time of year, things go wild pretty quickly if you don't keep an eye on them,' he shrugged. 'Not a big deal.'

'Oh, right.' Now Bel thought she shouldn't have made such a fuss about the flowers, but it had been a sweet gesture. 'Look. I just made a coffee. Do you want one?'

'I'd love one, if it wasn't any trouble.' Christian met her eyes and broke into a warm smile.

Bel felt a shiver run through her.

'It's no trouble,' she said, not wanting to look away, but knowing if she kept eye contact for any longer it would be... well, she didn't know what it would be. Sexy? Awkward? Odd? It had been quite a few years since Bel had been single. And she'd never been very good at it to begin with.

Part of Bel enjoyed flirting with Christian – if she could call what she was doing *flirting*, which she doubted. But a large part of her also wanted to run away from any suggestion of flirtation, and hide in the cottage until he went away.

I'm just not ready for it, she thought. *It's too soon. There's too much risk in putting yourself out there. I'd rather just stay hidden, away from it all.*

She turned to go back inside, grateful for the excuse of making coffee. This at least meant that she could escape for a moment and compose herself. She wasn't a shy person, but she felt awkward and overly aware of herself around Christian. What did that mean?

Nothing. It doesn't mean anything, she thought furiously. *You're definitely not going to look back at him as you walk away. Don't look back at him. Don't. I don't care how much you want to.*

She didn't look, but when she was back in the kitchen, Bel felt as though she'd cheated herself a little, and peeked out of the kitchen window at him instead. For a moment, she watched the muscles in Christian's back as he ran a strimmer along the edge of the lawn.

All right. I looked, she thought. *I'm only human. It doesn't mean anything.*

Clearing her throat, she flicked on the kettle and looked for the ground coffee. It was okay to look at the menu: it didn't mean you were going to order anything, right? It was hardly her fault that the menu boasted such prime beef, and right outside her window, too. Bel laughed to herself and poured some milk into a mug. She remembered Gretchen saying she wasn't dead yet, when Bel had caught her making eyes at one of the elderly men at the care home.

Clearly, Christian did things to Bel's brain that included making vaguely off-colour jokes to herself about his admirable physique.

Well, I guess I'm not dead yet, either, she thought. *And that can only be a good thing.*

TWELVE

Now that Bess had organised the new sinks and decoration, Bel began cleaning the stock room at the back of the salon. In fact, once she'd made the decision to take the salon, everything seemed to have happened incredibly fast: a sign that she felt the universe approved of her actions. Hal wanted a tenant to take over as soon as possible, as Curl and Wave had apparently lain empty for at least a year, and been very inconsistent for a couple of years before that. More or less as soon as she'd got the money for the first couple of months' rent to him and signed the agreement, he'd dropped the keys round to the cottage.

Bella, who had owned the salon before her, had clearly not had a good go through everything for quite some time. Though Bel had had the salon completely re-fitted, the two back rooms needed a lot of clearing. So far, she'd found hair dye going back to the mid-90s, and at least three litre-containers of conditioner that had definitely gone a colour it wasn't supposed to.

Bel climbed up the stepladder to clear the top shelves. She grabbed a stack of ancient hairdressing magazines and dropped them onto the floor: they could be recycled. Then, her fingers closed around another, smaller bundle of papers. Bel was about to drop what she thought was another papery, 1970s-era hair magazine onto the floor when she realised that wasn't what was in her hand.

In fact, it was a bundle of letters.

Bel held them up to her face and blew the dust from them. Coughing when she breathed it in, she climbed down the stepladder and examined them.

There were perhaps ten letters in all, and all to a Rose Macaulay at the salon's address: 12 High Street, Loch Cameron. Of course, then, it might not have been a salon; she wondered whether the property had been a normal residence in 1965, which was when the letter on the top of the bundle was dated. She guessed so.

At random, she opened one of the envelopes and started to read.

Dear Rose,

I can't stop thinking about you and our last night together. Please, don't go. I'll miss you so much.

I don't think I can go on without you. No one understands me like you do. When we're alone, it feels as though there's no one else left in the world and it's just us, alone in our beautiful cocoon of closeness and touch and sweet kisses.

No one in Loch Cameron is like us. I feel like I waited all my life for someone like you: you walked into my life that day and everything changed. I didn't know a love like ours could be so beautiful. I hate that we have to hide it, but I feel like I've had to hide myself all my life. Finally, with you, I can be free.

Rose, I love you. Please don't leave. I would do anything to make you stay. Tell me what I can do to make you happy.

Serena xxx

'Wow,' Bel breathed, sitting down in one of her white leather chairs and re-reading the letter. Serena, whoever she was, really had it bad for this Rose.

She opened the next letter in the bundle. All the letters had, presumably, been hand-delivered: none of them bore stamps, but they had obviously been opened and read many times: Bel could tell from the way that the paper unfolded in her hands.

Dearest Rose,

You're leaving tomorrow. I know we've said our goodbyes, but I had to write down something of what I am feeling. I want you to know what I couldn't say to you in person tonight. You've just left my flat, and my heart is in tatters.

You know that I love you. I know that your music is your life, and I would never want to stand between you and what you love doing. I would follow you anywhere, and be your support. I would happily stand at the side of the stage every night, for every performance, giving you my heart and filling you up with love. Holding your coat and waiting patiently as you sign autographs, pose for photos. I would do all that and more to be with you.

However, I understand that your life is the life of the lone wolf. You have made yourself clear. Perhaps I am just one of many loves, for you. But, please know that you are my only love. I don't give myself freely to just anyone. You were my first, and will be my only love.

I wanted to scream at you. I want to hate you for leaving. But I can't, because my heart won't let me. I am forever yours. You have marked me forever.

I know that you love me in your own way, and I don't blame you for being who you are. You have never been anything but honest with me about how much time you had, and how much of yourself you could give me. I am grateful even for the crumbs. They will sustain me. For the rest of my life, I will remember the moments we shared, and hoard them like the treasure they are.

I wish you all the happiness and all the success in the world, my darling.

Always, your Serena xxxx

Bel breathed out another long sigh after reading the second letter.

'Serena definitely had it bad,' she muttered, folding the letter and carefully sliding it back into the envelope. It was a flip comment, but her heart went out to the author of these desperate, passionate letters: Serena had been so in love with Rose, and Rose – Bel had no idea how she had felt, but it seemed that Serena was the one that had truly loved and lost.

The second letter had inferred that Rose had been a performer of some kind. Bel picked up her phone. She was intrigued about Rose: who was she? Who was Serena? It sounded like Rose would be the easier one to find if she had had some kind of fame.

Curiously, she searched the internet for Rose Macaulay, singer; nothing returned that looked like it was from the right time period. She tried Rose Macaulay music – again, nothing from anyone who looked as though they were youngish in the 60s.

'What else?' Bel mused. She typed in Rose Macaulay, actress to the search bar. It returned a few different Rose Macaulays who were actresses; maybe one of them was this Rose.

Bel took a different tack. This time, she searched Rose Macaulay, Loch Cameron and pressed enter.

There were several entries. Bel clicked through a couple until she found a black-and-white clipping from *The Scotsman*, a broadsheet newspaper. It was brief, but the hairs on the back of Bel's neck stood up when she saw the picture and the caption.

THE ROSE OF SCOTLAND: LOCH CAMERON'S BALLERINA ROSE MACAULAY CHOSEN FOR THE ROYAL BALLET

JUNE 10, 1965

Twenty-four-year-old Rose Macaulay of the village of Loch Cameron has been accepted as lead ballerina at the Royal Ballet.

Macaulay, who attended the Royal Ballet School, graduated in 1960 and has been pursuing a career in ballet with regional companies.

Robert Oliver of the Royal Ballet said:

"We are delighted that Miss Macaulay has joined us as Prima Ballerina. She has excellent all-round grace and lightness of expression, and we look forward to audiences around the world enjoying her performances. It is always a joy to welcome a Scottish ballerina to the corps, and we look forward to Miss Macaulay becoming a household name in the years to come."

Miss Macaulay will begin her tenure with the Royal Ballet with an international tour of Swan Lake.

'A ballerina.' Bel nodded. 'So, she had to go abroad to perform. Poor Serena.' Bel could see there would have been no way for Rose's lesbian lover to accompany her on tour, even if she had wanted Serena to go. That wasn't the way that the world was, then.

The second entry she read was a review of a show Rose had starred in, in New York. It was glowing. There were more, throughout the sixties – Rose had indeed travelled the world, so it seemed, dancing at all the famous venues.

Then, Bel clicked on an article from 1971. PRIMA BALLERINA IN HEALTH SCARE, the headline read. This piece was from *The Times*.

> *Rose Macaulay, the prima ballerina for the Royal Ballet, collapsed on stage at the Opera National de Paris last night during an ensemble performance of* The Nutcracker.
>
> *Miss Macaulay, 30, has been Prima Ballerina at the Royal Ballet for six years, and was participating in a number of shows in collaboration with the Paris Opera Ballet. Macaulay fractured her ankle in 1969 in a performance of* Giselle *and had a year off to recover: this was supposed to be her comeback performance.*
>
> *Audience members said that Miss Macaulay delivered a flawless performance in the first few scenes, but then seemed to stumble during a complicated set piece in the second act. Medics were called to the theatre, and Miss Macaulay was taken away by ambulance.*
>
> *A spokesperson for the Royal Ballet said:*
>
> *"Rose Macaulay is a consummate professional, and we know that she will not want to disappoint her fans. She will issue a statement shortly, and we can assure all interested parties that she is safe and well.'*

Bel raised an eyebrow. That quote sounded like some frantic "everything is okay" public relations, if she wasn't too much mistaken.

She flicked through some other similar entries – stories that recounted the same events, without any significant additions – until she found something that was rather different in tone.

THE TAINTED ROSE OF SCOTLAND: PRIMA BALLERINA GAY SHAME

Oh, no.

Bel's heart clenched. Even though she could see the headline was from a tabloid newspaper in 1981 – it was never going to be a sensitive or thoughtful piece – her heart broke for Rose even before reading it.

> *Rose Macaulay, a former prima ballerina for the Royal Ballet, has been having a series of affairs with women.*
>
> *Apparently, the ballerina's antics onstage weren't the only thing that were as gay as a picnic basket. A source close to the ballerina told* The Sun *that Macaulay was known to frequent notorious bars in Paris and New York where sapphic sirens are ripe for the plucking.*
>
> *The same source disclosed Macaulay had also been disciplined by the Royal Ballet for her perverted inclinations in the early 60s while part of the corps de ballet, for an affair with another female twinkle-toes.*
>
> *We'll think twice before taking the children to* The Nutcracker *this year.*
>
> *Macaulay, who retired from ballet in 1972 due to injury, was unavailable for comment.*

Bel was disgusted; she closed the browser window. How could people say those things? Ignorance wasn't an excuse. Rose hadn't done anything wrong, and yet her name had been dragged through the mud because some middle-aged man in an office somewhere decided that women loving women was deviant and somehow disgusting.

She looked at the bundle of letters. They were all in Serena's handwriting. Bel scanned them all briefly: they were much the same as the ones she'd read, filled with Serena's longing, and dated every year or so. Poor Serena had nursed her love for an absent Rose for over a decade, it seemed. It was tragic.

I'm glad I didn't live then, Bel thought. But perhaps the letters were also a cautionary tale: *don't fall in love, because this is what happens.*

Bleak, she thought. *But, not incorrect.* Looking at her own trash fire of a love life, Bel couldn't say that she really had the secret to a life of love and fulfilment. *I'm going to take it as a sign from the universe to stay away from love,* she thought. *Nothing good comes of it.*

Nonetheless, she carefully placed the bundle of letters in her handbag before she continued cleaning. They had been special to Serena, once, and maybe to Rose. Someone should take care of them, and it looked like that responsibility had fallen to Bel. She might not believe in love anymore, but she could preserve the intimate inner thoughts of someone who had lived here once. There was a strange connection through time and space in those letters: Bel felt honour bound to look after Serena's words as much as if they had been her own. They had been important, once. And, in a sense, they always would be.

THIRTEEN

'So. What are you cutting back?' Bel handed a mug of coffee to Christian, took her sunglasses off her head and put them on. As well as being bright and sunny, it felt like it was less obvious that she was looking at Christian's shirtless torso if she had her glasses on.

He'd stripped to the waist and was now wearing only his khaki shorts and work boots. *Dear lord*, she thought, as she took in his strong chest, defined stomach and arms that looked as if they could lift her over his shoulder without any difficulty at all. She supposed it was his job that made him so fit and strong, but she almost didn't know where to look.

Andy had not been a muscular man. He wasn't flabby; it was just that he had never been particularly into sports or fitness, and his job wasn't a physical one. She'd never even thought about wanting a man with a body like Christian's before: she'd always thought it was about the person. And that *was* true, but the thought occurred to Bel that maybe it was possible to be attracted to someone with a hot body who was also a nice person.

She blinked, trying not to focus on Christian's torso and failing.

'The rose bushes need pruning. These brambles are running wild too.' Christian turned away and grabbed a long, thorny stem from a huge bush in his gloved hand. 'Ideally you'd prune in autumn but I wasn't working up here then,' he gulped down a third of the coffee, wiped his glove over his mouth and set the mug down on an upturned wooden box. 'Thanks. Great,' he said, turning back to his task.

Christian mentioning roses made Bel think about the letters to Rose Macaulay she'd found at the salon, written by a lovelorn Serena. She'd brought them back to the cottage and re-read them a few times, and, though they were romantic, they made her sad. It was a wonderful thing to have experienced that kind of love, on one hand. But, on the other, it was so terribly tragic for Rose and Serena to have been separated in the way that they had been – and for Serena's love to have been so unrequited.

'Aren't you going to put your top back on? Those thorns look lethal,' Bel suggested, stirring herself from her slightly melancholy thoughts about love and focusing back on the present. In today's world, Rose and Serena's story would likely be very different, and she wished that they'd had a happier time of it.

'Nah. I got it.' Christian grinned at her, picked up some meaty secateurs and started cutting away at the bramble stems.

'So, what were you doing before you started working in Loch Cameron?' Bel asked, clearing her throat and making herself look elsewhere.

'Ah. Bit of a story,' Christian continued cutting back the brambles, tossing them to one side when he'd done so.

'You might as well tell me. I don't know anyone here. Well, my sister and her partner. That's all, pretty much.' Bel sat on the edge of a little wall that ran around some flower beds to the right of the bushes. She had changed from her crop top and shorts before coming out, putting on a peach broderie anglaise sun dress she'd had the foresight to stuff into her bag when she'd left her house in Essex. It was a little crumpled, but it was pretty. She had bare feet, and had actually painted her toenails the night before, having found half a bottle of gold nail polish in her makeup bag; gold looked good against her brown skin. She'd also detangled her curls and put some product through the ends to freshen them up.

Not that she was trying to look pretty for Christian McDougall. Not in the slightest.

'Hm. You might not like me if I tell you.' He looked over at her, flashing her a glimpse of that warm smile again; Bel noticed his gaze lingered on her toenails, which twinkled slightly in the sunlight.

'Who says I like you now?' Bel countered, a smile twitching the edge of her mouth.

'Ha. Okay.' Christian stopped working for a minute, picked up his coffee cup and drained the rest of it. 'Well, before this, I was an IT guy, if you can believe it.'

'I... do actually find that hard to believe.' She raised an eyebrow. 'You don't look like an IT guy.'

'What do they say about serial killers? They look just like everybody else?' Christian chuckled. 'Same about IT guys.'

'Are you saying that IT guys are serial killers?' Bel started laughing.

'No. Though probably a higher than average number are,' he chuckled. 'Anyway. I did that a long time but basically I sort of died inside while I was doing it. I gained a lot of weight, I was depressed, my mental health suffered. So, one day, I thought, sod this. Jacked it in, bummed around for a while not really doing anything and then I found the Warriors. I always rode bikes. It was fun, being part of a group. One of the guys worked for the Laird as a gardener, asked if I wanted to help him out.

Some of the other guys introduced me to the gym they go to. The rest is history.'

'A bike gang, though? Bit rebellious, isn't it?' she asked, a little archly.

'I always felt like an outsider. So it works for me,' he shrugged.

'Why? Feeling like an outsider, I mean?' she looked up at him as he bent to put the coffee cup down, watching his back muscles flex.

Damn.

'Ah. Just always did. My family were kinda the village outcasts. I never knew why. That was always just how it was. You know what villages are like.'

'I suppose. I mean, I grew up in Essex. So, not a village. But I can imagine being mixed race in some small places might have made me an outsider,' she reflected. 'Don't get me wrong. Sometimes there were still comments, you know? It still happens. People can be mean.'

'I'm sorry to hear that. People can definitely be idiots.' Christian squatted on his heels and met her eyes. 'Whatever I've experienced is no comparison, also. All right, I'm a bit alternative, you might say. But I'm still a big, strong, white guy. It's not like I have a lot to complain about.'

'Well, sure. But everyone has their struggles,' Bel shrugged. 'I didn't say that to override your story. I guess I was just saying, I can relate.'

'I know. But if anything, I'm very aware that I should be using all the privileges I've been handed to help others. I try to,' he shrugged, standing up.

'So, you prefer working outdoors?' Bel watched him as he went back to pruning the bushes.

'A thousand per cent. Yeah. Turns out I have ADHD, so sitting down at a desk isn't for me. I've always had a load of energy, so I need variety and basically hard physical labour.

Gardening's fun, I get an amazing view most of the time, I like plants and it's great in the summer. Plus, sometimes, a pretty girl makes me a coffee and comes and talks to me.' He turned his head slightly, smiling at her over his shoulder.

'Oh, my. That was you trying to be charming, wasn't it?' Bel giggled.

'It was,' he admitted. 'Did it work?'

'Absolutely not.'

'Oh, good. I felt I could do better.'

'I felt that too.'

They both laughed. Bel felt a sense of ease, talking to Christian. It reminded her of how she used to be, when she was hairdressing; she had loved the banter and the back and forth with customers. It wasn't the same at HandyPhone: when you were doing someone's hair, usually you were sending someone away feeling great about themselves. At HandyPhone, the best Bel could ever hope for was that she solved a complaint, but no one was ever *happy*. It was never *fun*.

'I don't know if I've met anyone with ADHD before,' she said instead. 'I've heard of kids having it. Is it common for it to be diagnosed in adults?'

'It's actually super common,' Christian said. 'It's one of those things where there were tons of kids like me who hated school and thought they were no good at it, because they were hyper, or they found it hard to focus or whatever. Later in life you realise: you're not thick, you're neurodivergent.' He shrugged. 'The medical community are catching up now and diagnosing a lot of adults who have been coping with it for years. It was a huge relief for me to know what it was, and, in my case, have meds that help control it.'

'That's good. You feel better, then?' Bel asked, interested. She wondered how many people she knew who might have an undiagnosed condition of some kind. She guessed it would be a lot.

'Sure. Day to day, the meds help. It's weird because if *you* took them, they'd make you so jumpy, because it's basically the equivalent of a really strong coffee. But the stimulant effect helps my brain focus.'

'So, if I took your meds by accident, I'd be wanting to go to an all-night rave?'

'Exactly. But when I take them, it's suddenly like, hmmm, I might sit down quietly and organise my diary,' Christian chuckled. 'Weird, huh. I guess it probably *does* make sense about being the outsider, right?'

'No. Not weird at all. I'm just happy you've found something that works for you.' Bel looked up at the blue sky and took in a long, grateful breath of the fresh air of Loch Cameron. For all the time she'd been here, she felt it had been cleansing her spirit. 'So many people suffer in silence in so many ways. At least you asked for help. And you got it.'

'I did.' Christian nodded, smiling in that particular way he had, that made Bel blush. It was somehow suggestive and wholesome at the same time, and she didn't know what to do with it.

'Still, there're a lot of upsides. Physical energy. I can hyper-focus on some things I find very interesting. I'm an interesting conversationalist, if you like sudden breaks in the conversation to look at squirrels,' Christian added, pointing behind her. 'Shhh. Look.'

'Squirrels?' Bel turned around, seeing the flash of a fluffy tail disappear up a tree.

'You missed it.' Christian shook his head, gravely. 'You've got to be more on the ball than that, I'm afraid.'

'Hm. Well, I don't have your powers of squirrel perception,' she shrugged, getting up. 'Anyway, I should get on. I've got a lot to do today.'

As much as Bel was enjoying talking to Christian, she was excited to get back to planning out what she needed to do for the salon; for the first time in maybe forever she had an exciting plan for her career. And not even a gorgeous, though rather rough-around-the-edges gardener, was going to distract her from that.

'Right you are. I've kept you for too long. I can go on and on. You just have to interrupt me.'

Christian handed his empty coffee mug to her; their fingers touched briefly, and there was that same frisson of energy between them as there had been before.

Bel shivered. It felt as though a line of pleasure zinged from her fingertips, through her arm, to her heart and down into her knickers. It had happened before, at the Inn, but it hadn't been like this. Suddenly, she felt hot all over. She realised her breathing had become a little heavier.

What is happening? she thought, aghast. *The man literally just brushed your fingertips. Victorian ladies needed more to swoon than you, apparently.*

'You okay?' Christian met her eyes with a concerned look.

She looked away, embarrassed. 'Yes. I'm fine,' she said, more formally than she intended. 'Of course, I'm okay.'

'All right.'

Christian looked slightly confused at her sudden brusqueness, but it was too late for her to do anything about it. She didn't want him to know that being around him made her melt; that brushing his fingers sent jolts of electricity through her. It was ridiculous.

'See you later, then.'

'Yes. See you whenever,' Bel replied, far more casually than she felt. Was it normal to be overwhelmed by feelings of lust for someone who had only casually flirted with you? *Don't turn into a bunny boiler*, she chastised herself, hating the phrase as soon as she'd thought of it.

Walking back into the cottage, she closed the front door behind her and leaned against it for a moment, trying to collect herself. She'd never been the kind of woman who lost her composure because of a man. In fact, she had always taken a kind of dim view of that kind of behaviour. Yes, she'd enjoyed the banter that came with hairdressing, but that was different. She'd never felt as if she was melting when she was shampooing someone's hair. Or felt an electric line of desire through her heart and straight into her knickers when she'd been rubbing styling wax through someone's fringe.

Andy had certainly never, ever made her feel that way. Unexpectedly, Bel began to cry at the sudden grief that this realisation unlocked in her. She had never even been aware that she had missed out on feeling this way, but she had. All those years with Andy; all those times they'd slept together, and it had been fine, but there was no sense of passion or urgency. Many times, she'd found herself irritated at the annoying sounds he made when he kissed her, and at other times, repulsed by the idea of having sex with him at all. She'd thought that was normal.

It wasn't normal, she told herself. *That, what just happened, felt more natural than eight years with Andy. Years when you had to talk yourself into wanting to sleep with him at all, sometimes. That, just then, with Christian – that was instinct.*

Bel let herself cry. She knew she needed to let out her feelings: feelings she didn't even know she'd had. She went into the bedroom and held the pillow over her face as she cried, paranoid that Christian, who was still outside in the garden, would hear.

It was sad that she had spent eight years of her life in a relationship with little sexual chemistry. Sad she had thought she was happy, when she was only half alive. But that had ended, and there was no way she was going back to that life.

You are allowed to be happy, she told herself firmly, as the tears gradually stopped. *You are allowed to feel pleasure in every area of your life.*

Bel took the pillow off her face and lay on the bed, listening to the sound of Christian whistling outside. She wasn't under any illusion that he was her soulmate. But he had shown her something important that was missing in her life, and for that she was grateful.

FOURTEEN

'I now declare Bel's Salon open!' Hal Cameron cut the pink ribbon that Fiona had helped Bel set up outside the salon. 'Congratulations, Bel!'

The crowd cheered, and Bel took a little bow.

'Speech!' Fiona called out, raising her glass of sparkling wine.

Along with Hal, his glamorous American girlfriend Zelda and Fiona – her new neighbour, as Fiona's Fashions was just next door – a small throng of locals had clustered on the street outside what had once been Curl and Wave, and which was now Bel's new salon. She could hardly believe it – it had happened so quickly, and yet, here she was.

Eric and Dotty from the Loch Cameron Inn had come along to celebrate the salon's opening, as had Sally and Bess, some of Sally's colleagues from the whisky distillery, Bel's Viking-esque neighbour Angus, who towered above everyone, and some of the other local shopkeepers.

'Thank you for coming, everyone,' she began, her voice quivering a little with nerves. 'I can't actually believe this is happening.' Bel took a deep breath and steadied herself with a sip of wine. 'But it is, and I wanted to say some thank-yous. First, a big thank you to Hal Cameron, who gave me a very generous deduction on the rent for this place. And made it really easy for me to set up the salon.' There was a cheer, and Bel raised her glass to Hal, who nodded a little shyly, obviously not loving being the centre of attention.

'I'd also like to thank my sister Sally and her partner Bess, who helped persuade me that I could do this. Thank you, guys. You've been so supportive.' Bel blew them both a kiss.

It was always hard for Bel to read her sister; Bess was the demonstrative one. As Bel looked over, she was wiping a tear from her eye. Sally, by comparison, stood quietly, with a faint smile on her lips. She nodded as Bel caught her eye, but Bel found herself wishing that her sister would do something more – a hug, perhaps, or say *congratulations*. Bel was grateful Sally and Bess had fronted her the money she needed for the salon, while she waited for Andy to come through with the cash, but, still, Sally was always so reserved with her. She wished her sister could be more like Dad. With Sally Bel always felt as if she were a little girl who couldn't do anything for herself, and that Sally was the grown-up.

I'm a grown-up too, Bel thought, as she looked back at the crowd. *I'm literally opening my own business. Why does she have to make me feel like a kid, still?*

'I'd also like to thank Fiona, who is an amazing business-woman herself, and who inspired and encouraged me to believe that I could do this. Thank you, Fiona,' Bel continued. 'And, thank you all! Please come in and look around, enjoy some free wine and nibbles, and take a voucher – if you book an appointment in my first month of business, it's half price!'

Everyone cheered.

Bel led the way into the salon. The previous dated décor had been stripped away and replaced by clean white walls with rose gold taps and mirror frames. She was so happy with the way it looked. Clean white shelving units held all of the organic, vegan product range she'd chosen to work with in the salon – it all smelt so beautiful that she had to make an effort not to use it all up herself – and she'd decorated with plants, loving the green against the clean walls and the metallic accents.

The salon's former chipped sinks had been replaced by new, clean white sinks with top-of-the-line temperature-controlled taps and rinse attachments. Bel had invested in four white leather ergonomic hairdressing chairs – two at the sinks and one each at the hairdressing stations – and set up a front desk, though, nowadays, there was no need for a till. Sally had helped Bel set up digital accounting software, and she had a small card reader to take payments. Finance was her sister's area of expertise, after all, and Bel had to remind herself that Sally's way of showing affection was in sharing her practical skills, even though they'd ended up having an argument about the software because Bel couldn't understand it, and her sister became impatient.

That was how things went, usually. Sally would get cross because she would say that Bel wasn't listening while she was trying to explain things. And Bel would quickly lose interest in anything if it wasn't fun or creative, or when Sally started lecturing her, which was often. Sally adored rules. Bel disliked them. They'd got there in the end with the accounting software, but it had taken all of Bel's patience not to retaliate at Sally's bossy tone.

Other than the card reader, on the desk she had a new box of appointment cards with her name and logo on them. She'd chosen the image of a green leaf on a white background, and *Bel's Salon* in a simple yet modern font. She was turning over a new leaf: that's what it represented to her.

'Congratulations, darling!' Bess and Sally approached, and

Bess enveloped her in a bear-like hug. 'We are so proud of you! I can't believe it. You're running a salon! Your own business!'

'Just like you.' Bel hugged Bess back.

Sally gave her sister a peck on the cheek. 'It's smaller than I thought,' she said, looking around.

Bess frowned and gave her a meaningful look. 'And...?' she prompted her wife.

'And, congratulations. Obviously.' Sally made it sound as if she was doing Bel a favour in saying anything at all.

'Your dad would be so proud,' Bess added, mistily.

Sally looked away, not saying anything at all.

'Do you think so?' Bel asked, the familiar feeling of missing her dad settling in her stomach.

'Absolutely he would. We are,' Bess said, holding her hand.

'Well, hopefully it will thrive,' Sally said. 'It's hard, running a small business, especially in rural villages. Even the distillery finds it hard, and that's been running for centuries.'

'I can only do my best,' Bel said, keeping her voice level, but wishing Sally could be more positive. 'I think it will do well.'

'Of course it will!' Bess said.

'You'll have to find somewhere more permanent to live than the cottage, though,' her sister added.

'I guess so. The laird says that I can have the cottage as a long-term rental for now, so I'll stay there and get the salon up and running first,' Bel said, looking around her proudly. *I did this*, she thought. *This is mine.*

It felt good.

'This is some place,' an oddly familiar voice said from behind her.

She turned around, and almost dropped her wine glass.

There, standing before her, was someone she never thought she would see again. Someone who had broken her heart, long before the slow disappointment of her relationship with Andy.

Someone who had made her realise what people were singing about in those love songs on the radio.

'Nate,' Bel murmured in disbelief.

'Hi, Bel. It's been a while.' The man smiled at her, and Bel felt her whole world crumble to the ground.

FIFTEEN

'Nate. I didn't think I'd ever see you again.' Bel realised that her mouth was open; she closed it, aware she probably looked like an idiot.

'Well, here I am. Like a bad penny.' Nate shrugged and shot her the *aw-shucks* grin she remembered so well. She hadn't forgotten his accent, either; Nate, a touring musician, was from Texas, and his gentlemanly mien had been one of the many things that had attracted her to him all those years ago.

Bel had met Nate one unseasonably hot summer when she'd still been at hairdressing college. She'd come to Aberculty to stay with Sally for a couple of weeks; Sally had just moved up to the little village to work at the Loch Cameron distillery. Neither of them knew Scotland, then, but Sally had wanted to get into the beverages industry for a while at that point, and she'd been offered a senior role at Loch Cameron. It wasn't anything she thought she could get elsewhere, so she'd moved from Essex: a nine-hour drive away from Bel.

Two years after Sally left, Bel had met Andy. *And the rest, as they say, is history*, Bel thought, taking Nate in.

But Nate was also part of her history.

A very different part altogether.

Bel felt a blush creeping over her cheeks as she looked at him. He hadn't changed at all, as far as she could see, though it had been ten years. Nate was tall, around six feet two or three, and she could see that he still worked out. He was tanned, sandy-haired, and wore a short beard now: that was a small difference. But his sparkling blue eyes were the same, and so was the way she felt when they met hers.

Ohhh, goodness. Bel couldn't look away. It was as if no time had passed, and she was twenty-five again. She remembered all too well what it was like, being in Nate's arms. Being kissed by him. The feel of his skin against hers.

'Why? Why are you in Loch Cameron?' she breathed, trying to remain composed.

Bel and Nate had spent the summer together, ten years ago. When Bel had gone back to Essex, Nate had promised to come and visit her. They could do the long-distance thing, he'd said. He'd told her that he wanted her; that he needed her, and that they'd make it work, somehow. *I think I'm falling for you*, he'd breathed as they'd spent that last, sweet night together. And her heart had leapt. Because Bel had fallen for Nate the first time they'd slept together: the first time he had looked down and met her eyes as they made love, holding her gaze as he pushed gently, deep within her.

Don't think about that now, she berated herself. Because she had fallen for Nate. But he had blanked her, ghosted her, when she had got back to Essex. She'd called him, but there had been no answer. She'd tried to find out where his band was playing, even, thinking that if he saw her, he'd magically remember that he loved her. That there would be some good reason why he had suddenly cut off all contact after being so sweet and attentive.

Sally had stopped that. *Bel. He knows where you are. He knows how to find you*, her sister had told her firmly. *I may not be an expert when it comes to sleeping with men, but I know how their minds work. For whatever reason, he doesn't want to see you anymore. I'm sorry, but you just need to forget about him and move on.*

When Bel had finally realised that Nate wasn't coming back, she had spent a week in tears, cutting out of her hairdressing course to spend her days sitting on the bathroom floor, weeping. Although she'd only known Nate a little less than a month, they'd spent every available minute together.

Their bond had been intense and electric; she'd felt she knew him, deeply, and that he'd known her. She'd told him things about herself she'd never told anyone else. There was something about Nate that made her feel she could expose the deepest parts of herself; whatever she told him, he understood. And their physical connection had been out of this world. Before Nate, when Bel heard people talk about the fact that they should leave their partners, but the sex was too good – she hadn't understood it. Sex was just sex. It wasn't all *that* wonderful.

After Nate, she had understood. Even though he had ghosted her and broken her heart, she knew that if he had ever found her again, she would have gone back. And she hated that knowledge, because it had made her feel weak.

'On a break between tours. I come back to the village fairly regularly to chill.' Nate's voice was lilting and deep; the sound of it moving memories within Bel. Things she had forgotten now flooded back to her: the way he smelled as she laid with her head on his chest, listening to him. Not caring about the words, but in thrall to the sound, and the music of his voice. 'I was just walking past, and I saw you. It's wild. You look great.'

Nate's fingertips brushed her hair gently; his eyes meeting hers as he touched her, so lightly. Yet, his touch reverberated through her, like a stone thrown into the smooth waters of the loch.

'Oh...' Bel didn't know what else to say. She looked up and caught Bess's eye, who gave her a curious look. Bel wished someone would come over and interrupt her and Nate so that she could escape the pull she felt towards him; and at the same, her instinctual self wanted to wrap her arms around his muscular torso and bury her head in his neck.

'So, this place is yours?' Nate picked up one of the appointment cards and turned it over in his long fingers. 'I remember you were training to be a hairdresser. This is so cool!'

'Yes. Opening day.' Bel couldn't say what she wanted to. She wanted to breathe him in, kiss him, hold him. But she also wanted to punish him for breaking her heart. She'd gotten over it, or so she thought. But seeing him again had ripped open her wounded heart.

'Your own boss, huh. That's awesome.' He looked around at the modern décor and smiled appreciatively. 'You've got great taste. I had my hair cut in here once, and it was not like this. I should come in and get a trim, now I know it's you.' He gave her that lazy smile again.

Bel's heart quickened. She cleared her throat and looked away. 'What about you? Still on the road?' she asked. Now she was older, Bel realised someone like Nate probably got a new girlfriend every time he went to a new town or city. He played the piano and saxophone and sang; as a touring musician, he could have his pick of the girls at the stage door every night, after they'd seen him stripped to the waist onstage, immersed in the music. He was a brilliant performer, and Bel knew as well as anyone that he exuded a raw sexuality onstage that was incredibly hard to resist.

'Yeah. Sometimes I think about settling down. But then, another tour comes up. I've just come back from one,' he named a well-known female solo artist. 'Six weeks in south America. It was an honour.'

Bel remembered how sincere Nate was when he talked

about his work. It was one of the things that had first attracted her to him.

'Right,' she nodded. 'Well, it was good to see you.' She wanted to keep her guard up around him; she didn't want to be weak again.

'Bel–' Nate reached for her hand, and caught it in his as she turned to speak to Dotty and Eric. 'I'd like to catch up. Sometime soon, when I can have you all to myself.' He'd lowered his voice so that no one else could hear what he was saying; instinctively, she leaned in towards him to hear. 'I... I always thought about you, Bel. I think there are things that need to be said,' he added, his voice husky.

'Sure. You know where I am,' she replied, a wave of desire flowing over her. His skin was warm; without meaning to, she squeezed his fingers briefly. It was odd; as soon as he touched her, Bel was transported back to their previous connection. There was an unspoken language between them that had been established all those years ago; one stroke of Nate's hand had awoken that intimacy between them.

'I do,' he said, tucking her card into the pocket of his jeans. 'I'll let you get on with your evening, Bel: you've got all these people to talk to. But... I'll be in touch, okay?'

'Okay.' Bel could hardly hear or see anyone else around her as she watched him walk out of the door. It was as if a spotlight shone upon him, and when he had stood next to her, she too had basked in its light, just briefly. As he walked away, she felt as though he'd taken the light with him, and, despite it being her celebration day, the salon felt a little darker without his presence.

It was ridiculous to feel that – *it was her day! It was an exciting, wonderful moment!* Yet, that was how she felt, just for a second. That something beautiful had spread its wings in her new salon, and now was gone.

Bel shook herself.

Remember where you are. Remember who you are. You are the new owner of your very own hairdressing salon. You are the centre of attention. You are killing it right now. Don't let a man take all that away from you, just with the click of his fingers. Don't do it, Bel.

Dotty pressed a glass of champagne into her hand, and Bel looked away from the door and back at the salon, thronged with people who were all there to celebrate her. This was her moment.

But, for the rest of the evening, she caught herself looking towards the door and wishing that Nate would come back.

SIXTEEN

'And that, my friend, is Rummy!' Gretchen Ross hooted in triumph and laid her hand of cards on the table. 'Oh, hello, dear. I didn't see you there.'

Bel had popped in to the care home to visit Gretchen and bring her some flowers from the garden. She liked Gretchen, and it wasn't a long drive to go and see her.

'Pure luck,' Mavis sat opposite Gretchen, frowning. 'Hello, Bel. Nice to see you again.'

'Hi, Mavis,' Bel grinned. She handed Gretchen the flowers: velvety pink roses and white sweetpeas, with some heavy, nodding-headed peachy peonies. The cottage garden was absolutely full of them at the moment.

'Ah, what beautiful flowers! Thank you.' Gretchen put them to her nose and took in a long sniff. 'I do miss the cottage garden, I must admit. This place has a nice enough garden, but it can't compare. Ohhh, smell those peonies,' she sighed. 'Mavis. Smell these peonies. And the roses!'

'You know perfectly well I lost my sense of smell in 1978.' Mavis refused to sniff the flowers that Gretchen held out to her.

'Deviated septum. I had it operated on, but it wasn't a success,' she added in a low voice to Bel.

'That's a shame,' Bel said, politely. 'Could you have it fixed now? I assume there have been advances in surgery by now... maybe...' she trailed off.

'Certainly not.' Mavis sniffed. 'I've got used to it now. There would be no point smelling everything again. It would be overwhelming.'

Gretchen caught Bel's eye and rolled hers. Bel tried not to laugh.

'Mavis believes that stoicism is next to godliness,' Gretchen commented, collecting up the playing cards from the table. 'God forbid she should enjoy anything. Ignore her.'

'Gretchen doesn't seem to understand basic politeness,' Mavis countered. 'Excuse her, please, Bel.'

'How's your grandson? The... legal assistant?' Bel changed the subject, though she was amused by Gretchen and Mavis' frenemy vibe.

'Oh, he's very well, thank you.' Mavis was immediately distracted, as Bel had hoped. 'Jonathan. He's hoping for a promotion soon.'

'That's great. Must be an interesting job,' Bel commented.

'Interesting if you like sticking your nose in other people's business,' Gretchen interjected.

'Are you trying to suggest that I do that? Do sit, Bel.' Mavis indicated an empty chair at the table.

'Wouldn't dream of it.' Gretchen raised one eyebrow.

'Well, since you mention it. Jonathan said that he'd seen Hell's Angels in court a lot recently.' Mavis pursed her mouth as if she'd just sucked a sour sweet. 'He says they're always there, walking around the building in their leather jackets with patches and what have you. Shaved heads, loud engines when they drive up. Jonathan says he has to put his hands over his ears when they arrive, they make such a din.'

'Hell's Angels? You mean the Warriors? They're a local biker gang,' Bel said, thinking immediately of Christian and his friends. 'I mean, it might not be them, of course.'

'Yes. The Warriors. I remember now, because Jonathan said, I wouldn't fancy going to war with them.' Mavis clicked her tongue in disapproval. 'He says they're very rough gentlemen. I suspect they've been involved in some criminal shenanigans.'

'Come on, Mavis,' Gretchen sighed. 'Jonathan would be intimidated by Harry and Roger if they put on leathers,' she nodded to a couple of especially geriatric looking older gentlemen who were dozing in armchairs nearby. 'This just sounds like gossip to me.'

'Well, how do you explain them being at the courts, then?' Mavis argued.

'I don't know, but, unlike some, I wouldn't make assumptions,' Gretchen said, testily.

'Hmm. If it walks like a duck and quacks like a duck, then guess what, Gretchen? It's a duck,' Mavis said, standing up slowly and gripping her walking stick, which had been lying at the side of the chair. 'Now, if you'll excuse me, I've got a massage appointment. Bel, it was a pleasure to see you again.' The woman bestowed a rare smile on Bel. 'Gretchen.' She frowned at her fellow card player.

'Ignore her, she's a bitter old vixen.' Gretchen shook her head as Mavis made her way out of the communal room, barking something at an elderly man in a wheelchair who didn't get out of her way fast enough. 'I don't think those young men are up to anything. They were probably just there to pay parking tickets or something.'

'Hmm. It's just that Christian is in that gang,' Bel said. 'I wouldn't like to think that... I don't know. He was up to no good.'

'Well, I'm sure it's nothing,' Gretchen said, carefully. 'But, of course, there is always the vague possibility that Mavis and her wet flannel of a grandson are right. My advice is, ask him. It's the simplest solution.'

'You're right. As ever,' Bel sighed. 'I'm sure it's nothing.'

'Then I'm sure too,' Gretchen squeezed her hand. 'Christian is a good egg. I've got a good sixth sense about these things. That's how I know Mavis is appalling,' she caught Bel's eye, and they both laughed. 'Still, I'm stuck with her,' Gretchen chuckled. 'Don't get old, Bel. One day, you're a captain of industry. The next, you're stuck playing rummy with Mavis Bottomley.'

'I'll try, but I think it might be inevitable.' Bel smiled. 'The getting older thing, anyway.'

'Hmm. Well, you're right there, I suppose.' Gretchen sighed. 'But you've got a lot of life ahead of you still, my girl. My advice is: live it, and ignore the Mavises of this life. I do.'

'All right. I will,' Bel said with a grin. Gretchen was probably right. There had to be a good reason why Christian and the Warriors were in court. And anyway, why should she care what Christian was up to? He wasn't anything but her gardener.

Still, on the drive home, Bel couldn't help but worry. If Christian was a criminal, then she wasn't sure how happy she was with him being around the cottage. Should she warn her neighbours? Should she do something?

Come on, Bel. Now you sound like Mavis, she thought. She would just ask Christian about it, and see what he said. That was the mature thing to do. That was what Gretchen would do, and what she'd advised.

And, Bel thought, thinking about WWGD – What Would Gretchen Do – before most decisions in life was probably a good idea. After all, it was Gretchen that had inspired her to open the salon. Everyone would probably benefit from being more Gretchen Ross.

SEVENTEEN

'Helloooo?' a voice called out in the shop.

Bel, who was finishing sorting out the stock room, heaved a sigh of relief at the interruption. She leaned around the door to see who it was. 'Oh hi, Fiona.' Bel wiped cobwebs from her sleeve, grimacing.

'Hiya. Just thought I'd pop over an' see how it was goin'. Bit of a slow day fer me.' Fiona came in and closed the door behind her. 'D'ye need a hand?'

'No, I'm fine, thanks. Still clearing out the stock room.' Bel sneezed. 'Ugh. It's so dusty back there.'

'No' the glamorous side o' hairdressin', eh,' Fiona laughed.

'Not really. But it's fine.'

In fact, Bel had been thinking about Christian and the Warriors. She hadn't seen Christian yet, but she was thinking about how to broach the subject of him being in court. She couldn't just bowl up to him in the garden and say, *So, Mavis at the care home's grandson Jonathan thinks you're a criminal.* It wasn't polite, *and* it made her sound mad.

'Hmm. Listen, that fella ye were talkin' to yesterday?' Fiona leaned against one of the white leather chairs. 'The bonny one, aye.'

'Oh. Nate.' Bel looked down at her grubby T-shirt and frowned. She had temporarily forgotten about him, having Christian on her mind. *One potential criminal, one nightmare ex. What a lucky girl I am*, she thought. 'Just someone from a long time ago.'

'Nate, is it?' Fiona narrowed her eyes at Bel. 'I've seen him around.'

'You have?' Bel asked, cautiously.

'Aye. With a couple o' different girls. He isnae married, I don't think. I looked at his hand yesterday.' Fiona raised a playful eyebrow. 'Game on, in which case, I'd say.'

'Oh, I see. Well, I'm not interested.' Bel shrugged, trying to appear nonchalant.

Fiona was having none of it. 'Ye had quite the chat. Somethin' was goin' on. Any longer an' I thought I'd have tae get the hose out and give ye both a soakin'. Come on. Dish the dirt.'

'There's nothing to say! We dated briefly, ten years ago.'

'Dated! He's hot. Well done.'

'Oh. Haha. Thanks.' Bel blushed a little, thinking of Nate and how it had been with him. How close they had been, if only for a brief period of time.

'So how come he came to the salon? Did ye look him up an' ask him?' Fiona asked. 'I would, I dinnae blame ye.'

'No. That was the strange thing. He said he just happened to be in the village, walked past the salon and saw me. Weird, huh. Apparently, he comes to Loch Cameron fairly often.'

'Quite a coincidence, but okay.' Fiona raised an eyebrow. 'So?'

'So, nothing.' Bel crossed her arms over her chest, defensively. 'He was crappy to me back then. I'm not interested in men right now; I've got the salon to focus on.'

'Hmm. Right ye are,' Fiona sighed. 'I'll watch this space.'

'Well, you can, but I'm telling you, nothing's happening between me and Nate,' Bel insisted.

'Hmm. Sounds like you're tryin' tae convince yerself more than me, lassie,' Fiona grinned. 'Anyway. I should get back. Let me know if ye need a hand, okay?'

'All right. Thanks, Fiona.'

Bel watched her friend leave, thoughtfully. It wasn't exactly a surprise that Nate had been seen with different women around the village. Why wouldn't he? He was single, attractive and he'd always known how to talk to girls. Plus, there was the musician factor, which made them putty in his hands. Still, seeing him yesterday and now hearing this from Fiona gave Bel a feeling she didn't like. It was jealousy, pure and simple.

That is a totally ridiculous thing to feel, she thought, going back to the stock room. *You don't own Nate; you were never even his girlfriend. You were a fling, ten years ago. That was all.*

She had managed to forget about Nate, eventually. Or, if not forget him, then push him to the back of her mind, and only think about him on rare occasions when she allowed herself to. Yet, she was jealous. Jealous of women who had managed to keep Nate's attention for longer than she had. Jealous of women who had kissed him, touched him, and felt his skin on theirs.

Bel. Get a hold of yourself, she rebuked herself firmly.

She thought about Serena and Rose. Serena had yearned for Rose – written to her, missed her – for ten years.

She and Nate had been apart for ten years. It was a coincidence, that was all. *I didn't yearn for Nate for all that time, like Serena did for Rose*, she rationalised to herself.

No. That wasn't honest. She *had* missed him, for all those years. His memory had always been there, at the edge of her consciousness. What was the phrase? *The one that got away?* That was Nate, for her, and now that he had reappeared in her life, it had put her on edge. Appearing in her salon and then disappearing, flashing her a tantalising glimpse of what she'd had, so briefly: that was Nate's style. And it had worked, because now she couldn't stop thinking about him.

What if Nate was "the one"?

If he was, then surely it was a sign that he had reappeared in her life, just when she had separated from Andy. If Serena's story was anything, then surely it was a reminder to be brave in love and to put yourself out there with the right person.

But, on the other hand, was love too demanding? *What should we give for love?* she wondered. She had sacrificed her wants and goals in the past for Andy: she didn't want to do it a second time. She was just starting to be happy again. She didn't want to put herself in a position where she started sacrificing her joy for someone else. Not that Nate had asked her to do that, but it was something she had done before. She didn't want to do it again.

Yet, more than anyone, Nate had been the man Bel had felt the most for, despite the fact their relationship hadn't lasted long. But the feelings were deep: deeper than she had known with anyone else.

Was this a second chance at happiness? Serena and Rose hadn't had a second chance – as far as Bel knew, anyway. But it seemed that she and Nate might.

She opened her social media app and scrolled to the tarot reader's account that had predicted big change in her life before. In the message for that day, it said: *Be open to surprises and messages from the past. Doors that you thought were closed are reopening.*

Online messages were hardly anything to base life decisions on. But maybe it was a small sign. As far as Bel was concerned, the biggest sign of all was her heart, and the feelings she held there for Nate. Were they supposed to reunite? Was this the great love she had always wanted?

EIGHTEEN

Bel. We need to talk.

Bel was taking a lunchtime walk alongside the loch when her phone buzzed in her pocket. She had been thinking about the letters again. She took the phone out and frowned when she saw who was calling.

Andy.

Whenever she saw his name appear on her phone, her tummy got tight and she felt anxious. What did he want now? Bel didn't want to talk to him. As far as she was concerned, she was moving on, and the whole sorry mess was starting – slowly – to take up less space in her brain. There were moments when she realised she had been concentrating so hard on doing some-one's hair that she hadn't thought about Andy and the day everything had fallen apart for her for more than an hour.

That was progress.

I don't need to talk to you, was what she wanted to reply, but she sighed and tapped out a more polite response.

Hi. What about?

The house he replied. Then, his face appeared on her screen: he was calling her. Bel hadn't got around to removing his photo from his contact entry yet. It was a picture of both of them from a long time ago, at a dinner party hosted by friends. They were looking into each other's eyes and laughing. Bel had thought she was in love with him, then.

'Hello?' she answered the call warily. She'd considered not answering it, but she knew Andy: if he wanted something, he wouldn't give up until he got it. It was better to deal with him quickly now, although she didn't want to.

Bel wondered briefly how many men would take the same kind of attitude in dealing with a demanding female partner. Not many, she thought. In her experience – even at Handy-Phone – men demanded time and attention to their problems, and women tended to accommodate them. Andy had always been demanding.

'Bel, I need to talk to you about the house,' Andy repeated, his voice tense. No asking how she was, no polite chitchat.

As soon as she answered the phone, she regretted it.

'What about it?' Bel stopped her pleasant amble along the cobbled lochside path and turned to face the Inn, which was opposite. It looked especially pretty today, bedecked with hanging baskets and window boxes full of bright flowers. It was nice to focus on something pleasant; it diluted the dread of hearing Andy's voice.

'Listen. I know you've signed the papers and everything. But... there's a problem with me buying you out.'

'What do you mean, there's a problem?' Bel asked, deliberately keeping her tone level. Inside, though, her stomach flipped in anxiety. 'I've opened the salon, Andy.'

The terms of the salon's lease meant that Hal had wanted her to get started before she had actually received the money from her half of the house, which was why Sally and Bess had given her the short-term loan. Since Bel had signed the legal agreement for the house weeks ago, she had thought it was simply a waiting game for the money. The fact that it hadn't appeared in her account yet had started to worry her, but she had resolutely pressed on with the salon. It was keeping her busy, and that was a good thing.

'Yeah. The thing is that the remortgage has fallen through. I can't pay you the money. Not right now, anyway.'

'What do you mean, it's fallen through? I thought you had it agreed.' Bel's legs felt wobbly. She reached for the railing behind her that stretched along the edge of the walkway.

'I did. But then the underwriter had a problem with some of the detail. My self-employed income, even though it's enough. They don't like self-employed customers if there isn't someone with an employer income on the agreement as well.'

'Isn't this something that should have been mentioned before now?' Bel was aghast. 'I've taken on the lease for the salon. The agreement is for a year, minimum. I've paid for refitting, stock, marketing...' she trailed off. 'Andy. I need that money.'

'Look. I'm doing my best here, but it's not exactly easy.' Andy's voice was plaintive. 'I've given you everything you wanted, Bel. Don't be like this.'

'Like what?!' Bel felt desperation rising in her stomach as she thought about having to go back on all the new plans she had: the new life she had started to build in Loch Cameron. In one phone call, Andy had threatened to pull it all out from under her feet.

Just like he had done before.

The memory of that day came back to Bel as she clung to the railing. She felt sick. For a moment, she held the phone away from her and took in some deep breaths. She let the cool, clean air fill her lungs, and then sighed all the air out again.

'Bel? Are you there? Bel?'

She could hear Andy at the end of the phone, but she

ignored him and took in another deep breath, letting it all go. She thought of what her dad had always told her: *you're stronger than you know, cupcake. Believe in yourself, just like I believe in you.*

When her dad had been alive, Bel had been so different. She had been the sassy girl, always speaking her mind, sometimes getting into trouble for being too outspoken. When he died, Bel had taken that part of herself and hidden it, deep inside her.

Believe in yourself. Don't let Andy walk all over you again.

When she felt more centred, she put the phone to her ear again.

'I'm here,' she said, her voice level. 'Andy, I've started a business up here and I need that money. So, I suggest you get it sorted out ASAP and give me what's mine, otherwise I will get solicitors involved.'

'You can't make demands on me. I'm doing my best here,' Andy retorted, raising his voice. 'I don't have to give you anything!'

Bel swore under her breath. Was he really *serious*? After everything he had done to her? He thought he didn't owe her anything?

'I think you'll find that you do, and you've agreed legally to give me half of the value of the house, Andy. And, by the way, you were also the one who cheated on me. I did nothing wrong, except stay too long in an unhealthy relationship. So, I'll wait to hear from you. But if I don't hear from you in a week, then I'm getting legal representation,' Bel kept her voice steady. 'One week, Andy. Goodbye.'

She ended the call, pleased she had been firm, but now her stomach churned and a wave of anxiety washed over her. Everything she had worked so hard for was in peril. *She could lose the salon.* Bel closed her eyes. She wanted the salon. More than she'd wanted anything for a long time. It was totally unfair that Andy could just sweep in and take it away.

Bel clenched her fists. *You are in the alternative timeline,* she reminded herself. *This is your new life, and you've got to fight for it.*

Bel's Salon was her baby, and she wasn't just going to let it slip from between her fingers.

But she was scared. She could lose it all, just like Sally had warned. And then, where would she be?

NINETEEN

'So, this Serena was in love with the famous ballerina?' Christian leaned on his spade, taking a break from digging a hole for a new rose bush he was planting in the cottage garden.

'Yes.' Bel sat down on the grass, crossing her legs. When Christian had turned up in his van that morning, she almost hadn't come out of the cottage at all. She'd hardly slept and she felt awful. But it was such a beautiful day that she had thought at least she should get some sunshine on her skin: staying inside and being stressed and anxious wasn't doing her any favours.

Bel had been super stressed since Andy's phone call the day before. The thought that she might lose the salon was becoming an obsession, even though she was trying to stay calm. Immediately, she had started to worry about the fact that she had borrowed money from Sally and Bess, and now she might not be able to pay them back. The thought was unbearable.

Instead, she'd found herself telling Christian about the letters she'd discovered at the salon. It was something else to focus on: a welcome distraction, for now.

'She was heartbroken when Rose left the village. I don't think she ever came back. At least, not for a long time.' It was another sunny day, so Bel was wearing denim cutoff shorts and a white crop top to stay cool.

Christian laid the spade down and joined her on the grass. 'So, what else did you find out about Rose?'

'Just what I told you. I think there's probably other stuff online. But it's Serena I'm really interested in.' Bel pulled her hair into a clumsy ponytail and let the air get to her neck for a minute. 'God, it's hot.'

'It is,' Christian gave her an unreadable look, then gazed down, plucking a blade of grass from the lawn and rubbing it between his fingers. 'I think I had a distant relative called Serena, you know. I think so, anyway. Couldn't tell you anything else,' he shrugged. 'Why her, anyway?'

'I don't know. I guess I feel for her. She was so in love with Rose, and Rose left her. I don't know that it was out of meanness or anything – Rose had a career path ahead of her. I don't know.' She wrapped a hairband around the ponytail.

'You do know.' Christian looked back at her. 'Be honest.'

'All right. I suppose it's made me reflect on my own love life.' *Specifically, whether Nate is The One*, she added, in her mind. Since she'd seen him again, she hadn't been able to get the thought out of her mind. What if they were meant to reunite? It seemed such a crazy off-chance that she would ever see him again. It had to *mean* something. But what?

Bel left it there, keeping her thoughts to herself – she didn't want to get into things too deeply with Christian. She had been thinking about how to broach the subject of the Warriors being in court, but she hadn't found a natural way to mention it so far. They hardly knew each other, though when she was with him, she felt strangely at ease. It was an odd feeling; she'd never felt that way with anyone before. Not even Andy, who she had shared a house, a bed and a life with for years.

She'd arranged to go over and see Bess and Sally later, to talk about the loan and see if it was possible to have longer to pay them back, if Andy didn't manage to come through with the money. She'd given Sally a quick summary on the phone the night before. Her sister had made a disgusted snort and said, *I knew he was an idiot. I guess I thought he'd do right by you, for some reason. No idea why. You really can pick them, Bel.*

Are you suggesting that this is my fault? Bel had asked her sister, irritated.

But Sally had just sighed. *Why would you think that?* she'd replied. *Why would anything be your fault?*

Yet it was her sister's tone that said everything. It implied that this *was* Bel's fault, and it was just another in a series of failures. Bel wished Sally could not act the big sister for once, and sympathise with her. But she was never going to do that. Her role was too firmly entrenched.

'In what way, reflecting on your love life?' Christian held the blade of grass between his thumbs so that it was taut in the small gap between them, and blew through the gap. The grass made a surprisingly loud fluted sound. 'Sorry. ADHD.' He shot her a smile, and made the noise again. 'Basically, a grown-up child. Well. That's just me. Not the ADHD.'

'Ha. It's resourceful. You never know when you'll need a grass whistle.' Bel smiled. 'Oh, I don't know. I've never had that big love, you know? I was infatuated with someone, once, but that's not the same.' She thought of Nate again, and how he'd looked just a few days ago at the salon. Her head was all over the place. On one hand, she was dealing with Andy and the house. On the other, she kept thinking about Nate. She had to admit she had been a little disappointed that he hadn't called, despite taking one of her appointment cards. Was he The One? Was this what him coming back into her life meant? Her head felt as though it was spinning.

'I find that hard to believe.' Christian stared at her. 'That you never had the big love. You seem like someone who would be fighting men off on a regular basis.'

'As appealing as that sounds, no.' Bel frowned. 'Honestly, I don't think any woman loves the idea of having to fight men off. Isn't that just harassment?'

'Okay, I phrased that badly. I meant you seem like someone who would have no shortage of love interests.' He held out his hands placatingly.

'Well, I haven't. I just came out of an eight-year relationship,' she explained, pulling a face.

'Something you want to talk about?' Christian raised an eyebrow.

'No. Thank you, though,' she added, hastily. 'I guess I almost envy Serena. She was heartbroken, but at least she had that love, once.'

'I don't know.' Christian looked away, a shadow of emotion crossing his face. 'Be careful what you wish for.'

'Have you had your heart broken?' Bel shaded her eyes and gazed at him. It was a forward question, but she felt comfortable enough to ask it.

'Yeah. Wasn't great.'

'Do you want to talk about it?' She watched him as he pulled his knees up to his chest, as if protecting his heart. 'I could do with hearing about someone else's problems, quite honestly. It would distract me from mine.'

'Hmm. Well, I'm happy to listen to your problems, but I'll tell you about mine another time, maybe,' he replied, shortly. 'Did you find out anything else about Serena?'

'No, but I'm going to see if I can.' Bel accepted his diversionary tactic: she knew all too well what it was like not to want to talk about something painful, although she had to admit she was intrigued about Christian's love life.

'You know who you should ask? Gretchen, who used to live here. She's a great lady, and she lived in the village most of her life. We've had some good chats, when I had to call her about the garden and stuff,' he suggested, picking a few more blades of grass.

'That's not a bad idea. I was up there yesterday, actually,' Bel said.

'Oh, cool. How is she?'

'In good form. I took her some flowers from the garden.'

Bel reminded herself of her new motto – What Would Gretchen Do? – and how she and Gretchen had been discussing Mavis's story about the Warriors bike gang being up at the law courts. She knew she should ask Christian about it, to sate her curiosity at the very least, but she was also partially distracted by the sight of his naked torso so close to her. Gretchen would definitely have enjoyed that too. He was tanned, and this close up she could see his tattoos more clearly. A bear's head roared on his right pectoral, and a winged figure adorned his belly, with the number 19 emblazoned inside it.

'What's 19?' She pointed at the tattoo.

'Oh. My racing number. In the Warriors,' he said, offhandedly.

'You race the bikes?'

'Sometimes, for fun. No biggie.'

'You know, I don't really know what a bike gang actually does,' Bel said, innocently. 'Is it racing, then? Touring, riding around on your bikes for fun?'

'Umm. Well, we do those things, yes, but there are other things.' He sounded evasive.

'Like what?' she probed. Maybe she could get Christian to tell her more about the Warriors without having to mention what Mavis had told her. Gretchen would have been able to get it out of him with no problems: she was a conversation ninja.

'Err. Well, it's sort of hard to explain.' Christian looked uncomfortable.

'You can tell me,' Bel pushed a little harder. 'I'm not going to tell anyone. I mean, you hear things about biker gangs,' she added.

'Do you?' He shaded his eyes from the sun and frowned at her. 'What would that be?'

'Oh, you know.' She felt a blush steal up onto her cheeks. This was awkward. 'They used to be criminal organisations, didn't they? Once upon a time. In America, anyway.'

'Yes. But that's nothing to do with what we do now,' Christian said, sounding guarded. 'Is that what you think? I'm a criminal?'

'No, I...' Bel trailed off. 'Someone told me that the Warriors were seen in court recently. I just wondered what that was all about,' she said, grateful to have said it at last.

'Oh, did they?' He raised an eyebrow. 'Sometimes I forget how much gossip there is in Loch Cameron.'

'I know. But, if you need help, I'm here,' she said, deciding to couch her language in supportive terms. That felt nicer than going in, guns blazing with *so, I hear you're a burglar or a drug dealer or both.*

'I'd prefer not to talk about it,' he said, slowly. 'Maybe another time.'

'Why?' Bel asked.

'It's complicated,' he sighed. 'Look, I'd tell you if I could, but I can't.'

'Oh.' Bel didn't know what to say, now. She'd expected him to tell her about parking tickets or something else as innocuous, and dispel her worries. But he'd made it sound as though the issue was a lot more serious.

Was Mavis right, after all? The thought filled her with disappointment. Christian seemed like such a good guy.

'I can't talk about it, Bel,' Christian repeated. 'I'd like to tell you. Really. But I can't. Legally. It's an ongoing case I'm involved in.'

'I see.' Bel didn't know what else to say. 'I mean, I don't see, but OK.'

'I guess you just have to trust me,' he said. 'But we don't know each other that well, so I get it if you don't.' He gave her a long stare. 'I'm used to people thinking the worst of me. Why would you be any different?'

'Christian... that's not fair. I—'

Bel's phone buzzed. She frowned, looking at the unrecognised number on the screen.

'Sorry, I'm just going to get this. It might be for the salon,' she said, pressing the green call button.

Christian nodded and stood up, picking up the spade. 'No worries. I should get on anyway,' he said.

Bel could feel that the energy between them had shifted. She wanted to go back to how they were before, but she didn't know how: If Christian refused to deny that he was caught up in criminal proceedings – he'd told her that he was involved in a court case just now – then how could she trust him?

Absentmindedly, she pressed the call button on her phone and held it to her ear.

'Hey, Bel. It's Nate.' His voice was as velvety as ever, and a thrill went down Bel's spine as soon as she heard it.

TWENTY

'It's a typical Isabel Burns situation.' Sally turned back to the stove and stirred a pot more vigorously than it probably needed. 'That's all I'm saying.'

'Sal. Come on.' Bess looked up from the counter where she was chopping onions. 'That's not fair.'

Bel had gone over to Sally and Bess's house for dinner. She had just told them that she wouldn't be able to pay them back as quickly as she had initially imagined, and knew her sister would be angry about it, because that was how Sally operated. She had always been a kind of protective tiger mom sister to Bel, and though Bel appreciated it, there were times like these when she resented being treated like an errant teenager.

'It is fair, thank you.' Sally frowned at her wife. 'I know you love Bel, but you weren't there when we were younger. You don't know.'

'What's that supposed to mean?' Bel stood with her arms crossed over her chest in Sally's new kitchen, feeling vulnerable. She hated it when Sally was cross with her. 'It's hardly my fault if Andy can't remortgage the house.'

'You know what I mean.' Sally stood with her back to Bel,

hands gripping the edge of the stovetop. 'You and Dad were always like this. There would be a plan, and then the plan fell through because you were both away with the fairies. Impractical. Then I'd have to sort it out.'

'I don't think you can blame me on this occasion. Don't bring Dad into it, either.' Bel had a twinge of grief like she always did when she thought of him.

'I can say what I like about Dad. More than you can,' Sally snapped.

Bel recoiled.

'Sally!' Bess interjected, her eyes wide. 'That's too far, and you know it.'

'Is it? He wasn't her biological father. I'm just saying what's true.'

'Wow. I can't believe you brought that up.' Bel felt Sally's words as if they were a slap in the face.

After their dad had died, Bel and Sally had found out that he wasn't Bel's biological father. He'd never said anything, and it was only when Sally had gone through some papers in a box under his bed that they'd found the letters from her real father – a previous boyfriend of their mother's. It seemed that, while their mother was married to their dad, and after she'd had Sally, she had got back in touch with her ex and had an affair.

The letters were brief, but Bel's biological father had apparently wanted to have contact with her. Repeatedly, he'd said: *She is my blood. I want to see her.* There were no letters in the box from Bel and Sally's parents to see their replies, but when Bel had looked at the dates on the letters from her biological father, they'd become less frequent as time had passed. He had given up on her, it seemed.

And Bel had never wanted anyone but her dad: the one that had cleaned her up when she skinned her knee, who told her stories, who baked cakes with her and told her funny stories and, still, appeared in her dreams. Biology meant nothing. Love meant everything.

'Why not? It's true. And you were his favourite, despite the fact that I was his flesh and blood,' Sally added, bitterly. 'I was never a part of your little gang. I was out there, being sensible.'

'Oh, for goodness' sake.' Bel raised her voice. 'How can you even say that? I can't help the fact that Dad and I got on better than you did. Maybe if you'd removed the stick from up your ass now and again and had fun with us, maybe you would have felt more included. And, just so you know, he never *once* made me feel like I wasn't his daughter. But you did. You've been weird about it ever since we found out. Like you're being weird now.'

'I'm not being weird, Bel. I'm trying to explain to you that I have been looking after you your entire life, and you are completely ungrateful for it!' Sally shouted. The cup that was in her hand went flying across the kitchen and shattered on the wall. Sally swore. 'Look what you made me do!' she shouted, and grabbed a tea towel.

'Babe. You need to calm down,' Bess warned, taking the tea towel from her and picking up the pieces of the cup gingerly with it.

'It's not my fault! What do you expect when she just creates drama wherever she goes?' Sally argued.

'Don't blame me for that.' Bel had, in the past, hunkered down and accepted Sally's anger. But she wasn't going to anymore.

'I *can* blame you, Bel!' Sally yelled. 'You blithely danced your way into leasing the salon from Hal, with me as guarantor. You know he called me up to check you were on the level, that he could trust you as a new business in the village? I said, *Of course you can, Hal. She's my sister. And if anything goes wrong, then you can come to me.*'

'I didn't ask you to do that,' Bel argued.

'You asked us for the loan, and we gave it to you in good

faith,' Sally argued. 'So, yes, you did, actually. Now you're telling me that Andy can't pay for your half of the house. I thought this had all been signed off, and it was just a matter of waiting for the money.'

'It was. We signed a legal agreement,' Bel countered. 'But that was with a solicitor. I can't help it if he can't get a bank to agree to what he needs. He says it's because he has self-employed income. Me being at HandyPhone was why we got the mortgage approved when we bought the house.'

Sally rolled her eyes.

'Bel, love, I think what your sister is trying to say is that we love you, and we're here for you always,' Bess interjected, walking across the kitchen to take both of Bel's hands in hers. 'But you know she's the money whiz around here, and we love her for that. And, basically, this is all making her pretty anxious,' Bess finished. 'So, we're happy to help you as much as we can, but I guess remember where she's coming from too.'

'Babe, that's very sweet. But it doesn't change the fact that I had to take out a loan to get that money for her,' Sally argued.

'No, it doesn't. But you need to apologise for what you said about her biological father. You know Bel is your sister, and that's that. We will never bring that up again.' Bess had a steely tone to her voice now.

Sally looked up and met her wife's eyes for a moment. 'Fine. Sorry. I mean, biology or not, she's just like Dad. He insisted on working at that bloody biscuit factory all his life, and it meant we never had anything. He had no idea about money and nor does she!' Sally raised her voice in exasperation.

'Well, thanks for that backhanded compliment and apology.'

'Bloody hell, Bel. I said sorry. What more do you want?'

'Yeah. You said it. I don't think you meant it.'

'What do you want? I said it. I meant it. I'm sorry.' Sally raised her hands to the ceiling in frustration.

'Please don't talk about Dad like that. He did everything he could for us after Mum died. No, the biscuit factory wasn't ideal, but it was a job. He had a job and he paid the bills and put food on the table, Sally. Don't ever say he didn't,' Bel repeated. Even more than Sally bringing up her parentage, it hurt when she was negative about their dad.

'Fine. But you were both dreamers. I dunno, Bel. This whole thing is just... classic *you*.' Sally sighed and sat down at the kitchen table opposite Bel. 'I wouldn't have signed a new lease without having the money in the bank. I'm more careful than you.'

'What do you want me to say? I'm sorry? I *am* sorry!' Bel was really trying to hold it together in the face of Sally's displeasure, but it was hard. Not least because Bel really felt like she could have done with seeing her dad, right now. No one else had understood her like he had.

'I know you are,' Sally sighed. 'Look, I am sorry. About what I said. I didn't mean it. And I'm annoyed at Andy too. Thing is, if he can't buy you out then he's going to have to sell that house. So, you'd get your money back then, but it'd take a while. And, okay, you've signed some piece of paper with a solicitor to say that you both get half. But he's in the house and you've left it. There's nothing stopping him just living there and not giving you anything.'

'He can't do that!' Bel felt a wave of panic engulf her.

'Possession is nine tenths of the law, as they say.' Sally shrugged. 'I hope he doesn't. But my point is, people change their minds very quickly in these kinds of situations.'

'She's not wrong, Bel,' Bess said, gently. 'How can we know what he's doing? Andy, I mean?'

'I don't know. We just have to trust him?' Bel knew that as soon as she'd said it, that she couldn't. Andy had proved that he couldn't be trusted the moment Bel had seen his half-naked lover walk into her kitchen. 'Oh, no,' she covered her face with her hands. 'I'm so sorry, Sal. What am I going to do?'

'I don't know!' Sally shouted, and banged the wooden spoon she'd been stirring the pot with down on the table. 'Can I please not constantly be the one that has to provide the solution here? It's your problem, Bel. You sort it out.' She walked out of the kitchen, a furious expression on her face.

'Sorry, Bel. She's just really stressed about this,' Bess said, looking concerned. 'I better go after her.'

'I know. Go.' Bel sank into one of the kitchen chairs. Why couldn't just one thing go right in her life? She had done the hard part. Wasn't it time for her new life to start? Wasn't she supposed to be *in the new timeline* now?

She took out her phone and started scrolling aimlessly, trying to calm the ball of stress in her stomach. She and Sally had had this tension between them for years, and Bel had never been able to figure out how to dissolve it. She had tried to go along with Sally's suggestions and plans, but she never seemed to get it right in her sister's eyes. And sometimes she'd resisted, knowing that what Sally wanted wasn't always the best thing for her. Whichever way, though, it always seemed to end up with Sally storming out and Bel wondering what she'd done wrong.

It wasn't her parentage, really, that was at the heart of the problem between them. It was that, for some reason, Sally had felt left out in their family, but Bel didn't exactly know why.

She found the tarot reader's account she followed on social media. *What wisdom do you have for me today?* Bel thought as she pressed the speaker to hear the woman's voice on the video clip. *Because I'm not far off from just running away again, at this point. The only problem is I don't know where I'd go this time.*

The woman was talking as the sound came on. *Sometimes things have to die in order for the new to begin,* she said. *Just hold on. Good things are coming for you.*

Bel watched out the window as Bess caught up to Sally on the drive. They started having what looked like a heated conversation, and the ball of tension in Bel's stomach tightened. She had caused this. She was causing nothing but stress for everyone, it seemed.

She couldn't deal with it, not right now. It was bad enough that she had messed up with the salon money, but she couldn't stand the fact that she'd made Sally and Bess argue, even though Sally had been such a bitch to her. The thing about Sally was that the tougher she was on the outside, the more Bel knew she was hurting inside. And, despite everything, she loved her sister. She didn't want Sally to be in pain.

She gathered up her coat and bag and let herself out of the side door. It would be better for everyone if she left, she thought. Perhaps she should never have come to Loch Cameron at all.

TWENTY-ONE

This is so stupid, Bel berated herself as she stood outside her cottage, trying to keep her hair tucked inside her jacket collar and away from the wind, which wanted to buffet it into a ball of fuzz. *Why did I say yes?*

But she knew the answer, which was that she couldn't say no to anything Nate suggested.

When he'd called that morning, she'd been in the garden. There was something in his tone, in his way of speaking, that turned Bel's legs into jelly and enact every other romantic cliché she'd ever heard of on her body. Even though she was stressed about the salon; even though she felt as if she was standing on a beach, watching a tsunami come in, powerless to stop its destructive force; and even though Nate was part of that huge wave of things she couldn't control.

But there was a part of her that didn't want to control Nate, and didn't want to control how she felt about him. Nate might be The One, and this might be her second chance at real love with him. You heard about these things, but you never thought it was going to happen to you: the love of your life, returning out of the blue.

Bel was a ball of nerves, waiting for him to arrive. No one else had ever had this effect on her. That had to mean something, didn't it?

Bess had called her a couple of times since she'd been at her sister's house the other night, but Bel hadn't picked up. She didn't know what to say. *Sorry for being chaotic. Sorry for making you and Sally argue. Sorry for blowing back into your lives and causing trouble almost immediately.* She felt awful about the money for the salon, but she didn't know what else to do other than to promise to pay it back as soon as she could.

And, as if that stress wasn't bad enough, here she was, waiting for Nate on Queen's Point, with a dry throat and her stomach churning and her heart beating wildly. *It's just a walk,* she told herself. *Calm down, for goodness' sake.*

But she couldn't calm down. At least this stress was somewhere on the "pleasant" spectrum, and it was a distraction from obsessively ruminating over what she should do about the house and salon situation. Nate's presence *did things* to her in a way that no one else ever had. There was something primal about the way he influenced her: a kind of haze of comfortable, strong masculinity that emanated from him like heat. When he'd stood near to her at the salon the other day, she had felt herself melting into him.

And I'm not a woman who melts, as a rule, she thought, hugging her new parka around herself and wondering if she should have worn prettier shoes. She did have a pair of espadrilles now, courtesy of Fiona, who had nipped into the salon the day before to tell Bel she'd just had a delivery in and the high wedge sandals were really nice. But wearing espadrilles on a walk around the uneven ground of Queen's Point, up and down the steep lanes and narrow, tussocky paths surrounding the loch, was asking for a twisted ankle. She'd put her trainers on instead. And, anyway, it wasn't like she wanted Nate to think she was trying to impress him. Even if she was.

Bel had, in fact, done her hair nicely with some of the new curl detangling conditioner she'd ordered in for the salon, and had applied fresh but pretty makeup. Under her parka she wore a white crop top and her nicest, tightest jeans that she knew showed off her little waist and generous bottom. Nate had always said he'd loved her figure. She remembered everything he'd said to her, and everything they'd done. Even though it had been ten years.

'Hey, you.' Nate approached, and threw his arm casually around her shoulder as if they were old friends. As if there hadn't been a ten-year gap of silence between them, like a wall, blanking out Bel's feelings. 'What a great day! What a view up here! You really chose a good place to live, huh.' He kissed her on the cheek, and Bel had to steel herself not to instinctively turn her face up to his and kiss him properly.

'Yeah. It's really pretty.' Bel self-consciously tucked her hair behind her ears. 'I thought we could walk down to the loch and over to the castle. I hear there's a public footpath that follows the edge of the loch, right the way around. If you're game? Might be kind of a long walk, though.'

'Sounds good.' Nate beamed at her. 'You look great, by the way. But you always did.'

They started walking along the dirt path at the edge of Queen's Point – as well as the dirt track that led up to the cottages from the high street, there was another way down to the loch at the other side of the rock promontory, further away from the shops and the little school and community centre. Bel had explored it a little, but not much so far.

'Thanks.' She didn't know how else to reply. She didn't even know if this was a date; it had been she who had suggested the walk. It seemed more innocent than a drink at the Inn – and there was less opportunity to be gossiped about by the well-meaning locals.

Nate had said, when he'd called, that it would be great to

catch up. *Like old friends. Was that the etiquette?* Bel wondered as they fell into step with each other. If someone broke your heart, once upon a time, was it okay to pretend that you were old friends if enough time had passed? Were you old friends, in a certain kind of way? She didn't know. Usually, friends hadn't done the things with each other that she had done with Nate. But it had been a long time ago. Maybe they *were* friends now. Or, something else.

'So, catch me up.' Nate pulled his khaki baseball cap down over his eyes to shield them from the sun.

It was another glorious summer day, and the sun glinted on the surface of the loch below them. In the sky above them, hawks circled lazily, scanning the long, green and yellow fields that stretched around the village of Loch Cameron for mice and voles. Bel liked the sound of their cries: when you were away from the high street like she and Nate were now, the sound of birds and the occasional splash of oars from a rowing boat was all you could hear. It was rare to find that kind of peace.

'You've opened a hairdressing salon. That's awesome,' he continued.

'Yes. Though I might have to close it.' Bel hadn't intended to say anything about it, and regretted doing so immediately.

'Oh no! Why on earth?' Nate turned to her with a surprised look.

'Ah, it's nothing. I don't really want to get into it now.' She made herself smile. 'Forget I said anything.'

'Well, it is somethin', but I won't push ya,' he said, kindly. 'Though if ya wanna tell me, I'm a good listener. So I'm told.'

'Thanks. But you don't want to hear about my money problems.'

Bel had decided that if she hadn't heard from Andy in a week then she would apply for a loan from her bank. She wasn't sure if she would get it – after all, she had no job apart from the salon, and no capital without the house money. But at least it was a plan. She hadn't told Sally yet, but she knew she had to. However, she was avoiding talking to her sister. Bess was always the intermediary between them when they argued, but Bel knew she had to talk to Sally eventually. She just didn't want to yet.

'Ah, now, missy. I'll decide what I wanna hear about.'

Bel remembered Nate's confident, intimate manner very well: it was all part of his considerable allure. But she wasn't comfortable talking to him about Andy and the house, mostly because – despite the fact that she had made a decision and had a plan – she still found it incredibly stressful.

'I appreciate the thought. Maybe another time.'

'All right. What were you doing before?' He nudged her gently with his elbow. 'Come on. Don't spare any detail. I wanna know all the good stuff.'

Bel jumped as Nate touched her.

'Did that hurt? Jeez. I don't know my own strength.' Nate frowned. 'Sorry, I was just being... stupid, I guess.'

'No, it's fine. I'm fine.' Bel blushed copiously. *Come on, girl*, she pep-talked herself. It wasn't that he had caused her pain: very much the opposite. Just an elbow nudge from Nate apparently still had the power to render her a hot mess.

Bel had to admit that Nate looked fantastic, even though he was just wearing a black T-shirt and black jeans with the cap. His longish hair was shorter than it used to be, so rather than have it tied back, it curled out from under the cap. His beard, which he hadn't had before, had a few light streaks of grey. His eyes were just the same: warm and melting with a sweet puppy dog expression.

Remember that those eyes – and the voice, and the muscles – are what turns women like you into idiots, Bel counselled herself. Nate was about as puppy-dog-like as a great white shark.

'Oh. Good. Was worried about my powers for evil there, for a second,' he laughed. 'So? Come on. Catch me up, I'm serious.'

'All right.' Bel climbed over a wooden stile at the end of the pathway that led into woodland: a small sign that said *Public Footpath* pointed into the forest. Nate followed; she tried not to notice the fact that his T-shirt rode up as he climbed over, showing off a washboard stomach and muscular waist.

Damn. She looked away, pretending to study the path and trying to get her thoughts in order. Being around Nate had the unfortunate effect of making her mind go completely blank. All she could think about was why he had walked back into her life and whether it was some kind of sign. What was she supposed to do? Did she have to do anything, if it was fated? There was that phrase, *what's for you won't go past you.* Was that the case with Nate?

'Well, I had some time out from hairdressing for a few years. I actually worked in telecoms,' she began, as the forest surrounded them. The smell of pine and damp earth was different to the clean, fresh air around the loch, but Bel liked it in a different way. The woodland was full of life: she could hear the rustling of animals moving in the bushes – foxes, perhaps, or mice. And there was birdsong of a different kind here: the tweeting of smaller birds, which was sweet and homely. For a moment, Bel listened to a series of chirrups that seemed to be two birds talking to each other in turn. She smiled, wondering what they were saying.

'Telecoms? I wouldn't have expected that.' Nate jumped from the top of the stile onto the ground. 'How come? You were so into the hairdressing thing. And still are, obviously.'

'Umm. It's complicated.' Bel held out her hand as three blue butterflies fluttered past, hoping one of them would alight on her palm. 'I was... I got involved with someone, and he didn't like me working in the salon. The job at Handy-Phone came up and it paid more, so I quit,' she shrugged. 'I shouldn't have. I learned my lesson. Albeit, it took me eight years.'

'Oh wow. I'm sorry to hear that.' Nate frowned. 'You were so talented. Artistic. I kinda always felt we had that in common, y'know?'

'Did you?' Bel turned to him in surprise. 'I never knew that. You were – are – so successful.'

'Nothing more successful in life than finding what you love and doing it.' Nate shrugged. 'I was lucky to find it early on, and luckier to be able to pursue music with a profound lack of responsibilities. I'm fully aware how selfish you need to be to do that, by the way,' he added. 'Travel the world for your work, avoid commitment. I know that's what I did with you, and I wanted to say, I'm sorry.' He reached for her hand. 'We had something really great. Unusually connected. But, at the time, I guess I thought the world was full of women like you. That I had unlimited options. Unlimited women.'

'Didn't you?' Bel asked, hyper aware of the feel of her hand in his. His palm was warm, and his long fingers entwined in hers. 'I mean, I'm guessing you did have a lot of women to choose from. The life you have. Being a musician on the road. And being... like you are.' She looked away, not wanting him to see the emotions that were battling for control of her face. Bel had never been good at hiding her feelings, and especially not with Nate. Desire flushed her cheeks, but sadness ached in her heart too. *We had something really great.* That was what he'd just said. She'd always known that it was something special; that was why she'd mourned the end of their brief relationship so hard.

'Like I am?' He smiled lazily, still holding her hand. 'How is that, fair Belladonna of the Scottish Isles?'

'Oh, don't make me tell you.' She returned his smile, despite her mixed feelings. 'Your ego is already way too big.'

'Ohhh... so, it's positive, at least. Y'all don't hate me.'

'No, I don't hate you. I'm not sure how much I like you, though.' Bel raised an eyebrow, extricating her hand from his.

'That's fair. We haven't spoken in a long time, and last time I saw you, I was kind of an ass,' Nate sighed. 'I'm sorry, Bel. You've been on my mind a long time. I wanted to make it right with you – I even tried to find you on social media, but you weren't anywhere.'

'Oh. No, I don't post anything, though I have a couple of accounts just to follow people I like,' Bel admitted. 'Although, with the new salon... I think I might have to create some content for it. Make posts. If I don't have to close.'

'Not a bad idea.' Nate nodded. 'I have a social media presence. I kinda have to. But the point is, I couldn't find you, and I wanted to. So, when I walked past the salon last week and there you were, suddenly, like magic... I knew I had to talk to you. Make it right.'

She wanted to say, but didn't, that she too had felt the magic of their connection, that she had wondered what significance Nate coming back had in her life.

'So, talk,' Bel said, aware she sounded slightly abrasive. Better that than let him know how she felt, for now.

'Wow. Okay. Look, I've grown up a lot since... since we were together. And I know that I cut you off cold. It wasn't an okay thing to do.' Nate sighed, and pulled at the branch of a nearby tree. 'I was young. And I'm not making excuses. I'm really not.' He held up his hand as if to ward off her protest. 'But I didn't know how to deal with my feelings then. I realised I had feelings for you, and I freaked out. So, I ghosted you. It wasn't the right thing to do, and I'm sorry, Bel.' Nate reached for her hand and squeezed it. 'Really, I am.'

'Well, I guess I don't know what to say. The normal thing would be to forgive you. So, I forgive you, then,' Bel shrugged. 'I mean, it's been ten years.'

She was masking her romantic feelings because she didn't

feel safe to express them. Not yet. Bess, if she were here, might have pointed out that not feeling safe to express one's feelings wasn't a great sign in a relationship, but Bel would have pointed out that she and Nate weren't in a relationship.

Not yet.

'Right. But y'all don't forgive me. I can see it in your eyes, and it's in your tone of voice,' Nate chuckled. 'It's okay, by the way. I can see you're still really pissed about it. I'm a grown up now; I know that just because I say sorry, it doesn't wipe away the memory for you. I value and validate your feelings,' he said seriously.

'Wow. You've been to a therapist, and I'm guessing an American one,' Bel said drily. 'So nice to have one's feelings validated.' She rolled her eyes. *Yeah. I am pissed*, she thought crossly. 'Not that I asked for them to be validated by you. Or that I need your validation in any way.' She swore under her breath and stalked off a few paces.

If Nate was The One, then he was making this hard. Yet the feelings he awoke in her were undeniable. Just looking into his eyes, and at the handsome profile of his face as they walked along, made her want to swoon. *Swoon*. Like the heroine in a romantic film. Bel was appalled at herself – no self-respecting woman should swoon over a man, she thought – but she felt it nonetheless.

The nerve of the guy. First, he turned up in her life without warning. Then, he asked her out and acted like they were friends. Then, he told her that he *valued her feelings*.

Not that there was anything wrong in that, of course. It was a thoughtful, sweet sentiment. But Nate had really broken Bel's heart, and here he was, swanning in with his charm offensive and his therapeutic buzzwords and expecting everything to be okay.

It wasn't okay. Bel's heart had yearned for Nate: being so close to him now was almost unbearable after all this time. But her feelings were deep, and steeped in ten years of longing. She felt as though her heart was made of broken, aged wood that she had pinned back together so gingerly over the years to resemble something heart-shaped again. Nate didn't know that: he didn't know how vulnerable her heart was, had always been.

'Okay, okay. You're really pissed, huh.' Nate jogged after her. 'I'm sorry. Yes, I see a therapist. I didn't think that was a bad thing.'

'It's not.' Bel strode on.

'What, then?' Nate matched her long strides. 'Look, I did genuinely want to go on a nice walk with you. It's gonna be awkward as hell if y'all ignore me for the whole route.'

Bel shot him a glance. She could see he wasn't sure whether to smile or not. She scowled.

'Unless you'd prefer if we just walked on in silence?' he asked cheekily.

Uh-uh. No. I'm not going to smile at you.

'Yes, I would,' she said, and charged ahead.

Nate had said that he had been too young when they'd known each other before. He'd had feelings for her, then. And, he seemed to have hinted that he still might. Hadn't he? Or had she filled in the blanks in what he'd said and heard what she'd wanted to?

So why didn't he tell me that ten years ago? she thought, angrily. She'd always wondered if Nate had felt their togetherness as deeply as she had. It had taken her so long to get over him. She wished he'd have been mature enough to tell her. She wished...

She exhaled. She still wished they had never broken up. That was the truth.

After Nate, she had been afraid of waiting for the right person, fearing it would never happen. She'd felt like she'd had the right person already, but Nate had ghosted her. Afraid of being alone again, she had accepted Andy, who wasn't right for her, but she didn't have faith in her judgement anymore. She had loved Nate. But Nate hadn't returned her love. At the time, she couldn't see it, but now Bel could see all too well that she'd chosen Andy as a kind of reaction. She couldn't trust her instincts, so she hadn't listened to her gut that had told her Andy wasn't the one for her. Andy was there; he stayed. And he seemed interested in her. That seemed like enough at the time.

Bel wanted to tell Nate all of this. She wanted to make him understand what his crappy behaviour had caused.

But, really, it wasn't Nate's fault, she thought, as an opening in the trees approached at the end of the path. Light streamed in as Bel walked towards it. *Those were your choices. That was your reaction. Someone else would have done something else. Sure, it was bad behaviour on his part. But you were the only one responsible for what you did as a result.*

She sighed. She hated it when this kind of realisation hit her: it was exactly what Sally would say if she was here. Sally had always been the critical, pessimistic one, and Bel and Dad were the emotional, sweet ones. Obviously, if Sally was telling it, she'd say something like *Bel and Dad were always the criers. I'm a realist.*

Despite the fact it annoyed her, Bel knew Sally would be right, this time. Whatever had happened after Nate had split up with her so cruelly, it was in the past. And being with Andy and working at HandyPhone had taught her a valuable lesson, which was that she never wanted to go back to either, and that she should have trusted her gut in the first place.

It had taken Bel eight years to put on her big girl panties (as Sally would have said) and commit to what she actually wanted to do, rather than let life just happen to her. And she wasn't going to make the mistake of not trusting her instincts again.

She had deep feelings for Nate. Yes, those feelings had blown her heart into pieces when he'd left her before, but having experienced what it was like to make safe choices, Bel knew that a broken heart was not helped by them, either. In the end, was there really a choice other than to follow your heart wherever it led?

She waited by the wooden gate that led out of the forest until Nate had caught up. As he approached her, he looked wary.

'You talking to me yet?' he asked.

'Yeah. Can't stand awkward silences,' she said. The sunlight outside the woods surrounded her in an aura. It was a beautiful day outside, and being in the forest made it seem as if she and Nate were the only two people in the world.

'Thank goodness,' he murmured. 'I was getting worried back there. Seemed like y'all wanted to punish me. Not that I don't deserve it. But...'

Bel, ignoring him, wrapped her arms around his neck and kissed him. This was what she'd wanted to do ever since she'd seen him at the salon. She couldn't quite believe what she was doing, but she also didn't want to overthink anything. *I'm not ignoring my instincts anymore*, she thought, a little wildly.

'But... I thought...' Nate pulled away from the kiss for a moment, confused. 'I thought you hated me, Bel.'

'I don't hate you,' she murmured, her lips millimetres from his. 'Just kiss me, Nate.'

'Yes, ma'am,' he murmured, and brushed her lips with his.

TWENTY-TWO

Kissing Nate was as remarkable as she remembered. As their lips met, Bel had the same sense of electricity as she had when he'd nudged her with his elbow, but magnified a hundred times over.

Nate's kisses were warm and soft, sensual and light. He was a good kisser. In fact, Bel tried not to think about all the technical expertise he had no doubt gained from the many, many women he'd kissed over the years.

But it was more than that. There was a connection between them. Kissing Nate just felt... right. He *smelt* right. His arm, which held her around the waist, felt good. And Bel had the overwhelming feeling that she wanted to dissolve into him, as they stood there in the forest. That they were both somehow part of the nature all around them. It was a perfect moment.

'Well... that was... not what I expected,' he murmured as he drew back, eventually. 'I mean, I *hoped*... but...' he looked a little stunned. 'Yeah,' he added, vaguely. He grabbed onto the gatepost and stared at her dumbly.

'I didn't plan it. It just happened,' Bel said, equally as distracted. Her heart felt as if she'd just run through the forest, instead of walking through it. She saw a group of ramblers coming up behind them on the path. 'Come on. We should get out of the way.'

'Sure.' Nate followed her through the gate and they emerged into an open field that sloped downwards, spreading out into lush green grass fields that waved delicately in the wind. 'Wow. This is some view.'

'It certainly is.' Bel nodded, gazing across the fields – some of which were dotted with cows – and over to a row of purple-heathered hills on the horizon. 'I haven't walked out this far before.'

The group of ramblers passed them, and Bel and Nate nodded and smiled. Bel had the disjointed feeling of acting normal on the outside, while her interior reality was a hot mess. Her poor, pinned-together, fractured wooden heart felt as if Nate had just set light to it with a blowtorch.

'It's weird that y'all don't usually talk to each other in the street, but if you're passing each other on some kind of country walkway, everyone says hi,' Nate chuckled.

'Hmm,' she replied, trying to compose herself.

'What? Y'all don't do that?'

'No, I disagree. You can't go two steps down Loch Cameron's high street without someone saying *good morning*.' Bel began following the footpath that led down the hill: she figured it would meet with the loch when the ground levelled out again.

'I guess in Loch Cameron it's different. Y'all say *hello* anyway, you're right. I was thinking more about the big cities. Or even the towns, y'know? People can be so standoffish.'

'Isn't it like that where you're from?' Bel asked, partially relieved they were having a sensible conversation now: as if the kiss hadn't happened. She'd just gone with her instincts, and it had been amazing, but she didn't know what to do now. It was far too soon to tell him how he made her feel. But she felt it, nonetheless: her heart burned.

'Ah, in Texas? Kinda. But I'm from a smaller town. Everyone's in your business.' Nate grimaced, adjusting his cap as he walked. 'It's not always a good thing. And in Texas we kinda have a thing where people say stuff that sounds like they're being sweet, but really, they're being kinda dismissive.'

'Like what?' Bel asked. She was resisting the urge to reach for Nate's hand as they walked along. She wanted to be close to him. She wanted to kiss him again, to bury her face in his wide, muscular, tanned chest. *Get a hold of yourself*, she thought, taking a deep breath and letting it out again.

'Oh, like, *bless your heart*.' He laughed as he said the phrase in a thick Texan accent. 'People say that when they think you're basically an idiot.'

'I'll have to remember that, in case you say it to me.' Bel raised an eyebrow.

'Ha. I wouldn't dare.' Nate's expression grew more serious. 'Anyway, I went back to live in Marlin a couple years back. Took a break from touring. It didn't go so well.'

They were walking downhill now, and Bel admired the wildflowers that grew among the long grass on either side of the dirt path.

'Marlin?'

'That's my home town. Marlin, Texas. Not famous for much, apart from back in the day, there was a natural spring. People used to come by if they were fixin' to take the waters as part of their health regimen.' Nate shrugged.

'It's a small town?' she asked.

'Uh-huh. Not much goin' on. Kinda place where people gossip.'

'What didn't go so well?' Bel asked. 'When you went back?'

'Ah, I shouldn't have said anything.'

'You should. You can tell me.' She reached for his hand and squeezed his fingers.

Again, it was instinct, and Nate looked surprised, but squeezed her fingers in response. Bel's whole body thrilled to his touch.

'Ah. You won't believe it, but I fell in love and was goin' to settle down. Well, I thought I was in love, anyway.' He pursed his lips, looking like he was thinking about what to say next.

'What happened?' Bel was enjoying the sensation of holding Nate's hand. It felt so natural, but just that small act of affection and touch made her more aroused than she had been in eight years with Andy.

'It was all going great. Then, three months in, she asked me to loan her twenty grand. She needed a new truck, and she couldn't afford one. Totalled hers.' He shook his head. 'I guess I should have heard alarm bells, but when you have feelings for someone, you just wanna help them out, right? So, I gave her the money. That was it. She left for work the next day and I never saw her again.'

The loch was suddenly visible in front of them, and Bel took in a breath as its gleaming expanse spread in front of her. She'd never seen this part of it so close before, and she realised there was a whole extra, longer stretch of water that looped off to the side of the land. She'd read somewhere that Loch Cameron had a tributary to the sea, but had never seen it. She didn't think that could be on this side, because of the fields and the distant hills she'd seen. It must be on the other side, somewhere.

'She disappeared with your money?' Bel asked, shocked.

'Yes, ma'am, she did.' Nate pulled on the brim of his cap.

'Couldn't you just go to wherever she worked and demand it back?' Bel was aghast.

'Nope. She was a self-employed beautician. That was why she needed a truck. She just took off and that was all she wrote.'

Nate shrugged. 'I went to her apartment, but she wasn't there. Turns out she'd defaulted on the rent for three months before she left. She was about to be evicted.'

'Ouch. I'm so sorry. It's a little like my situation, actually. Well, kind of.' Nate's honesty was making her feel safer about opening up to him a little.

'It is?' Nate loosened his hand from hers and jammed both his hands in his pockets. 'I guess it served me right. Karma, or something. What was your situation, if ya don't mind me askin'?'

'I won't bore you with the details, but basically I split with my partner of eight years, and we own a house together. He said he'd buy me out, now he says he can't get the money. So, it's not the same, exactly. But it's a similar money stress kind of situation with an ex, I guess.'

'Ah. That's why you were sayin' you might not continue with the salon.' Nate nodded. 'I'm sorry. I hope you do. It seems like a good thing for ya.'

'Thanks. And, nobody deserves to lose twenty thousand dollars,' Bel said, reasonably. 'Even if you have been a bit of a...' she trailed off. 'Playboy,' she added, trying to find a nice enough word.

'It's okay, Bel. You don't have to be kind. I know I've treated women badly over the years. I do actually think that was karma, and I'm kinda okay with it, in a weird way.' Nate kicked a stone as they reached another stile at the bottom of the hill. This time, he held out a hand to help her over it.

'You are?' Bel was grateful she was wearing jeans, what with all of this clambering around.

Nate vaulted the stile in one easy motion, after she had got to the other side. Bel pretended not to notice his easy athleticism.

'Yeah. I mean, no one's going to be *happy* about losing that kind of money. But it made me stop and think for once. I don't

think I had stopped and thought about what I was doing, ever. It
was all so easy, y'know? I'd meet new girls all the time. And I
was always moving on, place to place, for work. I didn't have to
commit to anyone.'

'It's a charmed life, all right,' Bel said, a little archly. They
began walking alongside the loch. Here, the dirt path was a little
muddier for being so close to the water, and dragonflies and
other, less pretty bugs, buzzed around them.

'I know. I guess I just never thought about anyone's feelings
too much. If I'm honest, though, you were the one I realised I
regretted the most. That's why I started coming back to Loch
Cameron when I could. It was my one link back to you. I
thought, if I came here, you might one day, too. And I could
apologise to you. Because I really am sorry for leaving you.'
Nate stopped and took both her hands in his. He sought her
eyes with his. 'The thing with Cara – that was her name – it
made me realise that you were the one I'd felt most connected
to. And I needed to find you, and tell you that.'

'Nate, I... This is a lot.' Bel felt herself blushing. 'I mean...
I'd be lying if I said I didn't feel the same way. But you really
broke my heart. It was the one time I allowed myself to open up
and be vulnerable to someone, and you stomped all over my
feelings. How can I trust you?'

'I know. I know, and I'm so sorry, Bel.' Nate pulled her
closer to him. 'But when you kissed me just now... I mean, has it
ever been like that with anyone else, for you? Because it hasn't
for me. Not even with Cara.'

'No. It's never been like that with anyone else,' Bel
confessed in a small voice. There was so much more she wanted
to say, but she didn't trust herself.

'Bel, you have this crazy effect on me,' Nate murmured, his
lips brushing her ear. 'I missed you. And when I saw you again
in the salon, I couldn't believe it. It was like... I was guided here

by an angel, or some such thing.' His Texan drawl was intoxicating, as was his immediate presence, holding her.

'I missed you so much, too,' she whispered back. 'I haven't been able to think about anything else since I saw you.' She hated admitting it, but it was true. She was making herself vulnerable again, just like she had before. She didn't know if her heart could withstand Nate again, but she also felt powerless to stop what was happening.

'Bel...' Nate murmured her name, and his lips met hers again.

This time the kiss was deeper. He made a sound in his throat as he kissed her: like a moan or a growl. This time, there was need in the kiss; he pressed her tight to him, and she wrapped her arms around his neck. Bel lost all sense of her surroundings, even the beauty of the loch was forgotten, while she was in Nate's arms.

She still couldn't entirely forgive him, but forgiveness seemed a lesser priority compared to the tornado of emotion that swept them both into its arms, and refused to let go.

TWENTY-THREE

Bel was carefully applying auburn dye to a customer's roots when the frosted-glass door to the salon opened, and Christian poked his head around it.

'Hiya. Am I interrupting?' he asked.

Bel shook her head. 'It's fine. You're not after a haircut though, I assume?' Christian had a shaved head and a short beard. 'Other than oiling your beard, I'm not sure I can be of much help.'

'Ah. No. Thank you,' he chuckled, pushing the door open. 'I was just wondering if you wanted these. For the salon.' Christian held a tree in a large terracotta pot. 'It's an olive. Looks pretty indoors, or you could put it in the doorway. We had a few spare and I was passing, so...' He set it down on the floor.

'That's very kind of you,' Bel peeled off her plastic gloves and laid them on the side of the sink. She went over to the doorway, where Christian had placed the tree. 'What do you mean, spare?' She tried not to sound suspicious, but her tone gave her away.

'Spare, from a job.' He shrugged. 'I was up at some big house in the next village and the woman ordered these for her conservatory, then decided they didn't look right. She still paid for them, and they're in my truck taking up space. Not off the back of a lorry.' He rolled his eyes. 'But if that's what you think, then I'll be on my way.'

'I didn't say that,' Bel exhaled. But what did he expect, after their conversation the other day? He had refused to tell her anything about the court case, and left her in the dark. As far as she knew, he was up for something awful like fraud, theft or – heaven forbid – assault. It was possible. Though she didn't want it to be, of course. 'It's nice of you to think of me. How much do I owe you?' She was on her guard around him now. She couldn't help it. It was the only reasonable reaction.

'Hello, Christian.' Sheila, whose roots Bel was colouring, gave him a little wave.

'Hey, Sheila,' he answered, giving a polite nod. 'Sorry, I'm interrupting your hairdo.'

'Quite all right. We can gossip about you when you're gone,' Sheila remarked, slightly archly.

'I bet.' Christian grinned. 'So? If you want them, Bel, I've got two more.'

'Well... yes, I do. You're right, they'll be perfect in the entry-way,' Bel stepped through the doorway and into the salon's wide, black-and-white tiled porch. It was easily wide enough to take a potted tree on either side. 'And I could have one inside, by the window. If you're sure?'

'Very sure. You'd be doing me a favour, princess.' Christian winked at her. 'But you have to give me a hand getting them off the truck.' He pointed to where his vehicle was parked, a few spaces away. 'Deal?'

'Of course. Let me just tell Sheila what I'm doing.' Bel nipped back into the salon and came out a moment later. 'Princess?' She followed Christian to his truck. She wasn't sure how comfortable she was with him flirting with her anymore. What if he was some kind of serial abuser? Her mind was racing with the possibilities, even though they seemed unlikely.

'Sorry. Turn of phrase,' he chuckled. 'It's not a bad thing. I enjoy a girl with princess vibes, but maybe that's just because I'm an old fashioned kinda guy.' He climbed up onto the flat bed of the truck and started to undo the protective netting around the pots.

'Hmm. I'd prefer Queen,' Bel raised an eyebrow. She wasn't flirting back – more, asserting herself. *Like that would make any difference if he really was a wrong 'un*, she reflected. But it didn't do any harm to assert some strength with him.

'Ah. Of course.' He grinned and handed her one of the pots. 'Your majesty.' He doffed an imaginary cap.

'Better,' Bel muttered.

'Her majesty can carry that one, and I'll take this one,' Christian instructed. 'All right?'

'That's fine. Her majesty is strong.'

'I don't doubt it for a second.' He climbed down from the bed of the truck, holding the other pot. Following her to the porch, he placed his by the front door.

'Thanks, Christian. This is so kind of you,' Bel caught his hand, instinctively. It *was* kind, and he didn't seem to have an ulterior motive. She wished he would just tell her about the court case and put her mind at ease.

'Aw. You're welcome, my Queen.' Christian looked a little self-conscious, but pleased. 'Might as well go where they're appreciated, eh?'

'Well, I appreciate you thinking of me,' she replied primly, though in truth it gave her a warm, fuzzy feeling to be thought of in such a nice way: the fact that Christian had made a special trip to bring her the plants was more than kind. He was trying to make light of it, but he'd still had to go out of his way. She wasn't used to anyone doing sweet things for her, and, in a way, the realisation of that made her feel sad as well as happy. Yet, she also felt anxious about him. It was hard, not feeling she could trust Christian.

'You're welcome,' he said, softening his tone and meeting her eyes with his green, long-lashed gaze.

A moment passed between them. *What is this?* Bel wondered, as she gazed up at him.

But she knew what it was: there had been several moments like this with Christian. And she didn't know if it meant anything, or it was just him being friendly. Bel had always had trouble being able to tell when anyone was flirting with her, and, more than that, even when someone else had told her it was happening, she tended to refuse to believe it.

If she asked herself why, truly and honestly, it came down to the fact that she basically didn't believe anyone would really want her.

That's messed up, she told herself.

But it was also messed up being so unsure about Christian. How could she relax in his company? What if he had done something awful?

He cleared his throat. 'Well, I better be off,' he said, his normal tone restored. 'See you on Thursday.'

'Thursday?' Bel asked, slightly befuddled by the sudden intimacy of the moment.

'That's when I'm next at the cottage,' he explained.

'Ah. Right. Yes.' She nodded, seriously. 'Okay.'

Christian looked a little confused at her changeable energy. 'See you, then, Bel,' he said, letting himself out of the salon.

Bel went back to where Sheila was waiting patiently in her leather chair.

'That was nice o' him, wasn't it? Bringin' ye a pressie for no reason,' her customer commented.

'Well, I think he was just being kind,' Bel said, taking a slip of foil from her dispenser and placing it under the next section of hair, ready to paste on the dye. 'Like he said, they were spare.'

'Hmm. He's a funny one,' Sheila commented. 'Wouldnae surprise me if they were hooky,' she sniffed.

Bel frowned. 'What do you mean?'

'Off the back o' a lorry.' Sheila raised an eyebrow. 'He's part o' that biker gang, aye. Ye want tae steer clear, is my advice.'

'You were quite friendly to him just now,' Bel said, painting the auburn dye on the foiled hair. She kept a calm look on her face, yet anxiety pinged in her tummy.

'Aye, well, I'm polite. I know he does the gardens okay. I'm just sayin', dinnae trust him. That gang're up tae no good, mark my words,' she tutted. 'All that ridin' around on those noisy bikes. There's lots o' rumours. Where there's smoke, there's fire,' she added.

'What rumours?' Bel asked, wondering if Sheila had also heard about the court case. When she'd seen Christian with his friends in the pub for the quiz, they had been quite rowdy. And she'd also noticed some of the locals giving them dirty looks. It didn't help that many of the villagers were on the elderly side and probably thought everyone under sixty having a few drinks were rowdy ruffians. Sheila's misgivings might just be that. It was a coincidence, probably.

'Ach. This and that. Since they've been around in the village, people say there've been more break-ins. And they're spendin' more and more time at the Inn. Some people have stopped goin' because of it,' Sheila lowered her voice conspiratorially, even though there was no one else in the salon.

'Is there any proof that they're connected to the break-ins?' Bel asked, choosing to ignore Sheila's comments about the Inn. It wasn't really anyone's fault if one set of people decided not to go because of another set of people. Apart from Dotty and Eric, no one owned the place. And Dotty and Eric seemed okay with Christian and his friends.

'Dunno, pet. But it's a bit o' a coincidence, isn't it? An' that Christian doin' the gardenin'. A few of them do. Gives them plenty of opportunity when people aren't aboot, slip inside, take stuff.' Sheila pursed her lips. 'Lot o' people in Loch Cameron never even lock their doors! It used to be the kindae place ye could just leave the door open an' pop tae the shop. Not anymore.'

'There aren't very many places like that anywhere. Loch Cameron is a special place,' Bel said, her mind whirring. Was the court case connected to burglaries? Her heart sank. She had really hoped that Christian wasn't involved in anything bad, but now, things seemed to be stacking up against him.

'Aye, well. Be nice if we could keep it special,' Sheila sniffed. 'No' that I'm one tae gossip, o' course.'

'Of course,' Bel murmured, continuing with Sheila's dye.

As a hairdresser, you heard it all. Bel knew that. She'd also worked in customer services for eight years, so she'd heard about as much gossip, accusations, threats and even tears as your average person could share in the space of a haircut or a phone call.

But Sheila's words troubled her. If what she was saying was true, then Christian definitely was mixed up in a criminal gang. *It's probably nothing. Gossip*, she told herself as she partitioned off more of Sheila's hair. *But what if it isn't just gossip?* Bel wondered. What if Christian was... what? Casing the joint? Planning to rob Gretchen Ross' cottage? Or, what if he was a *bad lad*, as they said in Yorkshire, where her dad had been from?

She wondered what her darling dad would have said about all of it. Likely, he would have given her a kiss on the forehead and told her to judge a person by what they did and not what they said.

Thinking of you. Can't wait to see you again.

Bel glanced at her phone. It was Nate. A glow of warmth flushed her cheeks and burned in her belly. It had been difficult not to think about him since they'd gone for their walk, and they'd talked on the phone a couple of times since, late into the night. He was doing some gigs in London, but he had asked to take her out when he got back the next week.

She couldn't reply with her hands covered in hair dye, but Bel allowed herself a small smile. She couldn't wait to see Nate again.

Still, Christian played on her mind. Could she trust him, or not?

TWENTY-FOUR

'Thanks for coming over, darling.' Bess put her arm around Bel's shoulder as she walked into the sitting room at Sally and Bess' house. 'We were worried about you. Weren't we?' she said pointedly at Sally, who was sitting on the sofa, holding a glass of wine.

'I guess.' Sally raised an eyebrow. 'Hi, Bel.'

'Sally.' Bel stood in the doorway with her arms crossed over her chest.

'Oh, will you both just knock it on the head? Come in, please, Bel.' Bess sounded tired. 'I love you both, but it's exhausting trying to mediate between you when you argue. We're going to get this sorted out tonight, okay?' She looked from Sally to Bel with the same gimlet stare. 'I am not kidding. I've had enough of this.'

'Fine. But I'm not the problem here,' Sally protested.

'Sal. Come on. We talked about this.' Bess was such a gentle person, and so loving, that Bel was always surprised to hear the steel in her voice. 'I'm patient, but you know it runs out eventually.'

'Sorry, babe.' Sally put her glass of wine down and stood up.

Bel was amazed to see an anxious look on her sister's face: she knew her sister and Bess were deeply in love, but she rarely saw Bess take charge with Sally like this.

'We're going to deal with this problem, just like we deal with every problem. By doing what we need to fix it.' Bess put one hand on Bel's shoulder. 'Sally and I have spoken about this, and can cope with the loan for a little longer, if we need to. You concentrate on keeping the salon fabulous, and we'll get a solicitor involved. There's no point this descending into family dramas from the past,' she continued. 'The thing to remember is that we're family. And family sticks together.'

Bess gave Sally a long look. 'And, to that end, Sally has something to say to you,' she said, meaningfully.

'I'm sorry about what I said. About Dad, and you not being his real daughter,' Sally said, in a low voice. 'I didn't mean it. He was a good dad, and he loved both of us. That's all that matters.'

'Thank you,' Bel said in a small voice.

'The thing is, Bel. It's a lot of money that we loaned you,' Sally continued. 'You know we can't take our holiday to the Maldives if we bail you out.'

'Sal. We talked about this,' Bess said, calmly.

'I'm not asking you to bail me out,' Bel protested. 'I'll pay you back. I can get a loan and pay you back if he doesn't come through with the money.'

'You won't get as good rates as I could,' Sally sighed.

'Maybe. But you've got to let me do it. It's my choice, my business. If something doesn't turn out the way I expected, then I have to find a solution,' Bel said, meeting her sister's eyes. 'Listen, Sally. I know that since Dad passed, you decided it was your job to look after me. And I've appreciated it. I know you didn't approve of Andy. And you were right. You might be right about this too, but you've got to let me do it my way, okay? So, I'm going to get a loan to cover what you gave me. And I'll have to work it out from there. Hopefully, we can either sell the house, or Andy will give me half. Or, I'll just make a big success of the salon. But I'll manage. Okay?'

'Okay, Bel,' Sally sighed. 'I understand what you're saying. Maybe I need to let you stand on your own two feet. I know I'm overprotective. It's just because I love you. And I don't want you to get hurt.'

'I know.' Bel reached for her sister's hand and squeezed it.

'I miss Dad, too,' Sally said, emotion choking her voice a little.

'I know,' Bel repeated.

'And I'm sorry, about the Andy situation. But I believe in you.' Sally squeezed Bel's fingers in return. 'You can do this. Whatever happens.'

'Family sticks together,' Bess repeated. 'We got you, babe.' She enveloped Bel in a hug, and then Sally. 'You two are awful. Thank God you've got me.'

'We are well aware,' Sally chuckled, and squeezed them both. 'I love both of you. I'm sorry for being... me.'

'Don't be daft. But also... thanks,' Bess replied, separating from the hug. She kissed Sally on the cheek, and then Bel. 'We've got to stick together. We can't let the world bring us down. Or the actions of some inferior men. We are so far beyond that. Aren't we?'

'Yeah. Men are awful,' Sally laughed. 'Well, some of them are, anyway.'

'There are some good ones,' Bess said, catching Bel's eye. 'But the thing is to know which is which. And stand tall in our own strength while we do it.'

'Amen.' Bel nodded. As ever, Bess was right.

TWENTY-FIVE

Bel tapped on the door to room 106 and waited, shifting the heavy tote bag she was carrying from one hand to the other. She'd phoned ahead to let Gretchen know she was popping in – Bel knew, from last time, that Gretchen was likely to be involved in a canasta or bridge tournament and she didn't want to get in the way. However, Gretchen had sounded pleased about the visit.

She'd gone to visit Gretchen to take her some of the packages that still arrived for her in the post; it was a Sunday, and though the salon's first week in business had been great, she was shattered. Still, she knew she needed to get out of the cottage for a while. The drive to Gretchen's nursing home, over the green and purple hills, was just the tonic she needed.

On the way, her phone rang. She put it on the hands-free speaker as she drove.

'Hey, baby. I got a break between rehearsals. I wanted to hear your voice.' Nate's low Texan purr filled the car.

Bel fought the urge to squeal with pleasure. 'Hey, you,' she replied. Just the sound of his voice made her feel as if she'd been dipped in honey.

'How's your day, sweet thing?' he drawled.

Nate had taken to calling her here and there, and sending her sweet little messages through the day. *Can't wait to see you. I miss you.* They would even exchange texts in the morning and at night before bed – invariably, when Bel went to sleep, Nate was still up: mostly, he went to bed in the early hours after a gig. But even though it had only been a few days, Bel had started to get used to having Nate's attention. It felt good. No, not good. It felt *wonderful.*

'Good, thanks. Just on my way to see Gretchen.'

'Gretchen?'

'The woman who used to live in my cottage. I'm taking her some post, and she's good fun. I like hanging out with her.'

'Cool. Where does she live now?'

'In a nursing home. But she's as sprightly as I am.'

'Sprightly isn't the word I'd choose to describe you.' Nate chuckled softly.

'How would you describe me, then?' Bel could feel herself smiling broadly.

'Enchanting. Howl at the moon gorgeous. That kinda thing.'

'Listen to you, trying to charm me,' she giggled.

'Uh-huh. Is it working?'

'I couldn't possibly say.'

'Ahh, well, I look forward to convincin' you of my ungentle-manly intentions sometime soon.' He made a growling sound. 'Bel, I can't wait to see you. You're keeping our date free, right?'

'Yep. It's in my diary.'

'I can't wait to see your pretty face,' he sighed. 'Okay. I've gotta go, baby. Have a good time with Gretchen. I'll be thinking of ya.'

'Okay. Bye.' Bel wished Nate was there with her and not just on the end of the phone line. She was trying not to get ahead of herself with it all, but it was difficult not to. Her dormant feelings for Nate had been awakened, and he was being very attentive to her. It was giving her The Feelings – or, reigniting them. She so wanted to believe what that online fortune teller had said: that someone was coming back into her life, and... what exactly had they said, again? This was the new timeline, and love from the past was coming back.

Bel, in her heart of hearts, wanted Nate to be The One. The letters had been a sign, of that she was sure. Somehow, it was like Serena and Rose were gazing through time, willing Bel and Nate to fall in love and end up happily ever after in a way that they couldn't. Bel and Nate could break Serena and Rose's sad curse of separation: another couple of lovers, who had been separated by time – Nate and Rose's lives had some definite parallels. But Bel and Nate had been reunited. Bel's heart sang.

Driving along the tiny, tree-lined winding roads, she had wound down her window even though the car's air conditioning had been on. She'd wanted to breathe in the clear Scottish air and smell its subtle, peat-and-heather smell. It was a comforting scent: already, she thought of Loch Cameron as home, even though she'd only been here a few months. But it was more than that. There was a kind of cleanliness to the air and the country-side that Bel couldn't get enough of. It made her feel... healed and whole.

She had so much on her mind right now – the salon, Nate, Christian. But at least some good things were happening. It was a relief to have at least come to some kind of agreement with Sally and Bess about the money. It had really killed her to have that tension between her and her sister; probably, it would happen again at some point, but this was the first time Sally had ever admitted she was at fault, too, and acknowledged Bel's feel-ings. That felt like a good development in their relationship.

However, as she drove along, she frowned, thinking about the odd thing that had happened that morning. Before she'd left, she'd pushed the blue ceramic flowerpot by the front door to one side with her foot, just to check – as she had got in the habit of doing – that the spare key was still there, and it wasn't. She'd lifted the pot and looked under it, smoothing the loose earth under it and chasing away the woodlice with her fingers, but there was no key. Would someone have stolen it? And, if they had, who?

She'd considered before taking it inside and putting it some-where safer, but the pleasant lull of Loch Cameron had taken effect and she'd stopped worrying about it. This was a place where people left their doors unlocked and trusted their neigh-bours, after all.

Bel wondered whether to mention it to Gretchen, but she thought there was no point in worrying her. The key would probably turn up.

However, as she waited for Gretchen at the care home the worry lingered in her mind. She felt a shiver of unease run through her as she thought about what Sheila had said in the salon. That since Christian and his bike gang had started hanging around in the village, there had been break-ins and crimes where there hadn't been before. And she knew he was involved in some kind of court case.

Christian was at the house, often. He would have had ample opportunity to take the key.

Come on, Bel, she cautioned herself. *You're being silly. There are probably a hundred explanations for a missing key. Why would Christian take it, anyway?*

'Just a moment!' Gretchen's voice trilled from inside.

Bel nodded to a care assistant who was pushing an elderly gentleman in a wheelchair in the hallway; they were having a good-natured argument about something and the assistant gave Bel a wry little shake of the head as she passed, as if to say, *these old people, eh?* But Bel could see there was genuine affection there.

'Ah, Bel! What a lovely surprise it was when you called. I

had my feet up with a murder mystery and a box of chocolates, so it was just as well. Come in, come in.'

Gretchen shuffled inside and Bel followed, patiently following Gretchen's slower pace.

'Oh, well, I don't want to distract you from your lovely morning. Or your chocolates.'

'No, no. Not at all. Diabetes, you know.' Gretchen rolled her eyes. 'They say I can't have too many sweet things. I say, you let me decide. I'm old enough.'

'Fair enough,' Bel chuckled. 'Where d'you want your packages? I assume they're books again.'

'Oh, I expect so.' Gretchen pointed to a chair inside her little apartment's doorway. 'Could you put them there, dear? I'll open them later.'

'Sure.' Bel put the heavy bag down and followed Gretchen into the small lounge.

'Tea?' Gretchen settled herself in an easy chair, adjusting it with a remote control so she could sit back into it with ease. 'If you don't mind making it yourself, dear, that would be best. I'm a little slow today. There's some lemon drizzle cake on the side: do help yourself.'

'Thank you.' Bel cut a slice of the cake and put it on a plate and made herself a cup of tea. Like at the cottage, Gretchen had a china tea pot and some mismatched but dainty tea cups with saucers on the worktop, and Bel spooned loose tea from a nearby canister into the pot. It seemed that no one in Loch Cameron made tea with tea bags. She had to admit that she'd acquired a taste for tea made the old-fashioned way: it really did taste better from bone china.

'Of course, I didn't make it. I don't cook,' Gretchen sniffed as Bel sat down in the easy chair opposite with her tea and cake. 'Jonathan brought in a vat of the stuff yesterday.' Gretchen picked up her glasses from on top of the pile of books next to her and pushed them onto her nose.

'Jonathan? The one that works at the court?'

'Indeed. Sneaky little worm that he is. Mavis thinks the world of him, but I can see right through him. The cake's all right, but I've had better.'

'In what way is he sneaky?' Bel sipped her tea.

'Oh, I don't know. For one thing, you shouldn't be gossiping about court business if you work there. It's supposed to be confidential, but I know for a fact that he's told Mavis all sorts of things she isn't supposed to know.' Gretchen tutted. 'Did you bring up the subject of the court with Christian, by the way? I was thinking of you.'

'I did, but it didn't go that well,' Bel sighed. 'He sort of refused to talk about it.'

'Oh. Why?'

'He said he couldn't. For legal reasons.'

'I see. Perhaps Christian would make a better legal assistant than Jonathan.' Gretchen rolled her eyes.

'Yes, but surely if he was innocent, he could have talked to me?'

'Not necessarily. Don't start thinking "there's no smoke without fire",' Gretchen counselled wisely. 'He might be testifying in a sensitive case, or even be on a jury.'

'Hmmm. Well, there's also something else.' Bel wondered whether to mention the key or not; perhaps she shouldn't.

'What?'

'Well, it's probably nothing, but the spare key to the cottage has gone missing.'

'And you think he's taken it?' Gretchen frowned. 'That would be very out of character for Christian.'

'Would it? How well do you really know him, Gretchen?' Bel persisted.

'Not that well, you're right. But I get feelings about people. He's troubled in some way, I can tell that. But basically good.' Gretchen looked thoughtful. 'Still, I could be wrong.'

'Well, I expect it'll turn up,' Bel said brightly, regretting saying anything. 'Don't worry. I shouldn't have mentioned it.'

'That's all right, dear. I know you've got a lot on your mind. Now. How's it been at the salon? First week opening, that's right, isn't it?'

'Very good, thanks. The opening was lovely, and I've had a good number of bookings. Some drop-ins, but I think people are going to take a while to get used to the fact that the salon is actually open most days.' Bel took a bite of the lemon cake.

'Ha. They'll get used to it.' Gretchen smiled.

'One strange thing I did find at the salon were some old letters, though.' Bel had been thinking about mentioning the letters to Gretchen on the drive over. Gretchen had lived in Loch Cameron for a long time: she might remember Serena and Rose. 'I wondered whether you might remember Serena McKellan? Or Rose Macaulay?'

'Hmm. Was it Serena, you said?'

'Serena McKellan. The letters I found were dated in the sixties. Starting in 1965. She would have been in her twenties then I think, judging from the research I did and what the letters are about.'

'Well, I was born in the forties. So, I was about her age, I suppose.' Gretchen frowned and pointed to one of her bookshelves. 'Go and get me that blue photo album, would you, dear? See, on the third shelf down? That's it.'

Bel brought back the album and gave it to Gretchen, who flicked through the pages for a moment.

'Here. I thought so. Serena McKellan. That's her.' Gretchen tapped one of the black and white photos. It was a class picture: twenty girls stood in three rows, dressed in uniform. At the bottom of the photo, their names were printed in small black print against a white frame that had now become cream with age. 'I remember her. I can't believe I've forgotten her name for so long. Age does funny things to you. Of course, Serena,' she sighed.

'Is this you?' Bel leaned forward curiously, looking at the picture.

'Yes. Old school picture. This was 1960. I was, what. Fifteen or sixteen? She was in my class. Not a close friend, but a nice girl. Quiet,' Gretchen sighed. 'I can't believe I had to think about whether I knew that name or not, but of course, it's been so long since it happened.'

'Since what happened?' Bel asked, looking at Serena in the picture. She was petite, blonde, and looking into the camera with an unreadable expression. She wasn't smiling, like some of them. All the girls wore the same pleated shirt, blazer and blouse: Gretchen, in the row behind Serena, had long dark hair in two plaits and wore glasses. Bel thought how pretty Gretchen was; even so long ago, she thought she would have recognised the same impish twinkle in Gretchen's eye.

'Poor girl jumped off Queen's Point into the loch.' Gretchen blinked. 'You know, I haven't thought about Serena McKellan in a while. Must be going senile after all.'

'She... killed herself?' Bel almost dropped her teacup and saucer; as a precaution, she set them both on the side table next to her chair. 'Sorry... I just didn't expect you to say that.'

'Yes. Terrible business,' Gretchen sighed, looking down at the picture. 'When you're in your eighties, you look at pictures like these and wonder if you're the last one still alive. But that's normal when you're an antique like me.' She smiled up at Bel. 'It's less normal to still be a young woman and lose someone the same age.'

'How old was she when...' Bel trailed off, thinking about what Serena had said in the letters. How heartbroken she was that Rose had left her. Had she ended her life because of it?

'Hm. No age. In her late twenties, I think. She definitely

didn't make it to thirty.' Gretchen screwed up her face, thinking. 'I was away in Edinburgh by then, working. My mother called me at work and told me. I remember wondering what on earth had happened because we were strictly forbidden to have personal calls at work unless it was an emergency. There was just one office line, you see, and all our business came through the phone or the post. Fortunately, the phone was on my desk because I was the Editorial Assistant and I took all the queries from the other departments, and the calls from the authors wanting to talk to the editors when they were out having their four-hour lunches in the pub. I was actually relieved at the time when Mother told me it was Serena. I thought my father must have died.'

'Goodness,' Bel took in a deep breath. 'That's so shocking. Do you know why she did it?'

'No. No one ever knew. She was a very quiet girl, not many friends, and no one close that I knew of. I heard some rumours, but there's never been a lack of rumour in Loch Cameron, as you can imagine.' She raised an eyebrow.

'What were the rumours?' Bel asked. 'The letters I found... well, basically, she was in love with this girl, Rose Macaulay, who moved away to become a famous ballerina. But being gay at that time wasn't as acceptable, was it?'

'Not really, no. Yes, there were some nasty things said. By people who should know better,' Gretchen tutted. 'I didn't know if they were true, but I didn't think they should have been said, anyway. If you can't say anything nice, don't say anything at all.'

'Quite.' Bel nodded. 'So, it was hard for her, then. In the village? Might she have ended it because of that?'

'I don't know, dear. Perhaps. Or perhaps she was just so heartbroken about losing Rose. Or both, or neither and it was something else. I knew Rose, a little, too. Just from a distance, you understand, but of course I remember reading about her in the newspaper too. After Serena's death, though, the McKellan family moved away. They got a reputation in the village and I don't think they wanted to stay in the place their daughter had killed herself. I have to say, for years, when I came back to visit my parents at the cottage, I didn't like it. I kept thinking about Serena, jumping off the cliff, just outside. Took me years to get over it. I probably shouldn't have told you, in fact.' Gretchen pulled her lips into a tight line.

'I can't say I love the idea of someone... doing that, near where I sleep at night,' Bel said, her stomach churning at the thought.

'But it was a long time ago, dear.' Gretchen patted her hand. 'I know it sounds funny, but on Queen's Point many years ago we asked the vicar to come up and bless it. Sort of do an exorcism. Nothing funny was happening, but we felt like it needed to be done. Lay her to rest, as it were.'

'Did it work?' Bel shivered, thinking about Serena McKellan's ghost prowling Queen's Point in the middle of the night.

'I think so. Always felt very calm up on the Point after that. Not that anything bad happened anyway, apart from what Serena actually did. But I think we all felt a lot more at ease, after he did the blessing or whatever it was.'

'I see.' Bel wondered what other dramatic secrets Loch Cameron held in its long history.

'Hm. What is interesting, though, is that Serena's sister Alison married and had children. I kept in touch; she was the year below us at school but she was a nice girl. Two boys and a girl. But even though they moved villages, they sort of grew up with this shadow hanging over them as a family, the McKellans. Or, the McDougalls, as she is now.'

'McDougall?' Bel gave Gretchen a quizzical look.

'Yes. Alison McDougall, nee McKellan. She had children, well, they must be in their sixties or so by now. Had their own children, in some cases.' Gretchen adjusted the glasses on her nose. 'Funnily enough, Christian is a McDougall. I've always thought it was funny that he ended up back on Queen's Point. Serena would have been... what. His great-aunt, I think?'

'Christian McDougall is related to Serena?' Bel's mouth gaped open.

'Yes, dear. I know, it's strange, isn't it? Since we were just talking about him.' Gretchen made a *hmm* sound under her breath. 'Very strange. But, then, those things often happen in life. Synchronicities.'

'I guess so,' Bel said, trying to line everything up in her mind.

'Yes, dear. That's Loch Cameron for you,' Gretchen replied, breezily. 'Everyone is related somewhere down the line. You should show him those letters. I expect he'd like to see them.'

Bel didn't know what to say. She nodded, mutely. She hadn't expected the situation with Christian to get even more complicated than it had been half an hour ago. And yet, somehow, it had.

Christian had talked about not feeling like he fitted in, being an outsider; that there had always been gossip about his family. Bel had witnessed him being gossiped about in the village; she had concerns about him, too. *Was* there smoke without fire, or was this a case of *if the cap fits, wear it,* to quote another old phrase her dad had used from time to time? She didn't know. There were usually two sides to every story.

Yet, what *was* true was that, years ago, Serena had fallen in love with Rose, and Rose had broken her heart. And, Rose and Serena had both become pariahs, in Loch Cameron and in the wider world. Was that persecution still being felt by Serena's great-nephew, Christian McDougall? And had he done anything to deserve it?

TWENTY-SIX

Any update?

Bel texted Andy. It had been a week, and she hadn't heard anything. Surprisingly, he replied almost immediately.

Sorry, no. These things take time.

These things take time was not the answer she was looking for. Bel felt instantly irritated. She'd deliberately given Andy space for a week to sort things out and at least get some further information or an update. She didn't necessarily expect the money to appear in her account in seven days – though that would have been amazing – but she expected *movement* of some kind.

No more information at all? she replied, cross. She had a break at the salon and was eating a muffin and sipping a cup of tea before her next customer came in: Kathy, a girl Bess knew from her crochet group, was coming in to have her bold two-tone hair colour redone.

No. Sorry.

Bel swore under her breath and pressed the call button. There was no point doing back-and-forth texting; it wasn't going to get her anywhere.

'Bel. I'm at work,' Andy answered the phone, sounding a little stressed.

'You didn't have to answer,' she pointed out, icily. 'Easier to talk in person. So, you can't get a mortgage agreed still?'

'No. I am trying.' His voice was tinged with a familiar whine. However, she'd never consciously recognised it before; now, she realised how annoying it was. *This is the opposite of absence makes the heart grow fonder*, she thought, with a wry smile to herself. *Absence makes the heart perceive all the bloody irritating things and be grateful you don't have to be around them anymore.*

'Have you spoken to a broker? They can look at deals from different providers.'

'Umm... no. I haven't tried that.' He sounded petulant. 'Look, I know you want the money, but you don't have to hassle me for it. I'm doing you a favour by offering to buy you out at all. Don't upset me, or—'

'Or what?' she interrupted him. 'If you want to make an empty threat, Andy, then go right ahead. I'm all ears,' she waited, giving him a moment to respond.

'I'm not threatening you,' he said, lowering his voice. 'Give me a minute, okay?'

In the background, Bel could hear a woman's voice saying something. Muffled, she listened as Andy said something in a low voice to someone else.

That would be her replacement, then. The woman she had seen that day.

At least Andy was making a go of it with her, then.

Bel took a moment to check in with herself. Was she jealous? Did she feel undone or destroyed, hearing the woman's voice?

Not really.

More than anything, Bel thought about Andy's whining tone and his *don't upset me*. She snorted, thinking about it. *Or what, you little whiny puppy?* she thought. *Or what?*

If anything, she felt pity for this new woman who now had to deal with Andy and his passive-aggressive suggestions. It had taken her all this time to realise that she didn't want or need Andy, but now, she felt free.

Plus, now, she had Nate. She smiled, thinking about the message he'd sent her this morning.

One more sleep until I see my Enchantress. Can't wait to kiss you, baby.

'Sorry about that,' Andy said, sounding vaguely contrite.

'No problem,' Bel said in an even tone. 'Get a mortgage broker, and call me back in a few days when you've talked to them. Okay? Otherwise, I *will* take legal advice. This is your last chance.'

'Sure,' Andy sighed. 'Sorry about just now, by the way. I find all this very stressful, but Rebecca has reminded me that I shouldn't take it out on you.'

Go, Rebecca.

Bel raised an eyebrow. 'That's her name? You're still together, then?' she couldn't help but ask.

'Yeah.'

Bel could tell he was really uncomfortable.

'Does she make you happy?' Bel asked.

'Yeah,' he repeated, and something came into his voice Bel didn't recognise. There was a brightness in his tone she couldn't remember hearing before. 'She... she doesn't take any bullshit from me. And I... kinda like that.'

'That's good,' Bel replied, keeping her voice calm. 'I hope Rebecca is good for you.'

'I hope so,' he sighed. 'This is still a super stressful conversation and situation, though.'

Cry me a river, Bel thought, rolling her eyes.

'Yes, Andy. I am also stressed. Don't forget that I've opened a new business up here. It's not exactly easy, especially with this kind of uncertainty. I thought I'd be able to make a new start up here with that money, but instead I'm worrying about where the rent's going to come from in a few months. So, please don't think that I'm doing this for fun. We agreed we'd split the money from the house, Andy, and I need it, to move on. You need to be able to move on too, and you can do that if my name isn't on the mortgage anymore. Until we dissolve our mutual interests, we'll always be tied together.'

'I know. You're right,' he said, quietly. 'I'll get a broker and give you a call back when I do.'

'See that you do,' Bel said, her tone brisk. Kathy walked in through the salon door, and Bel gave her a friendly wave and pointed to the phone. 'Okay. I've got to go now. Thanks for answering.'

'Thanks for calling,' Andy replied, quickly. His previous passive-aggressive tone was gone, and was replaced with something entirely more... *obedient*, Bel thought.

Maybe all this time, all Andy needed was a bossy woman to keep him in line, Bel thought. Was it a shame that she hadn't realised that until now?

No, not really, she decided. Rebecca was welcome to that job.

'Welcome. Bye.' She hung up. 'Sorry about that. The ex,' she said, in response to Kathy's inquiring look. 'You're Kathy? I'm Bel.'

'Great tae meet ye. Bess sang yer praises,' the girl said. 'Ah, exes. I can tell ye a few stories. All okay, hen? You're not upset? I can give ye a minute if ye need it.'

'No, actually, I'm fine.' Bel let out a long breath. 'Stressed, but fine. I think I just realised how much better off I am without him. You know? I knew it already, but...' she trailed off.

'Ah. I get ye. With break ups, sometimes ye dinnae want the guy anymore, but ye still miss havin' *someone*. An' ye still think aboot what might've been. An' then, one day, ye wake up, an' think, *ma gawd*, I'm so much better off without that negativity in ma life.'

'Ha. That's it, exactly,' Bel agreed. 'I've literally just had that moment. So strange that you should say that.'

'Ah. Synchronicity. I love it.' Kathy made the shape of a heart with her hands. 'Come on, then. Ye can tell me all aboot your ex, an' I'll tell ye all aboot the time ah dated an academic narcissist,' she laughed. 'Ah can laugh aboot it now, but, ohhhh. That was somethin' I'm not gonna repeat in a hurry.'

'Okay. Take a seat, and let me make us both some coffee first.' Bel grinned. 'Then let's get you back to your resplendent self.'

'Sounds like a plan.'

Bel went into the kitchenette and filled up the kettle. The money was still a source of stress for her, but at least she had made her position clear to Andy. She would do everything she could, and then, what happened, would happen. That was the only sane way to think about it.

I'm proud of you, cupcake, her dad's voice said in her mind. *It's not easy, what you're doing. Remember that I'm always with you.*

Bel gripped the coffee mug she'd just taken off the shelf and took a deep breath.

It isn't easy, she thought. *I wish you were here, Dad. I wish I could have one of your amazing hugs.*

There was no answer, now, and Bel took some deep breaths.

What else would Dad say if he was here? He'd tell her that she was stronger than she thought she was. He would remind her of how she was always so sassy as a kid. And that she should remember who she was, and walk tall.

It felt good to walk tall, after all.

She straightened her back, and walked back into the salon.

This was her place. And, here, she was Queen.

TWENTY-SEVEN

Bel dreamt of her dad again. This time, he was in the cottage garden, inspecting the roses.

Someone did a nice job here, he said, turning to Bel.

She had the same feeling she always did in dreams of her dad: relief that she was able to see him one last time. That he wasn't gone forever.

The gardener, she replied.

Got a gardener, have you? Her dad smiled. *Good for you, my beautiful belle of the ball.*

Well, he's not really mine. He just does all the cottages, Bel replied. She realised it was nighttime in the dream, yet they were still outside, looking at the flowers. *Come inside, Dad. There's so much I want to tell you.*

Good that someone's taking good care of the roses, cupcake, her dad replied, smiling at her. He took her hand and gave it a squeeze. *I can rest easier knowing that.*

Before she could ask why her dad was so worried about the roses in Gretchen Ross's old cottage, she woke up, still feeling her dad's hands in hers.

. . .

'I just thought you should know,' Bel said. 'You did say you had a family member called Serena. I think it was the same person. Your great-aunt. That's what Gretchen said, anyway.' Bel handed Christian Serena's letters. 'So, these belong to you.'

Bel had decided to broach the subject of Serena with Christian the next time she saw him. She was at home after a day at the salon and he'd sent her a message earlier to say he needed to pop round to pick up a couple of bags of compost he'd left in the cottage garden. She thought of mentioning the missing key, but she couldn't think of a way to broach the subject without it sounding like she was accusing Christian of stealing it. Plus, now wasn't the time.

In fact, Bel had been getting ready for her date with Nate when Christian had knocked on the door. She'd put on a pretty white cotton summer dress and sandals, and just finished applying light makeup when he'd arrived.

'I didn't mean to interrupt... you look like you're going out. You look great, by the way,' he said, smiling.

'Oh. You're not, it's fine,' she said, slightly awkwardly. There wasn't a reason for her not to be going on a date. She was allowed to. She and Christian were just friends. But, still, she didn't say the words *I'm going on a date*.

'So... For real? You think I should have these?' Christian took the letters and turned them over in his hands. 'This is... weird. But I asked my mum about it after we spoke, that time. She did tell me that her aunt was called Serena. And that she died when she was young.' Christian shook his head.

'Was this her?' Bel showed him her phone: Gretchen had taken a picture of the old school picture and sent it to Bel.

'Oh, wow. I think so.' Christian peered at the picture. 'Mum had a couple of old pictures she showed me. It definitely looks like her. And there's a family resemblance. I mean, I look more like my dad. But this could be my mum when she was younger.' He stared at the picture. 'I can't believe it.'

'Did your mum tell you what happened to Serena?' Bel asked, cautiously.

'No. I think she knew more than she said.' Christian frowned. 'Me and my mum have never been that close. She's great, but... I dunno. I was trouble when I was a kid. She didn't bond with me as much. Maybe it was the ADHD thing, though I don't think it was.'

'I'm sorry.'

'It's okay. I disappointed her when I didn't go to university, then did it again when I gave up working in IT to become a gardener. She finds me hard work, I think. My brother's very conventional. Married, two kids, office job. She never had to worry about him. My dad's the strong silent type. Never really had much input into my life apart from he was the one that got me into engines when I was a kid. I used to sit on a box in the garage and watch him tinker with the car.'

'I miss my dad a lot. He brought Sally and I up after our mum died when I was little,' Bel found herself saying. 'He was an amazing guy.'

'I'm sorry. I wish you still had him around.' Christian gently took her hand in his and held it.

Shivers consumed Bel as his large hand engulfed hers. It was a feeling both of being protected and being completely overwhelmed with... well, she knew what that feeling was. And she wasn't comfortable with feeling it.

Attraction.

She swallowed and cleared her throat, trying to get herself back under control, but the zinging, hot power that flowed between them – like the electrical current between two poles, positive and negative – wouldn't stop.

'Thanks.' She removed her hand from his. She had to focus and tell him what had happened to Serena: she was his ancestor, and Christian was living her legacy of inherited outsiderhood. Some things were more important than… whatever this feeling was.

Basic chemistry. Just chemicals in your brain, she told herself. *Nothing more than pheromones.*

And, don't get involved with a bad lad, she cautioned herself. That was what her dad would have told her. She thought of Nate: their chemistry was remarkable, but he too could be thought of as a "bad lad" – certainly if you had judged him on his past behaviour.

Maybe that's just my type now, she thought. *Bad lads. God, I hope not.*

'Okay. Listen,' Bel began, refusing to let herself get caught up in her thoughts. She told him Serena's story, as Gretchen had told her.

Christian listened, his expression growing more shocked as the story reached its dramatic conclusion.

'Wow,' he said, quietly, when Bel had finished.

'I'm so sorry,' she said, fighting the impulse to take his hand again. It felt like the caring thing to do, but Bel knew it wasn't that simple. She just wasn't sure of him. 'But if she's your ancestor – and I think she is? – then you deserve to know.'

'Thanks. I appreciate it.' Christian let out a long breath. 'So, she was gay? You think… that's why she did it?'

'I don't know. It might not have been. She might have been depressed for some other reason, or for no reason. Depression doesn't always have a definite cause you can point to.' Bel sat down on the pink chaise longue; Christian followed suit and sat at the edge of the large sofa opposite her.

'You know, I said our family were always treated like outsiders. I never knew why, but it was like there were rumours about us and I never really understood. Now, I get it. Maybe people remember Serena, even though we moved to Aberculty and it happened here. Like, the story of it all. You know what these small communities are like. We were tainted by what she did, or something. Crazy if so.'

'I know. As if you could think anything other than it being a terrible tragedy,' Bel replied. 'Gretchen told me that she and some of the other residents up here had Queen's Point exorcised. Blessed by the vicar at the time. So, I guess Serena is at peace, at least.'

'That's nice to know. A shame that the curse on our family can't be lifted,' he joked. 'It's one of those things that probably only people of my parents' generation remember. But even for people that don't know about Serena, we just have this reputation for being like wrong and odd in some way. I think that's why my mum's so annoyed with me about dropping out of work and joining the Warriors, you know? She was always so obsessed with us all being as normal as we could. I guess she wanted us to break out of that old reputation. Didn't work with me.'

'Hmm.' The mention of the Warriors gave Bel an uncomfortable feeling. 'Serena didn't fit the mould of her time either,' she said, tactfully avoiding the subject. Did she really believe Christian was up to no good? She didn't think so. But there were unanswered questions in her mind that bothered her, nonetheless.

'I feel bad for her,' Christian admitted. 'I wish I could go back in time and pull her back from the edge of the cliff, you know? Show her that life was still worth living. Or, that she could live now. And be married and happy like your sister and her wife.'

'I know. It's tragic.' Bel looked up as the doorbell chimed.
Damn. That had to be Nate.

'Um, listen. I need to get that, and... I'll be heading out, so...' she trailed off, not wanting to be insensitive but aware that Nate was at the door.

'Oh, sure. Of course,' Christian stood up, hurriedly. 'I really appreciate all of this, you know. Thank you, Bel.' He strode over and planted a kiss on her cheek.

'You're welcome,' she said, taken by surprise by the kiss. 'I should...' she gestured towards the door.

'Absolutely. Let me get it,' he said, striding down the short hallway before she had an opportunity to stop him.

'It's all right, let me.'

Bel followed him, but Christian had flung open the door, where Nate stood, holding a bunch of roses.

Oh, no.

'Oh. Is Bel around?' Nate asked, looking slightly confused.

'I'm here,' Bel practically ran up the short hallway.

There was a brief moment where no one said anything.

It looks like Christian and I are a couple, or something, she thought, standing next to him in the doorway. *This is not good.*

'Christian was just leaving,' she said, pointedly. 'He helps with the garden.'

Christian gave her a brief look that she could read clearly: *Is that all I am to you?*

Bel regretted what she'd said instantly, but there was no way to take it back now. Especially after they'd had the conversation they just had, which had been personal and meaningful. But, especially with Nate there, how else would she describe Christian?

Sometimes, I have awkward moments with Christian when I think he's going to kiss me, or I'm going to kiss him.

Christian tends the garden, and I try to look the other way when he takes his shirt off. Even though he is potentially problematic.

No. Neither of those.

Christian is a friend. She could have said that. Why didn't she say that?

'Cool. Take it easy, brother.' Nate nodded: his expression was open and his voice was friendly, but Bel could still detect a watchful note in his eyes. The two men were sizing each other up, like lions in the presence of a lioness. Or a gazelle.

'Anyway. I better be off,' Christian said, nodding to Nate, who stood back to let him pass. 'Good to meet you, man. Bel, next week as usual.'

'Okay. Thanks,' she called after him. Was she disappointed that Nate had turned up at all? Perhaps there was a part of her that was.

But, as Nate turned to her and switched on his million-dollar smile, Bel forgot about everything apart from kissing him again. Her heart erupted into the fiery state it had been in last time she had seen him, seemingly able to burn forever without being extinguished.

He stepped into the doorway and handed her the roses.

'Thank you,' she said, a little shyly. 'I should put them in some water.'

'I think they can wait a little longer,' he said, smiling that wolfish grin she remembered so well, and gathered her up in his arms.

TWENTY-EIGHT

'Nate, this is so beautiful,' Bel breathed, hardly able to believe what she was seeing.

He had driven her along the twisty, tree-lined roads from Loch Cameron out to the far hills, where she had thought there was nothing but farms and wide fields. Turning off the road, Nate had reached over and put his hand on her knee as the car slowed.

'Close your eyes, now, honey,' he'd drawled, and she had, feeling the sharp line of electricity slicing through her at his touch. Desire flooded her; she fought the urge to wrap her arms around his neck, then and there. He'd chuckled, perhaps sensing her inner struggle. 'C'mon, now. Don't be bad.'

She'd closed her eyes. Nate stopped the car and guided her out of it, holding her hand as she emerged into the evening air. The fields smelt different to the lochside air she had grown used to. The air around Loch Cameron was fresh and cool and clean. This smell was peatier and greener: dense with chlorophyll and the honey sweetness of heather. It was just as intoxicating, but in a different way.

They'd walked along what felt like a dirt path. The only

sound was the distant song of birds in the darkening evening: Bel didn't know what they were, only that their song wove through the twilight like a thread of gold in the dusk. All the time, Nate held her hand and guided her gently, his hand over her eyes to make sure she didn't peek.

Finally, they stopped and Nate removed his hand.

'Okay. You can look,' he said.

Bel had opened her eyes, obediently, not wanting to admit that she already missed the sensation of his hand on her face.

'Oh, Nate. Wow.'

They were standing in a field on a hill, looking down onto a green, grassy valley. To their left, a large farmhouse stood in the background, with a number of long white tent-type structures in the distance on the right.

Behind her, a baby-blue painted wooden summer house sat with its doors open, with two rattan rocking chairs nestled in front of it. Inside the summer house, Bel could see a day bed covered in a patchwork quilt, and a striped blue-and-white sofa with a cosy throw folded neatly over one arm. A wine fridge with a glass door displayed a selection of bottles, and a table to the side of one of the easy chairs held a brass tray with two champagne glasses and a tray of what looked like oysters on ice under a glass dome. To the right, a brazier burned, lending a faint charcoal smell to the air and taking the chill off the evening.

'You did this?' Bel gazed at Nate, her mouth slightly open.

'Well, the farm did it for me. I gotta confess.' He looked bashful, but pleased.

'It's beautiful.' Bel took in the fairy lights that were strung around the summer house and twined in the apple trees that lined the road up to this private little dell. 'I would never have known this was here.'

'It's pretty, huh. I got to know the owners a while back. It's a working farm, you can buy your fruit and vegetables up here.

Hell, y'all can even come here and pet rabbits if you wanted to. They have those, for the kids, I guess.' He stood close to her and looked down into her wide eyes. 'I thought it would be a romantic spot to uh...' he paused and touched her hair gently. 'Get reacquainted.'

Bel swallowed hard. 'Um. Well, it's lovely,' she said, knowing she probably looked halfway between a deer caught in headlights and a timid schoolgirl. Nate's presence was so magnetic that as soon as he'd walked her down the short pathway from the cottage to his car with his hand on the small of her back, she felt as though she was dissolving with lust.

'It is,' he said, his face excruciatingly close to hers.

She wanted him to kiss her so badly. She leaned in towards him, imperceptibly, knowing he must be able to read her body language. 'And you, also, are lovely.'

He kissed her gently, then: just a light brush of his lips on hers. Bel felt her whole body respond; she felt his arms around her, strong, pressing her to him.

'Oh, Bel,' he murmured. 'I missed you so damn much.' Nate broke the kiss and smiled down at her. 'C'mon. Let's pour a drink, huh?'

'Okay.' She didn't want to stop touching him, and, as if he knew, he held her hand and led her to one of the rocking chairs.

'Here. You sit and enjoy the view. I'll be Daddy and pour the drinks.'

Bel cleared her throat and sat down, trying to regain some composure. Nate calling himself *Daddy* wasn't helping her do that at all.

He went into the summerhouse and returned with a bottle of cold champagne, pouring it into the glasses and handing her one.

'To you. And to the salon,' Nate murmured, tapping her glass with his gently and maintaining eye contact.

'Thank you. Shall we have some of these oysters too?' she

asked, looking away a little shyly. She still wasn't sure where she stood with Nate. Yes, there was a powerful physical attraction between them, but he was still the one who had broken her heart all those years ago.

'Yes, ma'am.' He sipped his champagne and removed the glass dome lid from the plate. The oysters, piled up on ice, were displayed with wedges of lemon and sprinkled with fresh chillies. He placed a few on a plate for Bel and handed it to her.

'I hope you like 'em. Caught locally, I'm told,' he drawled. 'I developed a taste for oysters when I was touring the Pacific Northwest a few years back. The Kumos oysters on the Puget Sound blew my mind.' He took an oyster shell and tipped it into his mouth expertly. 'Mmm. So good.' He swallowed, catching her eye. 'I hope y'all don't think I'm the most awful braggart, goin' on about my travels like I do.'

'Not at all,' Bel said, taking an oyster from her plate and following suit after squeezing a little lemon on hers. 'I just don't have any stories to compare, really. I worked in a customer services department for eight years while you were off, travelling the world.'

'I'm sorry I missed you, then. I could've taken you with me. I was short-sighted,' he sighed and sat down in the rocking chair opposite her. 'Can you forgive me?'

'Maybe.' Bel took a sip of her champagne, feeling it loosen her up. 'You really hurt me, Nate.'

There. The truth of it was out there, laid bare.

'I know,' he sighed. 'I wish I hadn't. I wish there was a way I could take it back.'

'You can't,' she said, meeting his eyes.

'I know,' he repeated. There was a silence. 'I thought though... I could make it right. Make it up to you,' he said, quietly. 'You're such a beautiful, amazing woman, Bel. I realise now I was wrong to leave you. I should at least have broken it off with you properly and... talked to you. Told you what was going on with me. But I was young and stupid.' He leaned across the gap between their chairs and took both her hands in his. 'Bel, I'm sorry,' he said again, and gazed soulfully into her eyes. 'I should never have left you. You're the best woman I ever met.'

Bel didn't know what to say. She hadn't expected this confession from Nate. Frankly, she hadn't known what to expect at all.

She squeezed his hands. 'It's okay. We all do things we're not proud of when we're younger. It was a long time ago,' she said, and as she said it, she felt the truth of it. She felt herself forgive Nate: felt the tension unravel in her heart.

'Oh, Bel. Thank you,' he said, sounding genuinely relieved. 'You don't know what that means to me. It's been weighing on my heart a long time.'

He had been young. They both had. She couldn't really blame him for letting his opportunities go to his head. Perhaps she would have done the same if she was an international musician, always jetting off to somewhere new, with legions of adoring fans waiting at the stage door every night. Would she really have said no to that?

Yes, I think I would, she reminded herself. *Because I really did love Nate. And I never wanted anyone else.*

He put down his champagne glass and his plate and knelt in front of her, on the grass.

'You don't have to kneel, silly,' she felt slightly uncomfortable at the gesture. No man had ever knelt in front of her before.

'I do,' he said, taking her hands in his again. 'Bel. You're beautiful, talented and so special. I want you. I wanted you then, and I want you more than ever now.'

Gently, he kissed her, his hands leaving hers and reaching around her waist. She dissolved into the kiss, merging into him, finally letting herself go. If she could forgive Nate, then maybe they could move on. And the future with him she had dreamed about could still happen.

'I want you so much, Bel,' Nate breathed into her ear.

'I want you, too,' she murmured; she did. There was no denying it. Her body was crying out for his touch.

He nodded, his eyes hooded with desire. Wordlessly, he picked Bel up in his arms and carried her into the summerhouse.

TWENTY-NINE

In the early hours, Nate had roused Bel from her half-slumber. *We should be getting back*, he'd murmured in her ear. They were lying together, curled up on the day bed, limbs entwined.

Okay, she'd said, not wanting to move. Not wanting to leave their haven. It felt so magical to her. *In a minute*.

On the drive back, both of them had been quiet. When Nate had dropped Bel back at the cottage, the birds were just starting to rustle in the trees; the sun wasn't up yet, but it wouldn't be long, being summer.

Goodnight, sweet girl. He'd kissed her on the cheek, chastely. *I'll see you soon, okay?*

Okay, she'd yawned, and gone into the cottage to get a few hours' sleep before she had to open the salon. *See you soon*.

The whole day at work, Bel had been in another world, thinking about Nate and the night before. She had a few back-to-back appointments: a cut and colour for Dotty, a toddler haircut – which went surprisingly well, Bel had been dreading it – and, now, she was just finishing trimming Angus's long hair. Bel had persuaded him to shave up the sides again, and now she was finishing up with French plaiting the rest.

'There. How's that?' she handed Angus a hand mirror so he could see the plait at the back. 'Proper Viking.'

'Aye, woah! Looks stonkin', Bel. Thanks.' Angus examined the bottom end of Bel's careful plaiting. 'Getting a wee bit salt an' pepper, these days, though.'

'You still look great. Distinguished,' Bel reassured him.

She glanced at her emails on her phone, seeing she had one from the solicitor she had contacted about her situation with Andy. She wished she didn't have to go down the legal route, but he still hadn't updated her about the money, and so she hadn't really had a choice. At the very least, it would tell her where she stood in the matter.

'No' what a Viking should be though, is it? Should be pillagin' or something.' He grinned. 'Mind ye, I think ma pillagin' days are probably behind me.'

'Not such a bad thing, maybe,' Bel bantered back. 'Bit frowned upon, nowadays.'

'Aye. Better off mendin' things. An' potterin' in ma workshop,' he chuckled. 'How's tricks with ye? Stayin' at the cottage long term, then, since you've got the salon now?'

'Tricks are good,' Bel said, trying not to blush, thinking about the night before. She cleared her throat. 'Yes. I've got to talk to the Laird about renting longer term, but I think it will be okay. I could look for another place, but I like the cottage. Bess and Sally are having building work done on their house or I guess I'd be staying there.'

Even though she thought of the cottage as Gretchen's, Bel knew that it actually belonged to the Laird, like all the property in the village did. Hal Cameron relied on Gretchen to manage the rental of her cottage because he was too busy to do it, and Bel thought that Gretchen probably liked still having something to do with the place she'd lived in so long.

'Nice tae have yer own space, though,' Angus mused. 'Especially if you're seein' someone.' He gave her a shrewd look in the mirror. 'I wasnae bein' nosy, but I saw you had a gentleman caller last night. I was prunin' the roses at the front,' he protested, when Bel gave him a cross stare.

Trust Loch Cameron not to miss a thing, Bel thought. Now, her love life was likely to be the subject of gossip across the village by the afternoon.

'He's just an old friend,' she replied, not entirely truthfully. *But not completely untruthfully, either*, she thought.

'None o' ma business.' Angus held up both hands in mock protest. 'I'm no' surprised, by the way. You're a lovely girl. If I was younger, I'd have asked ye out too.'

Bel knew Angus was being kind; he had meant what he'd said to be a compliment and not vague sexual harassment, which she could have interpreted it as if she'd wanted to. She knew that older men, in particular, would say things like this in the spirit of kindness.

'Thanks, Angus.' She patted him on the arm. 'I don't really know what's going to happen there, if anything. But... I guess it's nice to have a good time with a man again.' She removed the protective cape from around Angus's shoulders and gave him a brush down. 'It hasn't exactly been the best of times, man-wise.'

'Hm. I'm sorry,' Angus rumbled. 'Life can be tricky when it comes to the opposite sex. Or the same sex. Or gender. I try and keep up with things, you know. Especially having been in the music business when I was younger. Artistic people are always very... expressive, let's say, aye,' he chuckled. 'But, I know. I had my heart broken a couple of times.'

'You were in the music business?' Bel walked to the counter where she had her card machine and laptop to manage her appointments.

'Aye. Played in a band for some years.' Angus named a band Bel had heard of, but wasn't familiar with. 'Came up here for a rest. Needed the quiet. Never left.'

'He's a musician too. The guy I saw last night,' Bel

confessed. She knew she shouldn't be talking about Nate to Angus, but something in her needed to.

'Uh-oh,' Angus tapped his card on the card reader when she pointed to show that it was ready. 'You watch yourself, lassie. Musicians are a funny breed. I can say it because I am one. There's a lot o' temptation. An' when you're young, that's hard tae resist.' He put his card back in his wallet.

'I know.' She didn't need the reminder. *Or do I?* she thought. *Look what happened last night. But he apologised. He missed me for all that time,* she told herself, aware that she was starting to have reservations about what had happened between them. She'd got carried away. She hadn't meant for them to sleep together, but they had. It had felt so right.

She thought again about the letters. What a strange gift they were: like a kind of odd presentiment. An omen, almost, that Nate – so like Rose – would come back into her life and reignite that intense love she'd felt for him, so long ago. Again, she felt a stab of terrible pity for Serena. She wondered if, on some other plane, Rose and Serena were finally together again. She hoped so.

After she waved goodbye to Angus, she checked her phone, expecting a message from Nate.

But there was nothing.

Bel frowned. Perhaps he was still asleep? It was possible; they'd had a very late night, though she thought they'd both dozed off in the summerhouse, after making love.

You slept with Nate, she thought, half marvelling that it had happened at all, and half in disbelief that she'd slept with anyone on the first date. But it wasn't a first date, she rationalised. It was a fifteenth or twentieth date. There had just been a ten-year gap since the last one.

She tapped out a message.

Last night was lovely. Speak later?

Bel pressed send. She watched the screen, but there was no response.

Fair enough. It was unreasonable to expect an instant answer. Yet, as she continued to stare at the blank screen, a twinge of misgiving unrolled in her stomach. Nate couldn't possibly experience the night before like she had and not want to be in touch afterwards.

He was probably busy.

He'd answer soon. Wouldn't he?

THIRTY

'How long has it been?' Sally frowned at Bel, who was sitting on the kitchen table on top of a sheet of plastic. The whole kitchen had been gutted and was slowly being rebuilt; Sally had excitedly invited her over to see the new kitchen units and the marble worktop that had just been installed.

'Five days,' Bel sighed and bent over to rest her forehead on the plastic sheet. 'Nothing. I called twice. No answer.'

'And no word from Andy either?'

'Not really. I called a solicitor this week. I've got a meeting in a few days.'

'Good. Glad to hear that, at least.' Sally swore under her breath. 'Bloody men,' she said. 'Come here, poppet,' she enveloped her sister in a hug. 'I'm so sorry.'

'I just... I really believed Nate, you know?' Bel felt the tears she'd been trying to hold back start to rise up in her chest and her throat. 'It was so beautiful. I...' She started to cry. 'Oh, for goodness' sake!' She tried to stop herself, but it was too late.

'And you... slept together?' Sally asked gently, leaning out of the hug a little to look at her sister's face. 'Not judging you. I just want to know what happened.'

'Yes. We slept together. It just... sort of happened,' Bel whispered.

'Were you safe?' Sally smoothed Bel's curly fringe out of her eyes. 'Again. Not judging. Just want you to be healthy.'

'Yes, we were safe,' Bel sighed. 'Maybe that was a sign. He was prepared. He planned it.'

'Well, it's not wrong to be safe, even if you did think you might get lucky,' Sally sighed. 'Honestly, it's better to think it might happen and it doesn't than the other way around. For you, anyway. With men, especially.'

And especially with men like Nate, Bel thought, darkly. Who knew how many girls he'd slept with just in the past couple of weeks? Again, it wasn't a judgement. People could have an active sex life and see multiple people if they were single and as long as everyone involved was on board with it. She'd watched a documentary with Bess about it just the night before: the new name for it was ethical non-monogamy. *Sleeping around, but everyone knows about it*, Bess had said with a derisive sniff. *Not for me.*

But Bel didn't want to be one of a number of Nate's *special friends*. She had feelings for him, and now it felt as though he'd trampled all over those feelings.

'He was... so sweet to me,' Bel tried to say it without sobbing. 'He told me that he regretted not staying in touch... since we were together, before. He told me I was the one he'd had the deepest connection with. That he'd always had feelings for me. I believed him.' She took in a deep breath. 'But what kind of person says all those things – and then does, what he did... and then ignores the person afterwards? I just don't understand it.' Bel fought the tears. She was miserable, but she was also angry, and when she felt the anger rise up, she caught hold of it like a rider on a horse. Anger was better than sadness. She'd read somewhere that anger was the protector of sorrow. If that was true, she could relate to it.

'You know what? I've heard of this so many times. That guy love-bombed you.' Sally released Bel from her arms. 'I'm going to make us a coffee. I'll make it extra strong, how you like it,' she added, going to the cupboard and taking out a cafetiere and two mugs. 'I've been keeping this in here for the builders since the cappuccino machine's out of action.'

'Thanks. That'd be great.' Bel watched her sister busy herself, spooning ground coffee from a jar into the cafetiere and holding it under the new boiling water tap she was so proud of. Sally was in her element when Bel had a problem, swooping in like a mother hen. But Bel had never minded that. It was nice to have that kind of support, when she needed it. It was more that Sally still had to learn to butt out sometimes. However, today, Bel was grateful for her protective older sister. 'Love-bombing? What's that?'

'Oh, it's one of those new phrases. Basically, it's when someone comes on very strong and showers you with love at the start of a relationship to get what they want – in Nate's case, I think that was sex – and then disappears or ghosts you, or tries to manipulate you after in some way. Becomes distant or withholding of affection as a manipulation technique, once they've shown you what it's like, being in the sunshine of their love for a while. It's a controlling thing.' Sally pushed the plunger down on the cafetiere and splashed some milk into both mugs.

'Oh... Did someone do that to you?' Bel asked, wiping her eyes. Sally had always kept her love life on a need-to-know basis, before Bess had come along. Not because she was ashamed of being gay – Bel had always been proud of her sister for being confident in who she was – but because Sally was by nature a very private person.

'No. But a friend had that happen to her. And I've read about it on Instagram.' Her sister handed her a mug of coffee. 'You should use it more. For the salon, if nothing else. Anyway, in Nate's case, it sounds like he's one of those guys who likes to cosplay being in love for short periods of time and then runs away from the realities of having to deal with an actual person.' Sally rolled her eyes.

'Bet it's a relief being gay.' Bel took a sip of coffee. 'At least you didn't have to deal with this crap.'

'What, because I dated women? Get real, Bel,' Sally laughed. 'There are just as many women out there with serious emotional problems as men.'

'Oh. Sorry. I guess there must be,' Bel blew out her cheeks. 'I guess I can't see beyond my own stuff right now.'

'That's okay. And I know. I get it.' Sally kissed Bel on the forehead. 'It's crappy, and no one should do it. But they do.' She was quiet for a moment. 'Am I being overbearing? Bess told me I need to remember to let you be yourself a little more. I know I can be... kind of bossy,' she admitted, though Bel could see that it wasn't easy for her to say it.

'No, today, I appreciate it.' Bel patted her sister's hand. 'It's just sometimes where you need to back off and let me make my own mistakes, I guess.'

'I know. I'm trying,' Sally gave her a wry smile.

'Just, with Nate... I just don't know what I did to deserve it,' Bel said, quietly. 'I'd just pulled my life back together again. And... *wham*. He blew it apart.'

Bel had thought that the letters were a sign that Nate was the love of her life. She had been so wrong. Her disappointment was so jagged, so sharp, that she felt it impair her breath. Her chest felt tight.

'I know, darling. But it's up to you whether you give Nate that kind of power in your life or not. Did he really "blow your life apart?"' Sally made air quotes with her fingers for the last part of the sentence.

'Yes!' Bel cried. A tear rolled down her cheek. 'I really... loved him, Sal,'

'Did you really? You've only been seeing him for five

minutes,' Sally said, concernedly. 'Look, I'm not trying to devalue your experience here. But I also don't think you were in love. Lust, maybe. Infatuation. You didn't know each other.'

'We knew each other well enough,' Bel sobbed. 'I thought he was the one.'

'Ah, love. I'm sorry. But you have to realise what happened here, Bel. Which is that he ghosted you after you slept together. Babe, don't lose focus here. You're the one doing amazing things. You left Andy, you left HandyPhone – which was a terrible job, by the way, I have no idea why you ever did it in the first place – and you started up the salon. You're happy, Bel. Don't let some idiot make you think you're not.'

'But... Nate was the love of my life,' Bel whispered, hating the truth of it. 'If I can't make it work with him, then maybe that was my last chance. I'm not going to feel that with anyone else.'

'Oh, can you hear yourself?' Sally shook her head and made Bel stand up. 'Come on. I know you feel crappy, but retain a bit of perspective here. Nate what's-his-face was NOT the love of your life. He was just some guy who romanced you when you were too young to know any better, and then took advantage of you at a vulnerable point in your life. That *is not* love, Bel.' Sally took Bel by the shoulders. 'Believe me, okay? Love is security, knowing you can be yourself totally with another person, and that they will love you whatever happens. That they *know* you are the most brilliant and wonderful person in the whole world, and they make sure you know it every single day. What you had with Nate was not love. It was just great sex and a lot of insecurity.'

Then what did the letters mean? Bel thought. She'd spent all this time thinking that they were some kind of sign or portent: something about great love, meant to be. But what if they were exactly what she'd originally thought: a sad tale about love gone wrong? A cautionary tale? Of course, they didn't have to mean anything. But, somehow, finding them at the salon had felt like the letters were a personal message for her. If the message hadn't been a sign that Nate was the one, then what *did* they mean?

'Well, if it wasn't him, then where am I going to find someone to love? When's it going to be my turn?' Bel shrugged off Sally's hands from her shoulders.

'I don't know, sweetie. No one knows,' Sally sighed. 'All I can tell you is that, one day, when you're not looking for it, it walks in. And your life is changed forever.'

THIRTY-ONE

'Ah. Sorry. I didn't know if you were in.' Christian was sheltering at the side of the cottage from a sudden summer rain storm that had blown in. He was wearing a T-shirt and shorts, and the T-shirt was fairly drenched already. 'I hope you don't mind. I'll just wait until the worst of it has blown over.'

'Ah,' Bel had heard a noise outside whilst she was ordering in supplies for the salon and come out to investigate. 'Look, you might as well come in, rather than cowering under the tiles. It's not very dry here, either. Ugh,' she jumped as a sudden heavy rivulet of water soaked her shoulder.

'Well, okay. If you're sure.' Christian shivered. 'It is a bit cold.'

Bel still felt uncomfortable around Christian. The lost key still hadn't turned up, and he hadn't told her anything more about the court case. It continued to bother her. But she wasn't so heartless as to make someone stand out in the rain when she was nice and cosy inside. 'Looks like the British summer has caught up to us.' Bel tutted. 'And it was going so well.'

'Well, y'know, a Scottish summer is sixty per cent rain instead of eighty.' He shrugged, grinning.

'Come on. You'll catch your death out here.' She wrapped
her cardigan around herself and headed back into the cottage,
wishing she'd put some makeup on. Though she didn't know
why. 'Tea?' She walked into the kitchen.

'That would be great.' Christian followed her and leaned
against the old leather sofa. 'Sorry to ask, but do you have a
towel?'

'Oh. Sure.' Bel lit the gas under the old-fashioned copper
kettle and went to the airing cupboard to get a towel for Christian. 'Pink. Sorry,' she said as she handed it to him.

'S'okay. I don't mind pink.' He rubbed the towel over his
wet T-shirt.

Awkward. She remembered all too well what she'd said to
him about him being a criminal; accusing him of things she had
no idea whether he had done or not. Now, here he was, doing a
real-life wet T-shirt situation in her kitchen.

'Actually, I'm going to take it off, if that's okay? It's just
going to be cold wearing it, otherwise,' he sounded apologetic.
'Is that weird?'

'No... that's okay,' Bel said, glad she had her face turned
away so he didn't see her almost immediate blush at the thought
of his shirtless torso. It wasn't like she hadn't seen it before, of
course, but, every time, it made her weak. 'I put the Aga on
earlier; it's gone really chilly. If you hang it near there, it'll dry.'
She pointed to the old, black iron door of the ancient stove.
'Heats slowly all day and I can cook on it later.'

'All right, then. If you don't mind.' He peeled the wet cotton
over his shoulders and handed it to Bel, who was standing in
front of the old stove.

'I don't mind.' She hung it on the oven door, trying and
failing not to look at him.

Goodness, he was beautiful.

'So. How's things?' he asked, clearing his throat.

There was a slightly awkward vibe in the air and she could tell he could feel it, too.

'All right. Just ordering in some supplies for the salon,' she replied, relieved at the mundane conversation.

'Even working on a Sunday, eh?' he asked.

'Yup.' She took the kettle off the heat and poured the water into the teapot. It splashed onto the counter, and she swore under her breath.

'Hey. It's okay.' He handed her the pink towel he'd just used. 'Here.'

'Thanks.' She wiped the surface clean. *Get it together, Bel*, she thought.

'You're not your usual self today.' Christian folded his hands over his chest. 'What's up?'

'Oh. Nothing.' She put the lid on the teapot to let the tea steep. She didn't want to talk about the Nate situation, but it had been playing on her mind.

'Did you have a good time the other night?' he asked, his tone neutral.

'What other night?' she asked, knowing that he meant Nate. A coil of irritation unrolled in her stomach. Like it was any of Christian's business what she did with Nate, or anyone else? But there was also that disappointment there too: a layer of nausea and hurt. She was humiliated at having been used by Nate. At not having seen through him. Again.

'On your date. I assume it was a date.'

'It was, and it's none of your business,' she snapped. Talking about Nate felt like she had stepped into the stream of her emotions and stepped on hidden broken glass. It hurt, and she wasn't expecting the sudden stab of pain Christian's words caused.

'Wow. Okay,' Christian looked surprised at her change of tone. 'I was just being polite.'

'Right.' Bel laughed derisively, under her breath.

'What's that supposed to mean?'

'It means, don't pretend that you weren't asking for another reason.' She stopped herself from saying *you were jealous*, but that was what she meant.

'What reason? I was just being nice. I thought we were friends.'

'I don't think we're at the stage where you can ask me about my love life.' She turned her back to him and poured the tea. 'We're not that good friends,' she snapped. As soon as she'd said it, she knew it was unfair. It had been her hurt talking, and she was lashing out. Not at Christian, but at Nate.

'Oh. I'm just the gardener. Right. I forgot.' The tone of his voice was suddenly cold.

'All I'm saying is that I hardly know you. For all I know, you're casing the joint so you can rob it when I'm not here,' the words slipped out before she could stop them.

'Excuse me?' Christian looked at her, askance. 'What the hell does that mean?'

'Nothing. Forget it.' She handed him his mug.

'Umm... no, I don't think so. You just called me a thief.' He took the mug and placed it on the wooden kitchen table. 'You can't do that and pretend nothing happened. And, it's incredibly rude, not to mention untrue.'

'Well, what am I supposed to think?' She turned to face him, her hands on her hips. She wasn't angry at Christian. She was angry at Nate, and she knew it, but she still couldn't help the wave of anger that overcame her. 'You're involved in a court case and you won't tell me why. You start working on the garden, and the spare key goes missing. You could be... dangerous... for all I know, and you could have the key to this cottage and...' she trailed off.

'And what? Attack you in the middle of the night?' Christian swore under his breath. 'Jesus, Bel.'

'You had more opportunity than anyone else to take it,' she argued. 'What am I supposed to think?'

'Why would I steal the bloody spare key? Bel, if I wanted to break in, I could have done it ten times over already. I've literally got a whole van full of tools out there.' Christian gesticulated towards the front door. 'Be reasonable! I don't even know why you're saying this.'

'What am I supposed to think? I hear about your gang doing shady things... break-ins happening... and now this?' Bel argued back. 'I just don't like dishonesty.'

'Neither do I,' Christian said, levelly. 'And I think we both know that you're not being honest, either. About what's going on here.'

'What does that mean?' she shot back, angrily.

He shook his head. 'You know what I mean. You know there's something between us. And now, for whatever reason, you're trying to push me away. I don't appreciate it.'

'*You* don't appreciate it? I'm not the one in a criminal biker gang,' she spat, losing her temper.

'What the...' He looked at her, aghast. 'Is that what you really think?'

'I think there are things you're not telling me. And the only reason I can think of is dishonesty,' she countered.

Christian stared at her for a moment. 'I like you, Bel, but you've got some serious things to sort out. That's all I'm going to say,' he said, getting up. 'I think it's time I left, before someone says something they'll regret.'

I have things to sort out? The cheek, she fumed.

'How dare you? Don't turn this back on me. You're the...' she trailed off.

'The what?' He met her gaze, his expression grave.

The criminal.

This time, Bel didn't say it. A niggling voice inside her said, *Don't: you'll regret it*, and she listened.

'Nothing.' Bel felt her anger receding, though the jagged pain underneath it was still there. *Anger is the protector of hurt*, she reminded herself. She was lashing out because she was still in pain.

'Right. Well, I guess I should be going. Don't worry about the tea.'

'Christian...' She reached for his arm and caught his wrist. 'I'm sorry. I didn't mean that.'

'But you did mean it, Bel,' he said, coldly. 'And I mean it when I say that you're an amazing woman, but you really need to adjust your perceptions of the world a bit. I'm not the bad guy here.'

He walked out, and Bel's heart plummeted. Had she just made a huge mistake?

THIRTY-TWO

Bel was in the middle of colouring Dotty's hair her signature platinum blonde when the salon's phone rang. She continued painting the dye onto Dotty's hair, knowing her message service would pick up; also, she didn't want to interrupt Dotty, who had just started telling her about the previous owner of the local bookshop, a young Irishman called Ryan, who had left the village with a cloud over his head. The shop was now vacant, which Bel had commented on: when she'd opened the salon that morning, she'd noticed that the shop had a sign in the window: CLOSED UNTIL FURTHER NOTICE.

'So, this guy was the owner?' Bel asked. She had been in the shop a couple of times and bought a couple of novels, but she hadn't had time to read either of them yet. This Ryan hadn't been there, either time – since she'd arrived in Loch Cameron, the book shop had only been open sporadically – and both times Bel had been in, there had been a rather sullen girl in her twenties at the till. She hadn't engaged Bel in conversation, which was unusual for Loch Cameron, where it seemed standard for everyone to be loquacious.

'The nephew o' the original owner, and he inherited the

shop when his uncle passed away. Ryan O'Connell,' Dotty made a distinctive tutting sound. 'He was a bad 'un, aye. Charmin' as ye like, but there were a couple o' incidents wi' local girls. Zelda, the Laird's girlfriend, even.' Dotty purse her lips disapprovingly. 'Course, I made sure she didnae get sucked in. She's a sensible girl.'

'No competition with the Laird, anyway, I'd have thought,' Bel said, smiling at the idea of Dotty going to war with a local lothario. He wouldn't stand a chance.

'Exactly,' Dotty agreed. 'Anyway, I s'pose he had enough o' Loch Cameron. Shame that there willnae be a book shop open, but I can't say I'm unhappy tae see the back o' that lad. Ye know, before he tried his luck at Zelda, he had a young lassie wrapped round his little finger, an' she ended up badly injured.'

'Goodness. Why? Did he hurt her?' Bel was shocked at the thought that something so violent could have happed in Loch Cameron.

'No' exactly. She was very keen on him, an' he didnae treat her very well at all. Then when he was done wi' her, just broke it off without warnin' and the poor thing was heartbroken. She took to standin' outside the shop at night, watchin' him in the flat upstairs. Anyway, one night, a big truck came along the road fast, knocked her out of the way. Broke her leg, an' it didnae heal very well. Poor thing was laid up a long time.'

'Oh, no,' Bel breathed. 'Is she okay now?'

'Aye, well enough, I think. Her mum and dad come into the Inn sometimes,' Dotty sighed. 'Still, it's a shame, an' the girl's still cautious about men, her mum says. Or leavin' the house, even. Poor lassie. I mean, I know she shouldnae been watchin' his flat at night. But ye do think, if he'd have been a bit more considerate in the first place, he couldae broken things off a lot better.'

'Sure.' Bel raised an eyebrow. 'I'm glad I never met the guy, now.'

'Och, aye. Bad news,' Dotty tutted. 'Some men, they just never learn that women are human bein's, eh? Think we're tae be hunted for sport, or somethin'.'

'Hmm,' Bel said, noncommittally. Ryan sounded exactly like Nate.

Part of hairdressing was gossip, and she'd learned a long time ago to remain neutral about what people said. You were never going to agree with everyone, but that was okay. And, in fact, Bel had always enjoyed listening to people talk about their lives. It was interesting to get different points of view. However, in this case, she agreed with Dotty that this Ryan sounded like bad news. And, now that she'd had a little distance from Nate, she could see that he had been toxic, too.

The thing with *bad lads* – as her dad had called them – was that they were also very seductive.

'Bear with me, Dotty? I just want to check that message.' Bel walked over to her reception desk, thinking about her appointment later that day and wanting to make sure they hadn't cancelled.

However, when she heard Nate's voice, her heart started beating wildly.

'Hey, sweetheart. I'm so sorry it's been a while since we spoke. Things got kinda crazy with work. Give me a call.'

Bel stared at the phone in disbelief. Nate's tone implied that he thought everything was normal between them, but it had been two weeks without any contact from him since they'd slept together.

Speak of the devil, she thought. It was as if Nate had a sixth sense that she might have got over him a little, and knew he needed to reinsert himself in her life, or risk losing his power over her altogether.

Without thinking about the fact that she was in the salon, Bel pressed Nate's number on her mobile phone and waited for him to pick up, anger coiling in her stomach like a snake.

She put her hand over the mouthpiece and called over to Dotty, 'Dotty? I'll be right with you. I just have to make a call.'

'Right ye are, lassie.'

Nate picked up on the third ring.

'Bel! So good to hear from ya, sweet girl.'

His warm tones filled her ears, but Bel was too angry to be charmed.

'Who the hell do you think you are?' she asked, in a low but furious voice.

'Awww, come on now.' Nate's voice remained calm, as if he had been expecting her outburst. 'Listen, baby girl. I said I've been busy, okay? Don't be mad at me.'

'Nate. I can be as angry as I want, thank you. And I think it'd perfectly normal to be upset, in the circumstances.'

'Well, I didn't know I was gonna get called away, sweet thing,' he drawled.

'Don't *sweet thing* me and expect me to be all right about you sleeping with me and then not calling me for two weeks,' Bel hissed, mindful that she didn't want Dotty, Loch Cameron's premier gossip, to hear her conversation. 'After everything we said to each other! After you knew how badly you hurt me when we were together before. Nate, you looked in my eyes and you told me that you'd always missed me. That I was "the one that got away". We connected, deeply. You know that.' She was trying to keep her voice low and firm, but it was wavering and she couldn't stop it.

'Awww, Bel... you know, I didn't mean anything by it... That's how my work is, you know? I thought you were cool about that,' he wheedled. 'Don't be angry, now. You're so much prettier when you're smilin'.'

'I'm not cool about being used. Again. No,' she replied, shortly. 'Don't try and pretend that we didn't connect, deeply. Otherwise, I would never have slept with you.' She lowered her voice. 'I don't do that with just anyone.'

'Come on, Bel. You don't need to be so precious about your body. It was just two adults, enjoyin' a beautiful moment,' Nate replied.

Bel could hear in his voice that he believed what he was saying, and she sighed, realising how wrong she'd been to imagine a future with him. Someone like Nate would never change, and he could never be what she wanted him to be. Maybe there was a woman out there who could deal with him disappearing at a moment's notice, or with him being terminally unreliable or unavailable. And, most likely, seeing other women. But it wasn't her.

'I meant what I said to you that night,' she replied. 'I can see now that you didn't, but that's fine. Or, you meant it in the heat of the moment. I can't believe I was willing to look past such a big flaw for the prospect of having a relationship again. I must have been crazy.' She let out a short laugh.

'Bel... I don't think we ever discussed a relationship,' he said quietly. 'I was honest with you about my feelings. We had – have – a deep sexual connection, and you don't find that every day. I value that.'

'Excuse me?' Bel felt disbelief well up inside her. Had she just imagined everything they'd said to each other? 'You told me that I was *the one,* that you'd been coming back to Loch Cameron on the off-chance of finding me again. That you'd never felt the same about anyone else. Not even Cara.'

'That wasn't a lie, baby,' he replied, sighing. 'I'd still like to see ya. I think you're great, and we had an awesome time together. I can't give you a relationship in the normal sense of the word, though, because of my work,' he said. 'We have a strong connection. You know that and I know it,' he continued, his voice caressing her ear. 'Physically... you know that was good. Don't throw that away.'

Bel took a deep breath, feeling the emotion well up inside her.

The truth was that when she and Nate had made love, it *had* been amazing. She couldn't deny it. She knew she would never forget the way he'd made her feel. And they *had* connected – reconnected – heart to heart, as they made love. She had felt Nate open his heart to her as he looked deep into her eyes as they moved together. It had felt like they were one person. One perfect union. She knew it was good. And never once in all her time with Andy had she ever felt anything like it.

'No,' she replied, feeling the anger surge into her heart. She was protecting herself, and she was grateful for it. 'I can't do that, Nate.'

'But why not, honey?' Nate sounded genuinely confused. 'Nowadays, people are so much more open about relationships. I wouldn't want you to think you had ta just wait around, when I was away. You could see other people too, I wouldn't mind.'

'Dear lord. Nate, I don't want to see other people. That's... that's not what I'm looking for,' Bel sighed, exasperated. She wondered whether Serena and Rose had had a conversation like this before Rose had left to embark on her ballet career. Of course, in those days, open relationships hadn't existed – and it was a whole different world when it came to lesbian relationships, too. Bel felt a pang of extra sympathy with Serena. Of course, she and Rose had been deeply in love: it was a different situation. But Bel could relate to the problem of having feelings for someone who was never around.

'All right. Well, ah guess we can just be friends. Maybe friends with benefits, every now and again,' Nate drawled.

Bel wished that Nate was in the salon, suddenly, despite Dotty's prying ears: in that moment, she would have loved to slap him. Friends with benefits, indeed!

'Goodbye, Nate,' Bel said. If she had yearned for him over the past two weeks, and thought about him and mourned for what could have been between them, then now the feeling was thoroughly and deeply excised, like a surgical cut. She no longer wanted anything to do with Nate. She pressed the call end button, and slid her phone into the back pocket of her jeans.

Perhaps that was the real message of the letters: self-reliance, Bel thought. Serena had loved Rose more than she had loved herself, and that was what had caused her to jump from Queen's Point. Serena's letters were a gift: they were a reminder not to give yourself up for love, and to remember who you were.

Bel could have pursued a relationship with Nate, but an open relationship with a terminally unfaithful man wasn't something that would make her happy. She knew that in her heart, and if she had said yes to that just now, then she would have been compromising herself. It might be all right for someone else, but it wasn't what she wanted. She wanted a love that valued her and made her feel secure and happy, and she was willing to wait for it. She was luckier than Serena and Rose, and she was deeply grateful for that.

'All right, dear?' Dotty enquired.

Bel knew Dotty would love nothing more than a blow-by-blow account of what had just happened, but she wasn't going to comply.

'I'm fine,' she answered. *And I am*, she thought, relieved at the sense of closure the conversation with Nate had given her. He'd upset her, but she was grateful for it. Now, she could move on, and put him in the past, at last. Where he should have been for the past ten years.

THIRTY-THREE

'You'll never guess what I heard about your gardener.' One of the ladies at what Bess only half-laughingly called the Crochet Coven, sat down next to Bel on a plastic seat and rested a cup of tea in a saucer on her knee. 'You're staying up at the Ross cottage, aren't you? Hello, by the way. I'm Mina.'

'Oh, hi, Mina.' Bel was halfway through a decadent slice of carrot cake and attempted to reply and keep her mouth closed at the same time. 'Bel. I'm Bess's sister-in-law.'

On the way in to the community centre where the crochet group was held every week, there was a trestle table that held a couple of Tupperware containers of cakes, a large stainless-steel teapot and a hot water heater with a tap and a stack of mugs next to a box of tea bags and a carton of milk. Bess had explained to Bel that the group met weekly for a chat and to provide a low cost, donation-based lunch for anyone in the village that wanted it. They were also, apparently, always open to teaching anyone how to crochet. Bel had decided, on a whim, to drop in for some cake.

'Oh, I know, darling. Bess has told us all about you,' Mina trilled.

Bel caught Bess's eye, who frowned and shook her head.

Mina caught the gesture and tutted. 'Bess, don't be a meanie. You have told us about Bel, over the years. Though you are terribly secretive.' Mina rolled her eyes.

'My gardener?' Bel asked, prompting Mina. She felt a slight sense of unease.

'You know. The shaven headed one. He does a lot of the gardens on Queen's Point,' Mina sniffed. 'Of course, I live in the newer development,' she said, as if it was understood that 'the newer development' was superior to everything else in Loch Cameron.

'What did you hear?' Bel hadn't heard from Christian since their argument a week ago. The garden had been done – the lawn mown, the shrubs tidied – when she had been at work the day before. Bel had wondered if he was avoiding her.

'Well,' Mina leaned in towards Bel conspiratorially, 'my husband Sanjay was at a business meeting in Glasgow – we have a jams and chutneys business, you know. Very successful. Anyway, Sanjay was walking past the courts of justice, and he says he saw the gardener—'

'Christian,' Bess interjected, frowning.

'Oh, yes. Christian. Sanjay saw him coming out of the court building. He knew it was him because he was wearing that leather jacket with the logo on the back, like they all do in that gang.' Mina's nose wrinkled with distaste.

'The court?' Bel asked, her stomach sinking. She already knew, of course. But, somehow, she still hoped that she was wrong about Christian being a criminal.

'Yes. The burglaries in the village, you see. I knew that they were connected,' Mina crowed.

Sheila, who had been the one to mention the rumour to Bel at her salon, was sitting in the circle of chairs, crocheting what looked like a jumper. She nodded sagely. 'I told you, didn't I, Bel? Cannae be trusted. Those biker gangs're renowned fer bein' criminals. In America, in the seventies and eighties, the Hell's Angels, all that.' Sheila made a dismissive motion with her hand. 'You only have tae look at him tae see he's a wrong 'un.' She pursed her lips with satisfaction at being proved right.

'Come on, ladies,' Bess interjected. 'First of all, there's any number of reasons why someone could have to go to court. He might be involved in a custody battle, or be a witness to a crime, or be filing some paperwork. A divorce, even. And, second of all, it's none of your business.' Bess raised an eyebrow, as if disciplining her friends.

'Well, he hasnae got any children or been married, that I know,' Sheila sniffed.

'It's very suspicious, is all we're saying,' Mina added, nodding primly. 'Bel, you should be careful, up at the cottage. Keep the door locked. Hide your valuables, hmm? And if you feel unsafe at any time, you can call me and I will send Sanjay in the car.'

'Oh, for goodness' sake.' Bess rolled her eyes. 'You two are the worst curtain twitchers I've ever known.'

Kathy came to sit on the other side of Bel.

'Hi, Kathy. How's the hair? Looks good.' Bel cast an appraising eye over her recent handiwork.

'Bonny, thanks. I'm gonna rebook in a few weeks if that's okay. And I've recommended you to a few friends who do extreme colour. If you dinnae mind.'

'Of course I don't mind. That's awesome.' Bel was pleased.

Kathy took a bite of a large home-made chocolate chip cookie. 'Did I hear some gossip just now?'

'We were just telling Bel to be careful of those bikers that have infiltrated the village,' Mina said, with an air of self-righteousness. 'Sanjay saw that Christian coming out of the law courts in Glasgow yesterday with a whole gang of them. Up to no good,' she sniffed.

'Well, they would be at the court. There's been a big case

they're involved with.' Kathy frowned. 'But they're no' criminals. Far from it.'

'What are they, then?' Sheila asked, imperiously. ''Cause I cannae think o' a good reason for them tae be there otherwise.'

'Well, I suppose I can say somethin', now that the judgement's finally come through.' Kathy wiped cookie crumbs from the side of her mouth. 'I've been on jury duty on the same case for a couple o' months. Jury duty's only supposed to be two weeks, but I got lucky, I guess.' She rolled her eyes.

'What was it?' Bel asked, her heart beating faster.

'Oh, it was a terrible child abuse case, actually,' Kathy blew out her cheeks. 'It was really tough to listen to the details. That poor little lassie.'

'And... Christian?' Bel tried to prepare herself for the worst. But Kathy had said that Christian *wasn't* a criminal. What, then?

'The Warriors were there throughout the trial to support the kid. It's a voluntary service they and a number of other biker gangs provide.' Kathy looked from Mina's face to Sheila's and back again. 'No? Biker Buddies? It's a charity that supports children in the legal system. Christian and his friends weren't there because they've done anythin' wrong. They're there tae be a supportive presence for that poor lassie that has tae be in the same room as her abuser. So that she knows someone's got her back, even if her own family didnae. And they're also there to scare the livin' daylights out of anyone thinking they can hurt kids,' she added, fiercely. 'Good for them, as well.'

'Is that true?' Bel's heart started pounding now.

'Aye.' Kathy nodded. 'Salt o' the earth. They do all the charity work unpaid, out o' the goodness o' their hearts. Ye should be ashamed o' yerselves fer gossipin.' Kathy glared at Mina and Sheila.

'But what about the burglaries?' Mina asked, mulishly. 'They started at the same time the gang got here.'

'No, they didnae, Mina.' Kathy sighed with exasperation. 'There havenae been any more house break-ins than usual over the past three years. My brother heard those rumours and he's friends with someone on the police so asked about it. They told him the crime numbers an' burglaries are exactly the same as usual. Which is about two a year.'

'Why has this rumour been going around, then?' Bess asked. 'Two isn't exactly a lot. Sounds about right for Loch Cameron.'

'Well, I dunno exactly, but I'd guess that someone decided they didn't like Christian and his friends, and maybe at the same time they happened to hear about one of the burglaries. Put two and two together an' made five.' Kathy shrugged. 'You know what people are like.'

Oh, no.

Bel stood up hurriedly and dropped her piece of cake.

'Sorry. I have to... I have to go,' she said, picking up the plastic plate and scooping the cake off the floor with it. 'Oh, damn.'

'What's up?' Bess handed her a napkin and Bel wiped the cake smear off the varnished wooden floor. 'You okay?'

'Yes. It's just that... I think I've made a terrible mistake.' Bel got up and threw everything in the nearby bin. 'Bess. Do you have your van outside?'

'Yeah. Finished for today, I was going home after this. Why?' Her sister-in-law looked confused.

'I need you to drive me somewhere. Can you? Now?' Bel pleaded. She had to make things right with Christian.

'Of course, love.' Bess grabbed her jacket. 'Where are we going?'

'Queen's Point. Hurry, please.'

THIRTY-FOUR

'Oh, thank goodness. I thought I might have missed you,' Bel
panted, finding Christian mowing the lawn outside Angus's
cottage.

Bess had driven her smart little handywoman van along the
high street and up the dirt track that led to Queen's Point, with
Bel urging her to go faster. Bess had pointed out that she
couldn't put her foot down on the high street: it was a strict
twenty mile an hour limit. And it would be suicide to try and
speed up the narrow lane.

Christian frowned and took off his ear defenders. 'What?'

'I thought I missed you,' Bel repeated. She'd run from the
top of the lane, making Bess stop the car in her impatience.

'Well, you found me.' Christian gave her a guarded look.
'What's up?'

'I need to talk to you.' Bel realised she had no idea what to
say to Christian. She'd been in so much of a rush to get up here
in case she missed him that she hadn't thought about how to say
what she needed to, and now she was standing here with no
clue how to begin.

'So, talk. If you can bear to be around a criminal. Careful no one sees you talking to me. They might get the wrong idea,' he said, drily.

'They might, but I don't care if they do.' Bel thought there was a very distinct possibility that word might get around the village about her running after Christian McDougall, but, frankly, the village gossips could, as they said in Essex, *do one.*

'I'm sorry,' Bel blurted out. 'I've been a complete idiot.'

'Hmmm. Go on.' Christian raised an eyebrow and let go of the ON button on the mower, cutting off its comforting whine and plunging Queen's Point into its customary tranquillity, apart from the squawk of some nearby seagulls.

'Everything I said the other day. About you being... a thief.' Bel swallowed uncomfortably, but she knew she had to be honest and open if Christian was ever going to forgive her. And she wanted him to, very much. 'I was wrong. I know that now.'

'What changed your mind? You were very certain, before.' Christian frowned. 'Are you sure I'm not that evil, deviant criminal you thought I was? Stealing the spare key, etcetera?' He gave her a look that said, *Come on now, Bel. Try harder.*

'Kathy told me about your charity work. You could have said something.' Bel felt her high ponytail falling down – she hadn't tied it very tightly that morning and the running hadn't helped. She took out the hair elastic and twisted it around the ponytail again with a few expert movements. 'It's an amazing thing to be doing. I'd be shouting it from the rooftops if I were you.'

'I don't do it to impress people,' Christian said quietly. 'I do it because I know what it's like to feel like you don't have anyone in your corner. I know what it's like to feel like the pariah. The one left out. If I can do that for a kid that needs it, then that makes me happy.'

'You couldn't say anything for legal reasons. I should have just had faith in you.' Bel felt absolutely awful. 'I'm so sorry, Christian.'

'Thank you, Bel. I appreciate that,' he replied.

'How long have you been involved with the charity?' she asked.

'More or less since I joined the gang and found out about it. Biker Buddies can take a lot of time when you're involved in a case. It depends how much you want to be involved and how much time you can give. Apart from work, I don't really have a lot else going on. So, I've always tended to volunteer quite a lot.'

'What do you actually do? I mean, Kathy told me about being in the courtroom to support children.'

'Yeah, there's that. We go in our bike gear and sit in the gallery so the kid can see us, and so can everyone else. We do a lot of arm folding and looking stern. Kinda to make sure whoever's been making the kid's life hell knows they've got family that's gonna look out for them.'

'Family?' Bel asked.

'Yeah. That's part of what we do. We work with social services and with their permission, and with the permission of whoever's looking after the kid – foster parents, usually – we visit and get to know the kid. Give them some stuff with the club logo on, so they know they've got a family for life. If they need us, we're there. Within agreed limits, but that can mean taking kids out to theme parks, days out, that kinda thing, going round for dinner, chatting on the phone if they need someone to unload on. A lot of us had it tough growing up, so we get it.'

'Wow. Christian, it's just the nicest thing I think I've ever heard.' Bel felt all the more stupid for ever thinking that Christian could have been a criminal.

'Yeah, well.' He kicked a tuft of grass.

'I'm sorry. Again. For what I said,' Bel repeated. 'The thing is that... I like you. I liked you from the beginning. And I think you like me. And... I... I'm so sorry.' She faltered. How did anyone do this?

'Bel...' Christian stepped closer to her.

She stopped talking and took in a deep breath. As ever, his presence had the effect of making her feel lightheaded.

'I'm sorry. That I pushed you away. That I thought I had a future with Nate. Sorry that I ever thought you were anything less than... a great guy.' Bel gazed up into Christian's clear green eyes. *A great guy.* Goodness, she was making a hash of this.

'That day when Nate came to the cottage and I was there. It kinda broke my heart,' Christian confessed. 'We'd just had that real heart to heart, about my family history... that meant so much to me. I know it wasn't fair of me to feel jealous, but I was... you and I had a connection the moment we met. And every time I saw you, it just intensified.'

'I know. I'm sorry. I really was an idiot to think Nate was... well, anything, really.' Bel looked away. 'I'm sorry. I don't want to talk about him now.'

'Look, Bel. You were – are – perfectly within your rights to go out with whoever you choose. It was never up to me. I'm just...' He sighed and shook his head. 'I'm powerless when it comes to you, okay? I always was. From that first day when you came out and yelled at me in your pyjamas.' He placed his fingers under her chin and gently tilted it up towards his face.

'Really? The pyjamas?' She giggled, a little nervously. Was Christian going to kiss her? It certainly felt that way. She didn't know whether to kiss him. She definitely wanted to.

'Yeah,' he said, quietly, gazing into her eyes. 'Rendered me completely weak at the knees.'

'Weak?' Bel breathed, a smile playing around her lips. 'I'd hope that you could be the powerful one, when it came to... you know.'

It was a cheesy line but Christian grinned wolfishly and brushed her lips with his.

'Oh, don't you worry about that,' he murmured, and, softly, his lips met hers.

Bel had never experienced a kiss like this before. Nate had

been a good kisser, but this was different again. With Christian, there was something else going on, other than pure animal attraction. It had been a long time – perhaps never – since she had been kissed with such affection and tenderness.

Christian's mouth was soft on hers, the tip of his tongue on her lips. It was relaxed, sensual, yet confident: Christian was in no hurry, and slowly, his hands found her hair and then her waist. Bel could feel herself leaning in towards him; he gathered her gently to him so that she could feel his chest against her and the warmth of his body in the afternoon sun.

He smelt of cut grass and soap. She felt herself let go, surrender to the kiss, to his body. It was... lovely. It felt right, and wholesome. There was no worry in her mind like there had been with Nate: no sense of feeling slightly off-kilter or being unsure how to feel.

She knew how to feel with Christian. And it was nothing but good.

'Why don't we go out on a proper date?' he said, pulling back from the kiss and tucking an errant piece of hair behind her ear. 'That feels like a good place to start. Somewhere that isn't your garden, maybe.' He grinned a little self-consciously.

'Maybe somewhere not in Loch Cameron at all,' Bel suggested, a little impishly.

'Oh. Are there other places? I had no idea,' Christian chuckled. 'Okay. Tonight? Is that too soon?'

'No. Tonight's perfect.' Bel looked up to see Bess driving off, waving out of the window.

Her phone buzzed.

I'm off to tell your sister the good news. Catch us up when you're free xx

Bel smiled to herself.

'Anything important?' Christian asked.

'Oh, no. Just Bess,' Bel laughed. 'I'm so grateful for them, you know. Family's so important. If it wasn't for Sally living up here, I would never have come to stay. And you and I would never have met,' she leaned in and kissed him gently.

'Mmm. That's nice. And I've got you to thank for making me more connected to my family.' Christian touched her face. 'I showed the letters to my parents, and we ended up having a huge heart to heart. They knew about Serena but they'd agreed not to tell me and my brother. They thought they were doing a good thing, keeping us away from the scandal and all that. But they had no idea that we'd always just grown up confused, knowing we were being gossiped about but not why.'

'Oh, wow. So, they understand how you feel, now?' Bel asked.

'I think so. We haven't been close for a long time, but I feel like, at least communication is open, now. I'm hoping we can get closer, over time. Those letters were a real gift, even though Serena would have had no idea that they would be.'

'That's great. I'm so pleased for you.' Bel melted back into Christian's arms. 'And I'm happy for Serena, too, in a funny way. At least you know about her now, and you can remember her. I feel that's important. She deserves to be remembered.'

'Yeah. Definitely.' Christian kissed the top of Bel's head, and they both looked out onto the loch.

'Gretchen told me that her and Angus and some of the others had a vicar do a blessing up here, after Serena died. Remember? I told you,' Bel said, thoughtfully.

'Yeah, I remember. To stop them feeling like her ghost was haunting this place,' Christian said. 'Hard to imagine that on a sunny day, isn't it?'

They strolled to the edge of Queen's Point, where the cliff dropped away towards the loch. Christian stood behind Bel and wrapped his arms around her. Together, they both stared out at the water. Bel thought about Serena and Rose. Rose had had a

similar life to Nate, travelling around the world. She had no
way of knowing whether Rose had loved Serena in the same
way that Serena had loved her, but she hoped so. She hoped
that Rose had truly kept a place for Serena in her heart.

'You know, we could put a memorial for Serena up here.
And Rose,' Bel said, suddenly. 'I think if the Laird knew Serena's story, then he'd let us. What do you think?' She looked up
at Christian, who cuddled her closer to him and rested his chin
on her shoulder.

'I think that's a lovely idea. I think you're lovely, Bel,' he
murmured.

At that moment, Bel's phone pinged. She reached into her
pocket and took it out.

Money should be in your account today, Andy had written.
*Sorry for the delay. Paperwork will be with you shortly. Hope this
means you can make a go of the salon.*

'Bloody hell!' Bel had to look at the message three times to
take it in.

'What is it?' Christian looked down at her with concern.
'Are you okay?'

Bel showed him the phone screen. 'My ex had said he'd buy
me out of our house. It's been a real source of stress, because
then he couldn't get the money, and I sort of overcommitted on
the salon.' Bel let out a nervous laugh. 'It's been... interesting, to
say the least.'

'Wow. I'm sorry, Bel. You should have told me. I mean, I
don't know what I could have done to help, but I could have
listened, at least.' He peered at the screen. 'So, I guess he
managed to get the money. Mortgage?'

'Or someone took pity on him and bought out my share of
the house.'

Bel wondered if Rebecca had stepped in, and, if she had,
she thought for a moment about how she felt about that. Did
she feel weird about taking Rebecca's money? The woman who

Andy had cheated on her with? Bel searched her feelings, but she couldn't find any resentment in her. Rebecca was living in the house she and Andy had lovingly renovated; sleeping in her bed; making coffee in her kitchen. But the thing was, Bel had never felt at home in that house. If she was honest, it had never really felt like it was hers. And, Andy and her relationship, when she looked at it with the benefit of hindsight – it had never been about love. It had been about avoiding being alone.

And that was no way to live your life.

'Either way, this is a definite cause for celebration!' Christian took her hands and danced around in a circle with her.

'Waaaa! I actually can't believe it. Is it real?' She giggled.

'Check your bank balance. You've got a banking app, I take it?'

'I do. Wait.' Bel tapped her phone and took a moment to look at her balance. She looked up at Christian with shining eyes.

'It's there, isn't it?' he asked, grinning.

'It's there,' she replied. And, in that moment, Bel felt the weight of all the stress of the past weeks drop from her in a sudden autumn.

I'm free, she thought. *I'm finally free.*

THIRTY-FIVE

'Thank you, everyone, for coming today.' Hal Cameron stood next to a new wooden bench that looked out over the loch. The bench had a red ribbon tied around it, which would be cut after he said a few words. At the back of the seat, Bel knew that there was a copper plate which had been inscribed:

IN MEMORY OF SERENA MCKELLAN
DAUGHTER OF LOCH CAMERON
HER LOVE SHOULD INSPIRE US ALL

When she saw the inscription earlier that day, before the crowd had arrived, Bel had teared up immediately. She knew what it was going to say, having organised it with Christian and his family, the Laird, Angus and Gretchen two weeks before. But, still, seeing the bench with its dedication set in the tussocky grass of the point was very moving.

Hal wore a kilt with a red stripe on a black background with a formal black jacket with tails, white knee socks and a black shirt. The traditional ceremonial *sgian dubh* – a small knife, used nowadays only to be symbolic – was tucked into his sock, and he wore a traditional sporran around his hips.

Dotty, who was standing one side of Bel, gave her a nudge. 'Turns oot very smart, doesn't he? The Laird?' she whispered.

Bel chuckled. 'Yes, he does, Dotty. But so does Eric.' Bel nodded to Dotty's husband, standing on her other side and wearing a blue and green kilt, shirt and jacket.

'Aye, right enough.' Dotty rolled her eyes.

As well as Dotty and Eric, Gretchen sat at the front of the crowd in a wheelchair, with all of the crochet coven: Mina, Sheila, Kathy and June. Bess stood next to Sally and Bel, and Christian stood with Hal at the front, though he looked uncomfortable at being so visible. Bel thought how handsome he looked: she'd hardly noticed the Laird, by comparison.

Christian, who Bel was used to seeing in T-shirts and shorts or work trousers, wore a burgundy and black tartan shirt with the sleeves rolled up, showing off his brown, muscled forearms. He wore smart black jeans and black boots. When he'd turned up just before the ceremony, Bel had done a double take.

That's my boyfriend, she thought proudly, still not used to the idea. It had only been a few weeks and she and Christian were very much at the beginning of their relationship. They were taking it slow, and that was fine with her. But, with every day that went past, she found herself feeling more and more for him.

Angus, who had agreed to play the bagpipes at the ceremony, also wore a kilt and a jacket, and Bel had done his hair for the occasion in the smart plait he liked, giving the sides of his head a fresh shave. Fiona from the shop was there, as well as a number of Sally's colleagues from the distillery, and all the Warriors, Christian's biker gang. Christian had also introduced Bel to his parents and his brother.

'Today, we commemorate Serena McKellan, a past resident of Queen's Point,' Hal began. 'Serena, the daughter of Bob and

Mary McKellan, lived in Queen's Point all of her life, which was sadly cut short in 1966 when she was just twenty-six.

'We don't know much about Serena, other than the fact that she fell in love with another local girl, Rose Macaulay, when she was just a teenager. Sadly, Rose left Loch Cameron for her ballet career and – as far as we can tell – never came back. We can't say for sure, but it's possible that Serena never got over losing Rose. It's certainly true that society didn't look kindly on same sex relationships at the time, but we can't say for sure that's the reason Serena decided to jump off this spot, on Queen's Point, all those years ago.'

Hal cleared his throat. 'What we can say is that Serena was part of Loch Cameron's community, however welcome she may or may not have felt in it. And, she is part of Alison, Christian, Rob and David's family. Serena was a friend to Gretchen. She belonged to this place, just as we all do. And, so, I'm proud to pass over to Serena's nephew, Christian McDougall, to unveil this stone in memory of Serena: a daughter of Loch Cameron who we remember with love and kindness.'

Hal handed Christian a pair of scissors, and Christian cut the ribbon.

'I now declare this bench open!' Christian cried, and everyone clapped. 'Thanks, everyone,' he added, as the clapping subsided. 'I just want to say thanks to you all, on behalf of my family. We really appreciate you coming here, and remembering Serena. And, Hal, thanks so much for funding the bench. It means a lot to us.' Christian shook Hal's hand.

'And, last, I want to say thank you to Bel Burns. Come up here, Bel,' Christian called out.

Bel shook her head, but Dotty elbowed her sharply in the ribs.

'Go on!' she hissed.

So Bel walked towards Christian and Hal, rather awkwardly.

'Hello, honey. Don't be shy. Bel was the one who found Serena's letters to Rose Macaulay, her lover, and gave them to me,' Christian told the crowd. 'I have so much to thank Bel for. But mostly, I want to embarrass her a little bit in front of all of you and tell her how special and beautiful and kind I think she is. And that I think she's a little like Serena. She has that amazing capacity to love. And that's a rare gift.'

Bel looked at the grass, deeply embarrassed. She hated being the centre of attention, but Christian's words made her feel warm and tingly.

'I just wanted to say, Bel, in front of everyone, that I think you're the most wonderful woman I've ever met. And I wish that I could have known Serena, but I'm so glad that I get to know you. That's it.'

Everyone cheered and clapped, and Angus started playing the bagpipes.

Christian enveloped Bel in a hug. 'I meant it, you know,' he whispered in her ear. 'Every word.'

Rather than reply with words, Bel kissed him. All her feelings were in that kiss: the desire she felt for Christian, the affection for him that was growing in her heart, and a thankfulness for all of the sweet things he continued to do for her every day.

But Bel realised that she had a new sense of knowing in her heart. Whatever happened with Christian – and she hoped it was all the good things – she had found something much more vital: herself.

The night before, she had dreamt of her dad again. He had been back in the little rowing boat, and she had been on the shore, holding the boat's rope in her hands.

It's time to let me go, cupcake, her dad had called out across the still, sparkling black water. *I'll always love you. But you're going to be okay now. You don't need me to watch over you anymore.*

But, Dad, I don't want you to go, Bel had called out.

You know you can make it without me, he replied, and held up his end of the rope. *I'll see you again, one day, a long time from now. Make sure you tend the garden together. Plant roses for me.*

Slowly, her dad had dropped the end of the rope in the water, and the boat started to drift into the darkness.

No, Dad! she cried out, and woke up, sobbing, knowing that he was gone.

And, yet, when the tears had run out, Bel knew that her dad had left her with a great love in her heart that would never run out. She knew that he had been with her, all this time, guiding her and protecting her. But, now, she could do it herself.

Bel knew she had returned to the core of who she was: no longer in an unhappy relationship or an employee in a job she hated. She had the salon, which she loved. Things were going well with Christian, who she felt her dad had approved of – he'd remarked on how well he had tended the roses, in that dream. Bel knew what that meant. She was close to Sally and Bess, and she had made new friends.

Serena's letters had reminded her never to compromise herself for anyone again. Self-reliance was a luxury that Serena hadn't had, in her passionate obsession. Bel could make other choices, and she had.

The moment that she had said *no* to Nate, Christian had stepped into her life clearly as a much better choice. That was the strange thing about life, like the tarot reader she followed online had said: *Sometimes things have to die in order for the new to begin. Just hold on. Good things are coming for you.*

Good things had come, in abundance, once she had been strong enough to say no to everything that was holding her back.

And all of it had happened in Loch Cameron, the first place that had ever felt like home.

A LETTER FROM KENNEDY

Dear reader,

I want to say a huge thank you for choosing to read *A Gift from the Cottage by the Loch*. If you did enjoy it, and want to keep up to date with all my latest releases, just sign up at the following link. Your email address will never be shared and you can unsubscribe at any time.

www.bookouture.com/kennedy-kerr

Women's stories are very important to me and I was keen to explore Bel's relationship with her sister Sally in this book as well as her experience of love and relationships. In the Loch Cameron books, as with my Magpie Cove series, female friendship and support structures are so important, and so Bel's story presented another opportunity for me to show how we can raise each other up.

Additionally, knowing several wonderful neurodiverse people, I was also interested in creating a romantic hero in Christian who had ADHD, which is so common and still under-diagnosed.

I hope you loved *A Gift from the Cottage by the Loch* and if you did I would be very grateful if you could write a review. I'd love to hear what you think, and it makes such a difference helping new readers to discover one of my books for the first time.

I love hearing from my readers – you can get in touch through social media, or my website.

Thanks,

Kennedy

facebook.com/kennedykerrauthor

x.com/kennedykerr5

instagram.com/kennedykerrauthor

AUTHOR'S NOTE

I have made a brief reference to the homophobia present in the tabloid press in the UK in the 1980s in telling the story of Rose's ballet career. I posed the tabloid article as being from 1981, as from 1983, the British media coverage of the AIDS pandemic would start to intensify greatly, and worsen the homophobia already present in the media. Colin Clews' excellent website Gay in the 80s (www.gayinthe80s.com) is a fascinating resource if you would like to look at example of homophobic press reporting of AIDS and more generally about gay communities at that time.

My thanks go to Shilara, a proud Texan, for her help with Nate's phrases and sayings, and her advice on a suitable small town that Nate could be from.

Christian's ADHD is inspired by a number of people – children and adults – that I know and love. Our understanding of neurodiversity as a society is still developing and all too often, it can take until people are adults for them to receive a diagnosis, whether that is ADD/ADHD, ASD, dyspraxia, dyslexia or a number of other issues.

This can mean that people have spent all of their childhood thinking that they weren't academic, or, worse, told that they were stupid or badly behaved, and punished for it. So many people, in the years where neurodivergence wasn't recognised, could have had a very different experience of school and early life if their conditions had been diagnosed, and if schools, workplaces and society had been equipped in those days to guide and support neurodivergent learners, employees, friends and family as we do now.

Biker Buddies, the Warriors' charity, was inspired by the charity Bikers Against Child Abuse International (www.baca world.org) who do more or less exactly what I have described in this book. I'm indebted to my cousin Chris who has worked with the charity in the past along with many of her fellow bikers – and I'm very grateful for all charities that exist to support children.

PUBLISHING TEAM

Turning a manuscript into a book requires the efforts of many people. The publishing team at Bookouture would like to acknowledge everyone who contributed to this publication.

Commercial
Lauren Morrissette
Jil Thielen
Imogen Allport

Cover design
Eileen Carey

Data and analysis
Mark Alder
Mohamed Bussuri

Editorial
Kelsie Marsden
Jen Shannon

Copyeditor
Claire Rushbrook

Proofreader
Tom Feltham

Marketing
Alex Crow
Melanie Price
Occy Carr
Cíara Rosney

Operations and distribution
Marina Valles
Stephanie Straub

Production
Hannah Snetsinger
Mandy Kullar

Publicity
Kim Nash
Noelle Holten
Myrto Kalavrezou
Jess Readett
Sarah Hardy

Rights and contracts
Peta Nightingale
Richard King
Saidah Graham

Printed in Great Britain
by Amazon